SHADOWS OVER AVALON

Curated by Nicole Petit

SHADOWS OVER AVALON
An 18thWall Productions book published by
arrangement with Nicole Petit
verba mea in minibus
desiderium meum
Cover by Johannes Chazot
Jacket Design and Book Design by Adventure on Earth Productions
Illustration by Sophie Iles

ISBN-13: 978-1-946033-17-8

CONTENTS

The DEATh. DROWNING AND REVIVAL OF SIR DINADAN

Dylan Freeman

The following text is a translation of an untitled manuscript of alliterative verse in Middle French, discovered in 1937. Though its exact provenance is unclear, radiocarbon dating has shown that the manuscript dates to the 15th century. The story appears to be set some time after the events of L'Morte d'Arthur, *but no exact date is given. An effort has been made to preserve the alliteration; other than associated corrections to punctuation, no further change has been made to the text.*

—-Allen Reid, Director of Literary Studies, Miskatonic University.

1. The Interregnum and the Entrance into the Dream

Sir Dinadan was dead, or so it was declared. The Knights of King Arthur had often said that Dinadan's joy and wit, even in the most dire and dark times, kept them hopeful for the future. Indeed, it had been said that if Dinadan's joy would die, so too would Camelot itself.

Sir Dinadan had survived the Strife, though the former knight wished he had not. His king and fellows were dead, and the next king, Arthur's cousin Constantine, could scarce keep the throne. Constantine was not a coward, but he lacked any loyal army—the knights that had survived had scattered to the four corners, with Bisclavret boarding a ship to France alongside Cai, Parcival travelling to the Holy Land with his half-brother Fierefiz, and Lancelot had defected back to Dolores Gard.

Britain at the time was battle-torn, with burning fields and

4

blackened skies. Just as Camelot's continuity had kept the climate fair, its downfall had been the decree for daily downpours, drowning the denizens of Britain. Constantine, while competent, could not properly distribute the kingdom's coffers to aid his citizens during a time which would be called the Season of the Fierce Floods.

Constantine would not have full control of his kingdom for another quarter of a century, during which time the surviving knights continued on their adventures, though there were few of them still in Britain. Some Constantine tried to locate, offer to lead them to glory and valor and virtue, but none heeded the call—they had seen sights otherworldly and unnatural, and had grown weary of the world.

Some have heard of Lancelot's madness in Dolores Gard, or of Cai's fight with the kraken off of Naples. Few, however, have attempted to retell the tale of the dour knight Dinadan, and how his heart hoped once again.

Sir Dinadan was dead, or so it was declared. In truth, his joy suffered the worst of his wounds, and it was during this joyless time that Dinadan travelled to Dover, on the coast of Kent, to see the chalk-white cliffs.

In those days, at the height of the cliffs of Dover, a dolmen sat, with a stone circle fractured around it. Those who still practiced the pagan ways would gather at the dolmen, offer libations to dark, dreaming things without name. In addition to his joy, hope, and the king's favor, Dinadan had lost faith in the Father, for how could something which loved all allow his fellows and friends to fight and die for a petty affair, a traitorous tryst?

And of Arthur himself...to Avalon, he had gone, an island, an apple orchard, an afterlife, to rise when Britain needed him most. "Is that not now?" Dinadan asked the ground. "Is now not the time when Britain needs a monarch, a merciful ruler, a savior? What more is needed to coronate the old King?"

The dolmen stood at the cliff, looking south towards the rest of the world. Dinadan was alone, the world dim and vacant but for him. Though the downpour had calmed to a drizzle on his walk to the dolmen from his horse, his inner flame, his joy, was still damp and withered.

The wise woman at the village of Hearth, twenty miles north, said this to him: "Lie upon the dolmen, dour Dinadan, and dream. Whether the dream be despairing or joyous, you will find yourself among friends once more."

Dinadan climbed upon the stone table, sword laying at his chest, hands across the hilt. He looked up into the rain and the roiling clouds. Sunshine seemed distant, but in a dream, daylight could last forever.

They said that Sir Dinadan was dead. He dreamt, and seemed to sink into the stone table.

2. The Shores of the Dream-Lands

It was the surf that awoke Sir Dinadan. He found his face sand-scabbed, with water in his hair. The sun shone overhead, and waterbirds, with a strange song, circled. "Tekeli-li, tekeli-li," they called. "Tekeli-li, tekeli-li."

Dinadan stood from the shallow water, finding himself garbed as he had been when he started to sleep, sword and all. The air of the island felt familiar—the smell, somehow, reminded him of better times. It carried the scent of apple-blossoms and ale and whetstones and wine.

Holding his head high and his hand higher, Dinadan turned to the horizon and gasped. "Good Lord alive." He strode forward. "Is this possible? Do I find myself at Corbenic? Is that the Castle Adventurous? Second only to Camelot in terms of splendor. I thought I would never see it, after the Grail was found and lost."

Indeed, before Dinadan's eyes, a great fortress, seemingly golden in the sunlight, stood tall above the shoreline. Corbenic had been the Castle of the Holy Grail, before it, and Galahad, had been taken away by angels upon high. Since then, Corbenic—also known as Castle Adventurous—had been lost to Camelot, but now he stood in its shadow.

"And—the apple orchards, dear Lord. These are the Fisher King's, from when the wound was healed! What is this strange, hybrid land of wonders?" He sighed. "Surely, a dream. One that I do not wish to wake from."

The sound of battle came through the apple orchard, and Dinadan stepped off of the shore. Through the forest he strode, stealing a fruit and biting into it; it tasted as sweet as any fruit he had ever eaten—the nectar of heaven itself.

The orchard gave way to a familiar tournament-ground, where the colors of Camelot flew. A joust was taking place in the field, with armor that gleamed in the sun and lances that shined like moonlight. The riders seemed familiar to Dinadan, somehow.

When the riders collided, the loser landed on the dirt, their helmet flying free. Below it was the massive, now-unmistakable form of Galehaut, the great wolf knight, whom Dinadan had mocked and made merry for in days long past.

Galehaut's opponent rode to the other side, dismounting from his horse, and offering a hand. Their helmet was also removed, and Dinadan's heart nearly halted, for the face beneath it was one he thought to never see again—Parcival, who had long since gone eastwards.

Dinadan came out of the forest, waving his hand. "Hallo!" He stuttered. "What is this place? What are you people? You resemble my friends, but this cannot be—you are either dead, gone, or both."

The riders turned towards Dinadan, their eyes growing wet. Galehaut gasped. "We thought never to see you again, Merry-Making Dinadan! You have never shown your face among the apple trees of Avalon, never taken part in the jousting, eaten at the table or hunted with Pellinore. We thought you worse than dead."

"And I thought *you* dead!" Dinadan turned to Parcival. "And you, with your brother!"

"Aye, we are all in those places, and also here, in Avalon." Parcival grinned and waved his arm towards a wooden pavilion, where the flag of Camelot still hung, its colors unmarred by time or war.

A man sat on this pavilion, astride a throne of gold and hope. His face was weary, his head of crimson hair crowned by a golden circlet. His eyes, tired though they were, became full of life when he set eyes upon Dinadan. "Why so dour, fair

7

knight?" Arthur asked. "You look as if you have seen a man rise from the dead."

"How can this be?" Dinadan laughed. "What trick of Morgan is this? My Lord, I heard of your death in battle, struck down by Mordred. You are dead, never to rise again."

Beside Arthur, a young man with white hair, his face unfamiliar and unpleasing, his ears pointed and perked, stood, and spoke. "If your liege is dead, loyal Dinadan, then it stands to reason that you are dead as well. But neither you, he, or I are dead."

A woman, whose face was similar to Arthur's in a fashion, appeared opposite the young man. "And that which is not dead can eternal lie."

The oracular and ominous tones of the speakers immediately told Dinadan their names— "Wise Merlin and Cruel Morgan." He bent his knee, head bowed in respect. "You then live, my king? Camelot is in disarray, but you still live? You live without ruling, letting your cousin drive Camelot into the dirt?"

"It is not yet the right time, Dinadan. The stars shall signal when I rise again." Arthur was by his side in an instant. "You are safe here, dreaming alongside me. Stay a while, fair knight, and learn to make merry again, learn to love fighting." Arthur's hand was around Dinadan's shoulder. "The things on Avalon, Pellinore enjoys them so, more than the Questing Beast itself. Come, we must meet the others at a feast."

Dinadan, stunned, stood and walked, but soon parted from his King. Merlin and Morgan stared at him, then at each other, their eyes uneasy. In the distance, a booming bellow echoed, like a weeping windstorm.

3. Dinadan Takes A Wager

Sir Dinadan's side had a wound in it that gave him searing pain. It was scarce but a scar at this time, but he still felt it burn and boil every other step. But now, upon the stones and earth of Avalon, his side did not sear. "Am I healed?"

"We can only hope, Hilarious Dinadan!" A voice over his shoulder bellowed with laughter. "That wound you took would make your wedding dress ill-fit."

A smile formed on Dinadan's face for the first time in an age as he turned. "And I suppose your casket was too uncomfortable, Gawain? Did Sir Marrock have to dig you from the ground, or did you actually rise from your respite under your own power, you lazy lout?"

Gawain, grinning, embraced his friend. "Avalon has been lonely without you, Dinadan! None can match your wit, though Pellinore has tried."

"Poor Pellinore. He may have stolen my planning diary—I had something in there about coating Cai in honey—"

"And leaving him in the forest for Sir Marrock to make a meal of while in the guise of a great bear!" Gawain laughed. "Come forth, we have much to discuss. But first, why not a wee little wager?" From his back, Gawain produced a great green axe that Dinadan found all too familiar, from a Christmas several years past at this point.

"The Green Knight's wager?" Dinadan took the axe. "Gawain, good Lord, you nearly were beheaded by it. Did you truly learn nothing from your lot in life?"

"I learned much in my life, Sir Dinadan, including how to wield this great weapon! In my hands, it can shear a single blade of grass in half as easily as it can cleave a great oak into ground mulch. Surely you possess some skill?"

"Do I appear as if I can walk on water, Gawain?"

"I do not see the connection, Sir Dinadan."

"I am a knight, not a carpenter. I would behead you as you beheaded the Knight if I took up that axe, and you are not a Fae like him—you would fall, dead."

"A scratch, Dinadan, is all I ask! Pity an old friend for this favor?"

How often had Dinadan done the same to his fellow knights when he was attempting to force a joke upon them? Gawain was a far less skilled fisher than Dinadan was at his worst, there was an element here he was not aware of—this was an attempt at revenge by Gawain.

"Very well." Dinadan took up the axe from Gawain's hand. "But this will be the lightest of cuts I can manage."

Before the next sentence was started, the axe had swung on its own, separating Gawain's head from his neck. Dinadan did not flinch, staring at both the head of the axe and the head of his friend, before shaking his own. "Merlin!"

From behind a great oak, a small, snickering form emerged— the mage himself, mirth on his face. "Aye, aye. I enchanted that axe to smite your friend. Do you not mourn his passing at my hand? Do you not wish to strike me down as well?"

"Why would I bother, when he still lives?" Dinadan delivered a slight kick to Gawain's legs, and his head cried out in pain.

"Damn it all!" Gawain's head laughed as his body collected it. "What gave away the game?"

"The knights are never subtle," Merlin admitted. "But how did you know he could not die?"

"Well, why would Gawain offer me an axe that could kill him, if there was not a trick to this? Have you forgotten the gamboling and capering I did in Camelot, at the expense of the other knights?" He handed the axe to Gawain once more. "And then there was what Morgan said—'That which is not dead can eternal lie.' Master Merlin, you once told me of a line in one of your books that began that way, and ended with: 'And with strange aeons, even death may die'. I dare say that what is happening in the waking world is certainly a strange aeon, if our King lives."

"Aye, aye." Merlin crossed to Gawain and got his head on his shoulders once more. "Now, no more of that, Gawain. If another arrives with less wit than Dinadan, you'll frighten them to…well, not to death."

"Yes, your point is taken." Gawain clapped Sir Dinadan's shoulder and began walking onwards.

"Be we in Paradise or Perdition, Merlin?" Dinadan walked a ways behind, talking to the wizard. "For we cannot perish, but several already have."

"The Northmen tell of a place called Valhalla, a massive mead-hall where a war is waged for sport, where the combatants cannot be killed. I believe that this Avalon is our own Valhalla, of a sort—we fight and caper and gambol, but we do not perish here."

"A strange aeon indeed." Dinadan looked up at the sky, unperturbed by the twin suns overhead. "Strange indeed."

The two walked through the apple orchard, to a destination that Dinadan did not know.

4. Dinadan Drowns

A full feast awaited Dinadan, Gawain and Merlin at what seemed to be a copy of the now-charred castle of Camelot. Surrounding the Great Table, dozens of knights, dead and living, stood gathered. Galehaut the great wolf and Parcival of the Grail were there, as well as Sir Marrock, Sir Cai, Sir Tristam, Bevdivere and Bleoberis, Lucan and Lamorak, Palomides and Pellinore.

Of these, Pellinore's presence perturbed Dinadan the most, for at an ale-house around Oxford, he and Dinadan had dined together, largely silent, for joy had left both knights. The Questing Beast, Pellinore's Purpose, was long-dead, and Dinadan's dreariness has been discussed. Surely the Proud Pellinore had not perished in the fortnight since they supped? Strange aeons, indeed.

Taking his place by Pellinore, Dinadan looked upon the table, his mouth watering at the meal before him. There was squab and salmon, mutton and mackerel and mince, sweet apples and strong cider, and ribs of beef and pork and plates aplenty to put it all on. "Who cooked this magnificent meal?" Dinadan asked, reaching over to acquire a single apple.

"It is not cooked," Pellinore chuckled. "It simply appears, and makes our bellies full in this realm. Some scarce need food anymore—such as his majesty there—but as I still live, finding adventure in Scotland, I feast in reality as well as in this dream-land."

"So, this is a shared dreaming? I live still?" Dinadan tried not to sour. "Then how come we here, Pellinore? How am I not come to Avalon before, in my dreams?"

"I do not know, Dinadan. I dare say that question is best left for after this feast—and after our hunt."

"You hunt still, proud Pellinore?" Dinadan's question was half-directed at a mass of mutton on his plate. "But the beast you quest after is at the bottom of a lake."

"You should see the beasts that threaten Avalon!" Pellinore laughed, piling his plate with pike. "The Questing Beast was but my first quarry, now I find things far fiercer and unfathomable to fight. I shall take you to the trophy room hall after we finish this feast."

After they had eaten their fill, and the good king said words of encouragement, Pellinore and Dinadan departed. The keep of Camelot was timeless, but somehow felt as if it were a facsimile—a gash on the armory's gate was gouged on every door in the castle, and the patterns of the tapestries, far from being the grand scenes of glorious battles, were spiraling shapes that Dinadan had to stop himself from staring at.

The trophy hall, at least, seemed similar to its counterpart in the Camelot of life. Half of it was lined by the heads of hinds, boars, bucks, and the odd wolf, but the rest of the walls were covered by things that Dinadan could only assume were demons of this dream land—among them was the upper torso of a being with wings, with its head horned but lacking a face, a wide worm that took up an entire corner of the room, a terrible two-legged toad-man with skin like the moon, and a great rat with what Dinadan thought was grass upon its snout—upon further observation, he saw that they were strands of flesh, and that it had the hands of a human.

"What manner of demons are these? Have the legions of the Goetia gotten loose in Avalon?"

"Nay, not demons. Dream-beasts. These and more are hunted in a place upon Avalon we know as the Hinterlands. A queer place, with squalling winds and ground that groans and gasps, but glory is to be found there." He turned towards Dinadan. "What say you, Noble Dinadan? Join me on a hunt in the Hinterlands this night? We seek a beast I know as the Top-Mouth."

"What in the name of Mother Mary does a Top-Mouth look like?" Dinadan laughed. "I must see this for myself. Pellinore, consider your hunting party expanded."

Avalon.

The mood at the Table Round was as dour now as Dinadan's had been when he had first entered this dream. Arthur, the King Eternal, scowled at Morgan and Merlin. Dinadan sat shielded by Gawain, while Pellinore tended to Marrock's apparent madness—he could not stop growling at himself, the poor knight.

"Sister mine," Arthur said to Morgan, "And Mage Merlin. What is the beast that assails Avalon at this time? How has it come to this paradise? My resting place, until England is in its greatest time of need? It comes to drive my men to madness, and I do not even know its name."

Merlin's head was hung in shame. "Avalon, as we know it, is an unreality. It does not exist outside of the dreaming, and it is in this dream that you all shall return one day. But this Avalon is not my creation."

"Nor is it even his dream, nor mine." Morgan circled the table, contempt on her face. "The fool found it when his fancying after the nymph Nimue left him sealed in a tree. He dreamed, half-dead, and in his eternal lie, he found a greater being."

"An intelligence, vast and terrifying. This is but a raindrop in its dreaming land, a single scar upon its *mēns*. Morgan found me in a patch of murk, drowning in the music of its mind. Terrible and beautiful, we knew it could be used."

"The two of us built Avalon, together, to save Arthur. We took from the dream-stuff of the intelligence, and from your own minds and memories. From Corbenic to Camelot, from the Castle to Caledfwlch, all of this is a shadow of the sun-lit lands of reality." Morgan glowered past Gawain, at Dinadan. "Your action has brought our ruin, for now an uncaring intelligence sees our scarring upon its mind, and it acts against us."

Dinadan sank into his seat. "The wise woman at Hearth told me to sleep and find you once more. I beg your pardon, Matronly Morgan. But Britain is burning. I simply want to awaken somewhere better."

"Foolish floundering child!" Morgan screamed. "You do

not simply sleep away your sorrow! Britain is better with men like you in it, Dinadan the brave, the joyful, the kind! From the minds of your fellows, I know of the merry that is made with you, of the jokes and tricks that are played. You've turned dour, Dinadan, last of the Round Table in Britain. Constantine cannot rule without knights. Your joyless heart is all he has in his kingdom, and you refused him."

Dinadan felt his heart tremble, a tear falling from his eye. A knight, he was, but also a fool. "What can be done to remedy this, oh Cruel Morgan?"

"I do not think there is anything to be done. The dreamer is not a river that can be dammed, it is a deep and dark ocean, unfathomable and unstoppable. Our only hope is that it returns to its timeless slumber once more, and that the King and Camelot both can survive its nocturnal turnings. Even the deepest sleeper can spare half a second of slumber to smite a gadfly. We may be able to open a window and throw out this fly instead."

"I do not see your meaning," Dinadan began, but before the sentence was said, he found himself on Avalon's shore once more.

"You are exiled, o Dinadan, Bringer of Disaster." Morgan's voice spoke in his mind. "We have to repair the damage done here. Perhaps when you truly die, you can find yourself here again."

And so, Dinadan, once more dour and dire, looked towards the sea beyond Avalon, and the shadows on the horizon. "Disaster-bringer indeed," he sighed to himself. "For if I had made more merry, kept a tighter brotherhood among Camelot, perhaps it would not have fallen. If I had talked to Lancelot, or given counsel to Gawain or Galehaut or any others, perhaps the kingdom would still be intact. Dinadan the Disaster-Bringer, I am. But I have been Dinadan the Dour for too long. When I wake, I shall cast off my mantle of depression."

The only answer he received was the seabirds above singing a sinister song— "Tekeli-li, Tekeli-li!"

In the distance, the Dreamer seemed to stare at him, with the same contemptuous disinterest—as if it did not want to notice Dinadan, but were forced to by fate itself. The gaze of the Beast pierced Dinadan, and while dozens of others would break from it, breaking into a series of gibbers and growls, Dinadan found himself growing—not in size, but in heart.

"Beast of the Bible, End-bringer, Evil Thing! Hear me! I am Sir Dinadan of the Round Table, Dinadan the Dour, the Disaster-Bringer, the Dead! I stand before you today and declare this: your awakening is inevitable, but if this be your dream, then when you wake, you shall drag my King and the Table Round from the depths of the dream-land with it, back into the world of the waking, onto the shores lit by a single sun! And when you wake, I know that England will need its True King! We shall not be cowed by your presence, o Beast! As long as you dream, Avalon will be in your dreams, and Camelot shall never die!"

While he was talking, the Dreamer stretched, and sank beneath the waves once more, with a spray of surf washing upon Avalon's shore. A rumble rose from the ground, and somehow Dinadan knew that the Hinterlands of Avalon had vanished. He turned, intending to head to the castle once more.

From the orchard, Dinadan saw Morgan and Merlin watching him. Their faces were wary, for they knew the truth of the matter—while Dinadan believed that his hope had driven off the beast, Morgan's metaphor of the gadfly was more apt—one could stir awake enough to swat at it, but if the fly did not buzz too loudly, it was easier to put one's pillow over a head and fall back asleep.

"Peace, Dinadan." Morgan held up her hand. "Though one day you may enter Avalon in dreams once more, you must wake for now. We have a task for thee—seek the Hermit Knight in Hearth, and join his quest to slay the Sons."

Before Dinadan could speak, he found himself once again in Dover, on the warm, dry dolmen, beneath the rising sun. He stood, stretched, and made his way to his mare, and began the ride back to Hearth.

6. Dinadan meets the Hermit Knight

The hamlet of Hearth today is lost to us, but in the time after Camelot's fall, it was a sort of home for vagrants and vagabonds, wanderers and mercenaries. It was here, in a nameless ale-house, that Dinadan found himself once again, his heart having been filled with hope once more. No longer would he be Dinadan the Dour—he thought he might dub himself Dinadan of the Daylight.

He knew not what this 'hermit knight' Morgan told him of would be, but the answer became clear within an hour of him having sat down to drink ale outside of the dream—a rainstorm had started anew, and from it strode in a man, soaked to the bone.

Dinadan recognized the knight, despite his bedraggled and battered appearance—though their once immaculate head of blonde hair had been muddied, a finger on their left hand had gone missing, and they lacked the perfect posture they had had in Camelot, he knew that this was Lancelot, the man who had committed the traitorous tryst that led to its downfall. Producing a hammer and a piece of paper, he nailed a notice to the wall, which read:

"A call to all knights and sellswords: the Sons of the bastard Mordred still live. In service to King Constantine, a sum of coin shall be paid to any who wish to aid in their extermination. If interested, contact Sir Lamentation."

Dinadan's now-grown heart started to harden—this man had a larger role in killing Camelot than Dinadan could ever have managed by himself. But Morgan had told him to seek out a 'Hermit Knight'—had she meant this man? This traitor, this son of the fae? Surely not. Still, Dinadan approached, hoisting his hood over his face—though now foes, perhaps a friendship could be kindled once more.

Dinadan made his way to the man calling himself Sir Lamentation, his voice mimicking the mysterious Merlin's. "Tell me, good knight—"

"Stay your tongue. A knight I am, but not a good one." Sir Lamentation held his hand up and shook his head. "Speak if you must, even if it is to mock me."

"It's just that I know of a huntsman in Scotland, by the name of Pellinore—I saw him there myself, but a fortnight ere now—who may be able to aid you in the hunt for the Sons of Mordred. Perhaps we can ride there, together, to seek him and his services?"

"You would ride with a lamentable hermit like me?" Sir Lamentation shook his head, not recognizing a former friend before him. "Why would you do such a thing?"

"Because, Sir Lamentation, I have dreamt of Avalon, and the redemption that awaits knights like us. Camelot is dead, but its dream is not— for when the End of Days comes, Camelot will be dragged up from the sea with it, and we shall drive our swords into the Beast's hide."

"You speak as if you have talked to the King himself, been among his court." Sir Lamentation looked upon him. "Do I know you?"

"Perhaps you did, in another life. Now, what say you? Do we ride to Scotland to seek the Huntsman Pellinore? Perhaps after you do, you too shall dream of Avalon."

"Avalon has no place for me—I know my fate, to be kept in Dolores Gard alongside my good friend Galehaut, away from Guenevere." He gazed out the window, into the downpour. "Then again, a Son is said to be in the lowlands of Scotland. Perhaps Pellinore will not recognize me, and give me aid."

"I believe that Avalon has a place for all who still remember the hope of Camelot." He extended his hand. "Call me Sir Daylight, for the time being."

"And I, Sir Lamentation." They traded grips. "You do seem familiar, in a way. On our ride, you must tell me of your Dream of Avalon."

And so, Dinadan the Dreamer rode towards Scotland alongside Lancelot, who might one day have dreamt of Avalon during his hunt for the Sons of Mordred. But this is a tale for another time.

Final note: After analyzing this tale, I re-examined the original journals of Gustaf Johansen, second mate of the

Emma *and the only person in the 20th century to have survived a first-hand encounter with the being described in this work. Francis W. Thurston's transcription of the journal left out approximately ten pages, recounting a series of dreams Johansen had of a land of apple orchards, where he was welcomed and congratulated for his efforts by a large group of English-speaking knights. Johansen closed this section by writing: "I know now that, though I suffer, there is a place for me where hope springs forth. When I die, I shall be greeted upon Avalon's shores." Then, the only piece of Norwegian text in the whole journal: "Rina, my wife, do not weep, for I shall greet you in the orchards when you pass on."*

—-Allen Reid, Director of Literary Studies, Miskatonic University.

IN THE BLEAH MIDWINTER

Richard Sheppard

Chapter One

I know what you're going to ask, because it is the same thing I'm always asked. I lost the eye in service to His Highness the King in the thirtieth year of his reign, and the twenty-fifth year of my life. I was holding on to a wooden shield while a Gaul hacked away at it in an effort to break the line. The shield splintered and a large needle of wood found my eye. Yes, it hurt a lot. Yes, I miss it. I can no longer shoot an arrow, let alone use a lance to dismount one of my fellow knights. Anything beyond the span of my outstretched hand wavers and twists in the sight of my one remaining eye. Am I bitter? Perhaps. Better to be bitter than to be amongst the fallen at the battle of Dungeness though. Merlin, who had seemed on the march to war as old as the marshes that lined the bloody shore, moved as fast as mercury when it came to plucking out the eye and stuffing the socket with a paste made from moss and figs. It was that foul-smelling stuff that stopped the wound becoming mortal, although I still maintain when I breathe in I taste figs on the back of my tongue. My eye was scooped out and thrown to the ground for some hungry seagull to squawk over, I assume.

On the long march back from the battle, home to Camelot finally, the King himself had given up his wagon for me to lie in. The fever that Merlin feared never came to me, and I was even able to walk the last ten miles unaided. I wanted to see Camelot again on my feet, like a true Knight of Arthur, and drink of its beauty. As I was gazing at the castle, I felt a hand on my shoulder.

"I thought I would never see it again." I turned to see who had addressed me. It was an old man, his face lined and his beard a yellow so light it would turn to grey as quickly as the rain could fall. With a shock I realised it was my King, Arthur.

"Yes, sire," I said, turning back to Camelot, a castle this man had built so other men would have something worth raising their eyes up to see. I felt a spasm of love in my chest for my King, who had sacrificed his health, his youth and any chance of a humble life in the name of virtue.

"Sir Ascamore, I hope with all my heart that these warlike days are over," Arthur said. "Perhaps they are for us anyway, yes? I grow old—"

"Milord—" I began.

"Please, Sir Ascamore, truth is a virtue, and truth with oneself a greater virtue for being so rare. I have grown old in years and battles, but before I lack all use there is still greater work to be done."

"My sword is yours," I said, falling to one knee.

"Your place is now away from the field, and nearer the throne. You may have lost an eye in doing noble service, but I shall require your clear vision in a greater work," Arthur said. For the first time I noticed Merlin had joined us in the clearing in the woods. He remained back in the shadows, as is his nature.

"The nation has wearied, like I have, through ceaseless battle. It lacks one head to think with, to speak directly to God with. I must remedy that before it is too late and an infection sets into the land."

"Yes, milord," I whispered. I would have cut my own throat if Arthur had told me my blood would refresh the ground beneath us. He talked like no other man. He never lied to me.

"And you, Sir Ascamore, shall share this burden." Arthur placed his hand again on my shoulder, and we gazed at the towers of Camelot until the sun went down, and fires were lit in every window to welcome home King Arthur and the heroes of Dungeness.

Chapter Two

It was fifteen years ago since we returned from Dungeness, when my King had told me that my days on the battlefield were over. I must wear a leather strap over my eye so as not to scare the cook's boys and scullery maids with the empty socket. Blood no longer stains my hands, but ink. My armour sits in one of the cavernous cellars that lay beneath all Camelot. I can't think about the armour too long, sitting there in the dark, rusting in the damp Cornish air that plagues us every Winter. Maybe it will be brought up and polished to impress the guests who were soon to arrive. Arthur may no longer fight in the field, what little fighting there is to be done since the Gaul stayed on their side of the water, but he knows the importance of appearance, and there is little appearance more frightening than his knights when armoured for battle.

Yes, the Gaul. That may be a problem, I mused. I held him in my hand and shifted him away from the Welshman on my desk. Each one of these small wooden markers represented one of the tribes who would soon be arriving in Camelot. The Gaul is carved with a long nose that threatens to topple him over, and a thin sword in his hand. I placed him on the map of Camelot I have unfurled on my desk. The map itself was a beauty. Each floor of the castle was picked out in deep, black lines of ink, with gold leaf used to show pathways and staircases. Another map, showing a smaller Camelot but with the grounds of the castle rendered in exquisite detail, lay above it on the desk. The map of the grounds was lush with the greens of the forest, since the map was created in Summer, when the whole land seemed drowsy with heat and fat with growth. Now it is deep Midwinter, and snow blankets as far as I can see from my window. The green of the map was almost painful to look at, as if it were all the colour and life left in the world. Now the monks who produced these beautiful things had to warm their inks over the fire before they could use them, and the vellum they draw on was brittle in the cold, dry air. I move the wooden Gaul to a meadow that separates the North tower from the orchards. The Gaul have decided they will not stay in the Castle for the duration of the meeting but will camp outside. They do not trust us. I do not blame them. Trust is the kind of currency first built with high walls and sharp steel. After that, trust can come a little easier.

Next in my hand was a smaller, wider piece of wood carving – a man with a beard reaching down to his grotesquely over-sized feet. His eyes bugged out from the wood as if he feared something. In his hand he carries what could be an axe, or more likely a miner's pick. The Welshman. Before I could decide where to lodge the Welsh, a hand plucked the wooden figure from mine.

"If you will permit me a polite suggestion, perhaps behind the sties? Although the pigs may complain of the stench...." Sir Hector de Maris said, staring the Welshman in his bulging eyes in a manner he would not dare to try with the real thing.

"I will not permit you, nor is that polite," I said as I plucked the Welshman away from his hands and placed them on the ground floor of the castle, in a large, airy room off the dining hall. "What brings a young gallant like yourself to this inky tower?"

"When there are battles, I carry no arms. When there are no battles, I carry messages." Hector passed me a scroll. All the young Knights talked like that, as if they were in a book, or constantly being overheard by the ladies of court. They were as quick with their words as they were with their swords, and Hector de Maris, by virtue of being Lancelot's younger brother, has more pressure on him than most to exemplify what being a Knight really means.

"And what do you mean by that?" I glared at him with my one good eye. The boy paled slightly. The problem with talking this new courtly speech is that you're bound to offend someone eventually by virtue of saying so much.

"My apologies, Sir Ascamore," Hector began. I could almost see him arranging the fancy words for an apology in his mind. "I realise some of us are blessed to have the choice to still go into battle and defend Camelot, whereas some serve

26

in other ways—" He gestured towards the maps, markers and scrolls that line my chambers.

"Peace, Hector. I jest. Given the choice, I would much rather do battle with paper and ink than sword and shield." Lying, like plain speaking, is also not part of Arthur's plan for his lands, but I think I had earned the right. And I despised the pity of others.

Hector relaxed and stretched himself out in the chair on the opposite side of my desk. He wasn't as handsome as his older brother, but nor was he as severe. Lancelot's fervour for Camelot and Arthur scares me sometimes; it often seems like the kind of devotion that masks a deep conflict. Hector has no such problems; he's happy just to be here.

I took the message and unfurled it. I could already tell from the blue tinge on the vellum that it was from the Picts.

"What news from the North?" Hector asked. He was eager to see a Pict in the flesh, especially their women. "Will they come?"

"They will arrive within a week. They have stopped in Sarum to pay homage to the stones. The writer of the note adds—'I, a poor monk of advanced years, have been made to write this message at the point of a spear by a woman covered in ungodly symbols and blue chalk. I advise your most gracious Highness, the Honoured Arthur, to put them to the sword when they arrive upon Camelot. Fear not for your servant, these pagans can neither read nor write my words.'" I said, rolling the scroll up and filing it away in the innumerable square holes that lined my walls.

"My lord Ascamore, what will we do?" Hector looked aghast. Whether for the safety of the monk who wrote the letter, or for the suggestion that we butcher our guests on arrival I cannot say.

"The tournament grounds, I think." I pulled another wooden figure from a square cubby, this one a sly looking fellow with daubs of blue on his face. I placed it on the empty patch of ground where in the Spring the grass would be flattened by horses whirling back and forth in the spectacle of a jousting tournament.

"But they're threatening our subjects, the people we have taken oaths to protect!" Hector said. He was a boy at twenty, who only took his oaths last Summer, and the Winter chill hadn't got to him yet.

"I realise that, Sir Hector, and I shall have words for them upon their arrival. However, please do not forget the sheer scope of what we are attempting here—for the first time, Arthur will sit down with the Gauls, the Picts, and even the Welsh and talk of peace, and of trade, and of the one God. They will sign their names, and the names of their sons and brothers to a pretty piece of vellum that will ensure peace in the Kingdom. There will be feasts. There will be diverse entertainments. I daresay there will be arguments. But there will be the signing of the treaty, I can promise you that. That is worth any disgruntled monk, or any amount of inconvenience here in the halls of Camelot." I sank back into my chair. It was the most I'd said to anyone since losing my eye at Dungeness. Odd that I should have spoken at such length to this boy I don't know. Odd that I should want to believe my own words so badly. Such an odd season.

Chapter Three

Seven days passed, and the snows deepened. From my chamber windows (and fear not, I will leave there soon, this is not the sort of story that takes place in one room) I could no longer see the nearby church that Arthur had built outside Camelot's walls. There, any of his subjects could find sanctuary and aide, should they be willing to swear oaths to uphold Arthur's laws and worship the one God. The former seemed to be no problem for most, the laws were the fairest this land has known, and yet the latter was more difficult. The common people seemed reluctant to give up their old gods, no matter how little joy and peace they may have brought them in return for worship. We gave them clean, well-hewn crosses and a loaf of bread for every effigy of their past they bring us. The few we had received are odd, misshapen things, hooved like goats, yet with scales like a fish. It was one of my many tasks to record these items on parchment, with some

28

indication where they came from, before burning them on my hearth. I wondered what the delegates arriving from every point of the compass would make of it all. Whether they worship these strange beasts as well, or whether they would embrace Arthur's religion as well as his ideal. Peace may be an easier thing to sell to them than the Prince of Peace, I suspected.

The Gauls represented the least problem and arrived before schedule. Their envoy was a serious looking fellow despite being only in his early thirties, who kneeled before our King in the throne room, then kneeled before the altar in the church. Perhaps realising how many good men they had lost at Dungeness, they now knew how weak they may appear to their crude barbarian neighbours in Germania, hidden away in their vast, dark forests and impenetrable mountains. Having friends of us Britons and our allies may be exactly what he was after. I vowed to make sure that envoy Cudius's stay here was uneventful, and that he may even be seen to enjoy himself and smile at some point.

I walked with Cudius over to the meadow outside the castle walls where they may strike camp. It was bitterly cold, but Gaulish Winters are harsher evidently, for Cudius didn't even seem to shiver in his grey robes. Flecks of snow fall into the long, black hair he wears pushed back from his high forehead, and his cold grey eyes chill me more. We talked of his journey, of the beauty of Camelot and neither of us mentioned Dungeness, or my missing eye. Once he had walked the perimeter of the meadow, noting with pleasure its proximity to the Church, Cudius declared it satisfactory. His contingent of twenty men started to erect tents and lay fires with whatever dry, dead wood they could find in the forest.

I hoped that all our guests may be so temperate, but the shrill sound of horns that woke me the next morning made me realise how vain that hope was. Quickly, the whole court dressed and assembled in the throne room, ready for the next envoy. Riders were sent out in the direction of the horns, to see them safely through the mists and snow to their destination. The way is hard though, and it is not until full noon that the riders return, escorting a train of caravans pulled by ponies so thick and stout they look more like boars. Despite having Camelot in their sights, they continue to blow ramshorns in a cacophony. The Welsh had arrived.

When their envoy stepped down from his caravan, I thought some enchantment had been woven. Ryrid Penbras, for that was his name, looked so much like the wooden marker I had placed on the hall on my map, that I thought It had come alive. Ryrid was as short as his beard was long, and his eyes bulged from his head like fried eggs. As he stumbled over to me, I could tell that he had been drinking. After almost falling on the slick ice under Camelot's great gate, he hugged me tightly to him.

"Camelot!" He exclaimed, in a thick, gravelly voice that could have travelled from one side of the valley, under a hill and then to the other side of the valley. "Camelot! And you, my boy? Are you my King Arthur?"

"I do not have that privilege, Ryrid Penbras of the Welsh. His Highness waits within." I gestured to the caravan to make their way through the gate, where Camelot's army of stewards would unload them and set them up in their hall.

Ryrid, who had not let his arms fall from my sides, pushed me back a little and gave me a shrewd glare. "I should have known! Too young to be a King, and one too few eyes! But you know my name, my boy, so you have power over me. Tell me yours, or damn you."

I pulled away slightly. Ryrid's breath was strong with what smelled like mead, and his brightly embroidered leather jerkin smelt like many long miles. I was not made for the diplomacy that Arthur had tasked me to, but with one eye what else was there?

"My name is Sir Ascamore, one of the Knights of Arthur's fellowship. I bid you welcome to Camelot. Please, let us go through to the throne room so you may meet his Highness, and then perhaps to chapel so you may pray?"

Ryrid finally stopped his embrace of me. Camelot air had never smelled so good as when I could take a few steps back.

"Pray?" Ryrid said, looking as vexed as if I had suggested

we kiss. "Why for, boy? Journey's over. The hard part is done, and the gods have been with us. No need to pray, my boy, we're all still alive."

With a shake of his head, Ryrid left me at the gate to join his men in preparation for their audience with the King. As it would turn out, the Welsh chieftain was wrong, there was to be plenty of need for prayer, and not all of us would live through the next few days.

Chapter Four

The Picts were the last to arrive, which I should have foreseen. Their journey must have been a hard one, for not only did most people fear their very appearance, but the Pict chieftain was an old man of seventy, who had to be helped down from his caravan by a woman I assumed was the chieftain's daughter. His name, I knew from messages, was Nechtan, and I greeted him at the gate.

"Noble Nechtan, of the mighty Picts, I bid you welcome on King Arthur's behalf to Camelot. I shall show you to where you may camp before escorting you to the King's throne room for an audience." Throughout this speech, this small, wizened man stared at me. His dull, green eyes were almost lost in a map of wrinkles and blue woad. He was beardless, but tufts of thick hair surrounded his ears and nostrils. When he didn't reply, I wondered if I must go through the whole damned speech again. Instead, his daughter stepped forth and took Nechtan's arms. She looked me full in the eye, which a woman had never done before, and gestured me to lead on. Without a word, the three of us led the Pictish caravans, which showed signs of many miles of hard travelling, to the snow-covered meadow where men would clash all of a Summer's day.

Each of the Picts were scrawny, yet none seemed to let the cold bother them. Like the Gauls, they were used to long Winters, and seemed amazed at the layers of fur I wore over my leather jerkin. None talked directly to me, but only to each other, using that strange, harsh Pict language. I could understand a few words, having been given quick lessons by

31

Merlin on each of the languages spoken by each envoy. They were pointing at the sky, which as far as I could tell was empty of all features. Maybe they saw omens in them that I could not. I did not bother asking them if they wanted to visit the church on the other side of their encampment, the circles and shapes they had drawn over themselves contained no crosses, only unending spirals and loops, ending who knew where.

"What is your name?" I asked the chieftain's daughter. They had finished breaking camp, their rude animal skin tents were now lit from within with campfires.

"Modwenna." The first word I had heard her speak. The Pict language sounded thick in my ear, like smoke and mud.

"Well, Mistress Modwenna, may I accompany you and your father to my King Arthur, who waits in the throne room?" I said.

"Aye, you may." She turned to me and smiled. I noticed with a shiver that her two eyeteeth had been sharpened into points. "But it shall be a task for the ages. My father was eaten by bears ten Winters ago. If you have a mind to, you may accompany myself and my man Nechtan to your Arthur."

I confess to a lack of discretion here, and I may have even gasped. That wizened old man and this young woman were husband and wife? My astonishment must have been as easy to read on my face as if it were written in woad.

"He may have seen a few more seasons pass than I have, but he's still strong enough to fill a belly, Knight of Arthur," Modwenna said. I swear she was enjoying seeing my discomfiture, and only put me out of my misery to assemble her aged husband and a few advisors together in a group to meet the King. I was struck by how much deference the men paid her, and not one seemed to chafe beneath her quick instructions. Picts had never had a Queen in all their history, it was only men who were considered fit to rule. Maybe Modwenna would be the first, I mused, watching the Pict envoy march over the tournament field to the gates of Camelot.

"There," I whispered under my breath. "Here are the last of

the materials, my King. Stitch this motley together as you see fit."

I should have been pleased. All the envoys had arrived safely and seemed ready to talk of peace. And yet, as I trudged my way back to Camelot, I could not help looking to the skies, as the Picts had done, and feeling as if it were going to crush us all at any moment.

Chapter Five

Perhaps this feeling of gloom was the recognition that my tasks were only half done. Whilst I would not take part in the negotiations in the throne room (that task would fall to wiser minds, thank the Risen Christ) I was still responsible for housing, feeding and entertaining the envoys. To that end, I made my way through the long, winding corridors that ran under the great halls of Camelot to the kitchens. The smell of roasting meats and stewing vegetables guided my route, and by the time I arrived in the kitchens my stomach was growling.

"Sir Ascamore! Greetings!" a man said, turning from one of many large cauldrons bubbling over the dozen fire pits that dotted the kitchen floor. Around each of these boys were turning spits of meat, peering into their own cauldrons and generally running about with platters and knives. Along the back wall, a hive of ovens kept in warmth in dark recesses, occasionally disgorging thick loaves of bread or spiced cakes. The impression was not dissimilar to a battlefield, with armies of boys running about their tasks, and once accomplished, running back to the man who had greeted me for more instructions. All was a whirl of heat, noise and barely controlled chaos.

"Greetings, Philip!" I said to the general of this sweating army. Philip had been with Arthur since almost the beginning, and rumour was he had witnessed the King as a boy draw Excalibur from the stone. Rumours that he had heated the stone and cooked bacon on it I did not pay any heed.

"How goes the preparations? The last envoy has arrived, so tonight we must welcome all with a great feast."

"I am well aware, Sir Ascamore. My boys were in a perfect fright when the news came that the Picts had arrived. I told them that their favourite meal is children who burn the bread, is that not so?" Philip asked me. He winked, playing to the group of children around him who were feeding the fire under the cauldron.

"Their teeth are certainly sharp enough," I said, thinking again of Modwenna. "And I doubt they will need little in the way of your napkins and knives."

"True barbarians, eh? I wonder what our King will make of that?" Philip said. I wondered too. Arthur always gave the impression of a man to whom dirt and grease would not dare stain. To sit down with drunken, puking Welshmen and flesh ripping Picts would be a trial for him. I do not mean to describe him as a prig, so don't take that as my meaning. It was merely that Arthur carried himself like a man who was not quite of our world. Too good for it, in all honesty. Even now, years after his death I can't help but think of what happened to him without tears. He had such hopes for all of us. Excuse me though, I digress. But that is an old man's prerogative and one I am lucky enough to be able to exercise. I was talking to the cook, Philip. He's long dead too.

"Our King will make of them a country, is the hope. Will you be ready to serve the feast at sunset?" I said.

"Of course, if only..." Philip trailed off, and waved his hands over the room. It was so full of noise and bustle he could have meant anything.

"Yes, Philip?" I asked, my mind already wandering on to the next problem to be solved.

"The damn fires keep blowing themselves out. I'm having to send boys down to the crypts every ten minutes to keep them burning," Philip said. I did not envy the boys sent to do it. Philip's kitchen, like everything in Camelot, was built to the most modern specifications. The floor we stood on was a false one, built over a low, dark room where fires were constantly kept burning through specially prepared sods of peat and a regulated influx of air. Like most innovations, it was Merlin's doing, and I was going to tell Philip it was

Merlin's problem to solve when I noticed a few of the kitchen boys standing around the narrow staircase that led to the fire chamber. They were nervously pacing around it, evidently deciding who would go down and stoke the fires or unblock the airways next. One boy was more vocal than the rest in his refusal, and he kept his arms crossed, the hands buried deep under his armpits.

"I ain't going down there again, I done my turn!" He was saying to another boy, who was nervously looking down the staircase into the black hole from which heat and a red glow wafted out.

"What's this boy, no courage?" I said, moving up behind him. He turned and paled a little, and I thought once again how much the eyepatch frightened people.

"No, milord. Even if I wanted to go down there I can't work the bellows or shift the peat," the boy said, quietly.

"Why on earth not?" I asked. The other boys had vanished back into the steam and noise of the kitchens, some ferrying trays of freshly baked spice cakes to platters by the windows to cool down. My nose twitched and my stomach growled.

"My hands, milord," the boy whispered. He drew them out from under his arms. They were wrapped in bandages of white muslin, through which I could see patches of black and red. I carefully unrolled the strips, revealing two fingers missing at the second knuckle on one hand, and one finger entirely gone on the left. The skin was cracked and red at the edges of patches of black flesh as big as a coin. In the middle of the black patches the skin had started to break, and bubbles of pus had leaked out. It must have been agony.

"I didn't burn myself, sir." He finally looked me in the eye, as if I were about to strike him for clumsiness.

"I know you didn't, boy," I said. I knew these wounds. Had seen them myself on men who had been caught out in the frozen wilderness when we had harried the Picts ten years ago. Somehow, in a heated kitchen surrounded by fire and steam, this boy had been afflicted with frostbite.

"Tell me, boy, have you ever met a wizard?"

35

Chapter Six

When Merlin planned the construction of Camelot, he gathered together stonemasons and carpenters from all over the country. The men who had designed the great church of Canterbury jostled over the designs with the men who had designed Arthur's long ships, neither sure if they were looking at plans for buildings or a fleet. All were puzzled. Masonry was supported by wood and vice-versa. Staircases, still a thing most people in the land had never seen before, were grand and wide, not tucked away. The throne room was to have a ceiling as high as the tallest tree in the kingdom, with intricate carvings covering every inch of the wood. The masons and the shipwrights shook their heads, anticipating the whole thing would fall like a house of cards, but for seven years Merlin fed them, paid them and whilst Arthur traversed the length and breadth of his nation (with a two-eyed Sir Ascamore in his retinue) Camelot was built beam by beam, stone by stone, with such art that when it was finished no man could believe it so.

The achievement that Merlin was most proud of, and he was a man to never hide his pride, was the eyrie that perched on top of the throne room. Built twice as tall again as that massive chamber, from there a man could see further than anywhere else in the kingdom. The tower itself was round and contained only one room at the top of a spiral staircase that could take the wind out of Arthur's youngest and strongest Knights. I had been neither of these things for a long time, and when I reached the landing that led on to Merlin's chambers, with the frostbitten boy in tow, I had to take a rest before even speaking.

"Boy," I managed to gasp, "bang on that door with all your might."

The boy looked at me strangely, and I immediately bit my tongue. Stupid. If that boy was to give the heavy oak door a whack his frostbitten hands might just fall to pieces.

"Give it a kick," I murmured. The boy smiled. He was a brave lad. Most of Philip's kitchen boys would have never come this near to Merlin's chambers. Even a few of Arthur's

Knights would have had second thoughts. When the church had been built outside Camelot and the alms had been distributed in exchange for old totems, most people assumed the old ways had given way to the new God, the one God. Where that left Merlin, people said, nobody knew.

"Entrate!" said a voice behind the door, and I stepped past the boy and into the wizard's chambers.

Merlin, as was his usual custom, was perched behind the round table that dominated the circular room. Every inch of the table was taken up with books, parchments and bowls in which foul-smelling bits of unnameable filth smouldered. Whether they were the natural experiments that Merlin so dearly loved, or food from the kitchens that had sat out for too long I would not like to say. The walls were covered with bookcases, with high narrow windows above to let in the rarefied air of this great height. He briefly looked up as we came into the room, then returned to reading.

"My Knight of Ashes, finally made it to the high nest, eh?" Merlin said, eventually. I knew the nickname was not a pleasant one. As I was responsible for burning the effigies of the old gods, Merlin would give me short shrift.

"As you see, my lord Merlin," I said.

"And have they given you a squire? I think that might be a little wasteful, no? Unless we are at war with the kingdom of the blind," Merlin said. I had thanked him many times over the years for saving my life at Dungeness, but both of us knew that some part of me would rather be dead than half a Knight. We had just never said that out loud to each other.

"Look at the boy's hands." I pushed the boy forward. Merlin, who had little interest in argument, immediately pushed on the tiny spectacles that lay on his desk and leaned in for a closer look.

"Well, we both know what this is, Ashes," Merlin said, after carefully unwrapping the bandages. I winced to see such damage again. The black colour of the rot was the colour of death.

"Aye, frostbite. Same as we saw plenty of back up North, fighting the Picts," I said.

"Who are now our honoured guests!" Merlin said. He searched amongst the jumble of his desk for something. "How goes the meeting of the tribes?"

"Not my concern, I am fortunate to say. I am merely responsible for getting them quarters to camp in and food in their bellies."

"And to entertain them, no doubt." Merlin looked up sharply. That reminded me, the actors would be arriving this evening, and it was my duty to greet them.

"Aye, and that."

"Too warm for frostbite." Merlin pushed aside a pile of papers and produced a small jar with a waxed seal.

"Exactly," I said. "And Philip doesn't let his boys out of Camelot to waste time. Especially not with our honoured guests around. He was injured in the firepits, below the kitchen floors."

"More of a place for heatstroke than frostbite." Merlin had taken the seal off this jar, and was rubbing a thick, oily paste over the boy's hands. The boy flinched at first, and then relaxed. Whatever else the paste did, it made the boy numb to the pain.

"Child, you're going to stay here and help me for a while, while this brave Knight finds out what did this to your hands, you understand?" Merlin asked. He started to search around his desk for something else.

"I can't move my hands, sir. But there's no pain," the boy said.

Merlin smiled sadly, his hand finally resting on a small curved blade that he held in the flame of a candle until it smouldered.

"There will be, child. There always is," Merlin said. I placed a hand on the boy's shoulder and gave it a squeeze. Frostbite was terrible, but the scraping away of the dead flesh would be even worse. At least the boy would have a story to tell and may even keep a few of the fingers he had left on his hands. I left the room as quickly as I could.

At the bottom of the staircase I could no longer hear the boy's screams, and I thanked God for it. Waiting for me was

Sir Hector, dressed in armour so polished and clean it could never be taken onto a battlefield, and a tall, thin man dressed in motley. I thought at first he was wearing a mask, his face was so pale and still, but as I spoke to Sir Hector I saw the mysterious man's face curve into a slow smile. It did not make him look any the less strange.

"Sir Ascamore, how goes it?" Sir Hector asked. He looked a little shaken. Maybe he had heard the screams from Merlin's chambers. It would have confirmed what a lot of the younger knights said about Merlin—he was a dangerous man, who clung onto old ways. I suppose they were right.

"Fair, Sir Hector. All of the tribes have arrived, as I'm sure you are aware. The preparations for the feast progress. And who have you brought me here? He looks chilled, does he need to sit by the fire?" I asked, turning to the grinning man in motley.

"May I present to you Master Bulvak, the leader of a troupe of actors who wish to provide diversions and entertainments to the King's honoured guests," Sir Hector said.

"And you will provide this good service for no expectation of reward other than serving the King? Or will you require payment?" I asked Bulvak. I hated actors, always had. I had seen them perform stories of old Kings that I knew to be untrue, and the way they wielded a wooden sword would have shamed a Camelot maidservant beating the dust out of a rug.

"We will perform for any reward you deem just, good sir Knight," Bulvak said. I had heard a lot of strange accents in the last few days, but his was the oddest. High, reedy, and yet clear as a bell. His face was of an unusual cast too – handsome enough, as befits an actor, but broad and flat somehow, with eyes that curved upwards at the ends. An odd fellow, but I did need to organise some diversions for the tribes.

"Where do you hail from, actor?" I asked. "I have been all over these lands, and I do not recognise your name, nor your accent. Are you a Norseman?"

"No, good Sir Knight, not a Norseman. I come from the

North, past the lands of the Picts, over the frozen ocean." He certainly sounded like an actor; I could tell Hector was impressed.

"I know no frozen ocean, but I have heard of a land of ice past the land of the Picts."

"Indeed," Bulvak said. "The Winters down here are like the summers to us."

I wondered what it was with our guests that they seemed to not mind the cold. My own bones ached for the warm sun.

"Excellent. You have a full troupe with you? Good. Sir Hector will show you where you can lodge, perhaps in the old stable-house?" I said. Both Hector and Bulvak agreed that this would suit, and I sent them on their way. That was my life now, away from the battlefield. Uprooting problems before they even became problems, and certainly before the King could notice them. There was an art to this diplomacy, much like in learning the sword or the lance, and most evenings I could tell myself that this new life was enough—watching and making sure everything fell into place.

Chapter Seven

That evening, I would see how all my arrangements could quickly fall apart. It began well enough—Philip and his boys paraded into the Great Hall with so many dishes and platters of good things that I could not keep track of them. I helped myself to some of the roast lamb and watched the Welshman, Ryrid, dig into a bowl of sheep heart's stew with glee. The Gaul envoy, Cudius, seemed most impressed with the lamprey pie that was laid before him, and I sighed with relief. The Gauls were notoriously particular about food and drink, and if we could impress him, the job would be much easier. The Picts were a little more hesitant, and sat at their long table constantly looking around, as if they were to be set on at any minute. I could hardly blame them, the Picts and the Welsh had warred for many years, and the fighting had not always been honourable. However, after Philip himself had poured a cup of hot, spiced mead to every Pict, they had seemed to relax. All except Modwenna, who stood behind her aged husband and seemed to fix each person she laid her gaze upon as if she were sizing them up for an arrow between the eyes.

And in the centre of it all sat my King. His table, at which I was honoured to sit with a dozen other Knights and Merlin, was against the far wall, facing the fire. From there, the three long tables were laid out, radiating from Arthur like rays of the sun. Each tribe could see the King, his crown and the elaborate tapestry that ran the length of the room. It depicted, with a little embellishment, the stories they had all heard – a boy drawing a sword from a stone in the middle of a dark forest, the same boy (a little older now) seated at the head of a round table, surrounded by Knights of the realm, and finally the same boy (now a man) slaying a dragon singlehandedly. Excalibur disappeared into the beast's throat with the ease a of a man carving a chicken. Power to slay a beast and unite men. I hoped the message wouldn't be lost on the visiting tribes—the King is a fair man, but one who would use force to ensure that fairness was triumphant.

Our hospitality was flawless, not one person had an empty cup or empty plate at any time. As the envoys ate and drank, I hoped they would reflect on this largesse, which held two important lessons for them. Firstly, that hospitality was a matter of great importance, and that the outsider, the stranger and the visitor were to be treated as well as the highest chief. Secondly, the abundance of food and drink spoke to the herdsmanship and farming skill that the new society could call on. By successfully harvesting a crop and gaining an excess of grain to trade or to store, we planned towards the future. By herding animals, and conserving the wild animals to hunt, we would never run low. Each tribe that signed Arthur's concordance were to be accompanied home by a priest, a mason and a clerk who would teach and impart the wisdom of Camelot to every part of the land. Would that cure man of his lust for war, I wondered? Looking around, I could see hopeful omens—Ryrid the Welshman was looming over Nechtan the Pict, Ryrid telling a story and waving a jug of mead around. I didn't know how much Nechtan understood, but he was smiling happily. Cudius and Modwenna stood to one side, talking. Neither looked happy, but they both seemed like strangers to happiness. That too, I hoped, was common ground. Cold fish were fine as long as they swam in the same direction, and in the same stream.

Merlin beckoned me over as I was making a round of the room, greeting a few there, instructing Philip's boys to replenish this guest or the other.

"Knight of Ashes! You are to be congratulated, everything seems to be sailing on smooth waters," Merlin said. He sat in front of an empty plate and cup; no man had ever seen him eat or drink.

"We shall see. They begin discussing the King's concordance tomorrow, and I think they will find more to disagree with there than they have with the meat and drink," I said. Secretly I was pleased with the praise, but humility was in fashion that year, and I demurred as often as I could.

"Maybe, but there is not a chief here who will forget this night, and when they return to their tribe they will try to do the same thing, if only to show off their largesse. Maybe we should send one of Philip's proteges home with each envoy, along with the masons, the clerk and the clerics?" Merlin pondered.

"Speaking of Philip's lads, did you manage to save the hands of that boy I brought you?" I said. Arthur himself was now walking through the great hall, and with a thrill of pride I saw him pay equal mind to Philip's boys, Welshmen of no real importance in Ryrid's retinue, and even the woman Pict, Modwenna. As she and Arthur spoke briefly, I may have even seen her curtsy a little. Never a ceasing of wonders.

"Hands, yes. Fingers…." Merlin trailed off, and I saw a quick grimace through his thick, grey beard. I know he would have done his best for the boy, but my spirit deflated a little. A kitchen boy needed dexterity, a quickness of the hands. A kitchen boy robbed of that was as useless as a half-blind Knight.

"What happened to him? He wasn't burned, those fingers were frozen off."

"I agree, and by something colder than anything a Camelot

Winter can provide. So maybe look beyond Camelot, Knight of Ashes?"

"The only thing that isn't of Camelot here is our honoured guests, surely you can't expect me to accuse them? Accuse them of what, more's the point?" I was getting angry. There were too many people milling around, the heat of the room grew unbearable and I couldn't stop thinking of the ruins of that boy's hands.

Merlin didn't reply, causing me more frustration. He turned from me and seemed to study the tapestry above us intently. I could waste no more time on him, the actors would need to be brought in before everyone was too drunk.

I found Bulvak and half a dozen of his troupe waiting outside the Great Hall, ready to go. They carried a rolled backdrop behind them, and wore dented, old armour that would probably dissolve under a heavy rain. Each of the troupe looked more or less like their leader, and all stared at me through those tapered eyes as I gave them instructions where they could set up.

"And what story do you have for us this evening, Master Bulvak? Nothing bawdy, I hope," I asked as his people set up the stage in the Great Hall. I was glad to see that the tables had been rearranged in lines in front of where the actors would perform, as per my instruction. Sir Hector shepherded the audience into their chairs, and the Great Hall became full of low murmurs of expectation.

"Nothing of that sort, good Sir Knight," Bulvak said. "A story from the bible. Very instructive."

I let them get on with it, and retreated to the rear of the room. Arthur sat directly in front of the stage, with Ryrid, Cudius and Nechtan behind him. Merlin was watching the actors very carefully, a strange look on his face. Perhaps even the great Merlin had never met men from the land of ice.

Their performance was a strange one, I am sorry to say. Their theme was the destruction of the temple of King Solomon in Jerusalem. I knew this story from the sermons given in the new church, of how the wicked King Nebuchadnezzar of the Babylonians had put Solomon's temple to plunder, killing the priests and looting the treasure. This was after a siege that lasted thirty months, in which the priests of the temple beseeched God for help, but to no avail. The sacking of the temple led to the burning down of most of Jerusalem. After the city was razed to the ground and its rulers had been taken into captivity, a few people had been left behind to till the land and grow what they could on the ruins of once-mighty Jerusalem.

It was a good story, and the actors performed their parts well, but as the performance went on I felt a sense of disquiet, which was shared by others in the audience too. It struck me as odd that Bulvak, playing the part of Nebuchadnezzer, should not be dressed in the finery of a warrior-king, but instead wore simple clothes, almost rags, which showed where his body had been painted a strange turquoise colour. Likewise, the three actors playing his army wore similar garb, and turquoise patterns were painted on their skin. They also carried spears, whereas I had been led to believe the Babylonians prided themselves on their skills with the sword.

The story itself was exciting enough, with attempts made by the priests inside to break the siege, each time repelled using brutal force by Bulvak and his men. Inside the partition on the stage that represented the temple wall, the priests practiced what I can only assume to be ancient Jewish rituals to prepare themselves for the inevitable. The three actors playing the priests crowded around a stone tablet (one of the commandment tablets of Moses, I thought) to which they prayed too, and even pantomimed the very realistic sacrifice of a white hare over. As the fake blood of the animal dripped down to the tablet, I assumed Nebuchadzeer's army was bedding in for the Winter, for horns behind the scenes blew strange, eerie sounds like a howling storm. Artfully, thick white furs were thrown over the besiegers, suggesting thick snow. I had assumed Jerusalem to be a warm place, given how often the priest would read to us of deserts, but I suppose each place must have a Winter and spring, and this Winter was evidently a bad one. Two of Bulvak's army did not rise from the white furs under which they were buried, but mimed a violent death through cold and exposure with a good many screams and contortions of the face. This did not deter Bulvak though, and with his one remaining soldier, they finally smashed through the partition and entered the 'temple.' The priests made no move to defend themselves, and were hacked to pieces through some deft spear thrusts and more than a subtle amount of fake blood. Once the priests were dead, Bulvak seized upon the stone tablet, whilst the horns representing the Winter winds grew in volume. It was all very exciting, but very strange, and I wondered if there were details I had missed in the Book of Kings, which told of Nebuchadnezzar sacking Jerusalem.

When the makeshift curtain descended over the bloody scene, the audience did not know how to respond. Arthur turned to his guests to gauge their reaction, and I moved with him, curious to see how they had enjoyed this queer tale. Ryrid the Welshman was asleep, but at least he was smiling. Cudius merely smiled politely, but his eyes remained cold. It was Nechtan that shocked me most of all. The Pict chief's eyes still gazed on the stage, as if there was going to be a second act, and yet his cheeks ran with tears, cutting through the thick woad on his face, and dripping on to the tattered robe he wore. How strange stories could effect people so, I thought. But one thing was for certain, this was not the ending I wanted for the first night of the meeting of concordance, and as my King swept out of the room followed by his personal guard of Knights, he did not look me in the eye.

Chapter Eight

Whether it was the heat of the room, the pressures of the arrangements I had been making, or the strange play by Bulvak's troupe, I cannot say, but that night I could not sleep. By rights I should have been exhausted, and glad of the brief snatch of oblivion, but instead I paced in front of the fire in my bedchambers and tried to order my mind. Why had Nechtan wept at the end of the play? Did he feel so strongly for the murder of Jewish priests over one thousand years ago? And what had happened to that boy's hands to leave them so

45

frostbitten and ruined? So many strangers walking the halls of Camelot. So many things that could go awry before the tribes agreed to be ruled by one King. And what if they refuse? What if they don't want a mason to accompany them back, set them to backbreaking mining for stone just so their rotten twig shacks wouldn't fall down in the storms? What if they didn't want our advice about what to plant and where, and how to treat a pig that had trotter rot? What if they would just prefer to steal from their neighbours until the whole land had a sword at each other's throats?

I felt myself as I often had in the midst of a battlefield, constantly looking around, knowing a threat could come from any direction at any time. I was the order in the chaos. The chivalry in the battlefield.

I was going to pace a trench in the stone flags of my bedchambers if I was not careful.

Time for bed, I decided, whether sleep would visit me there or not. I carefully unwound the leather strap that held my eyepatch in place, and started to undress. I had barely unbuckled my tunic, however, when the silence of the night was pierced by a scream, and a curious sound like bedclothes being folded and unfolded very rapidly. I went to my window, overlooking the main courtyard and the Great Hall. There was no movement, and the only other light burned high up in Merlin's eyrie.

Suddenly, the courtyard below began to fill with shadows, rushing towards something on the other side of the Great Hall. I couldn't see what the cause of this swarming was, but a dozen people were already making their way there. Shrugging a fur around my shoulders, I ran down the spiral staircase, my heart aching at the thought of yet another problem to deal with on the road to concordance.

At the bottom of the staircase I almost collided with Sir Hector de Maris, rushing out of the Knight's barracks.

"Did you hear that scream?" he asked me. Sir Hector looked flushed, his eyes wide.

"Yes, follow me, Sir Hector. Are you armed?" I asked. Chief amongst my concerns was the thought that some of the bad blood between the tribes had spilled out onto Camelot's grounds. If that was the case, the whole concordance would never happen—if Arthur couldn't ensure safety in his own home, no-one would trust him to rule the country.

Sir Hector reached under the wolf fur he wore around him and showed me the pommel of his sword. I hoped we wouldn't need it.

The two of us followed the shadows in the courtyard to the far side of the Great Hall, where a large group were massing. Torches had finally been lit and threw weird shadows on all sides of the courtyard. A light snow was beginning to fall. I pushed my way through the crowd, seeing a fair few Welshmen, Gauls and Picts amongst them. Lancelot represented the King, and he waved me over to what appeared to be a heap of rags on the ground.

As I got closer, however, I could see that sticking up from the rags were the spindly arms and legs of a man, patched here and there with woad. I did not need to remove the rags to identify the corpse of aged Nechtan; he was the only one of the Picts with the shrivelled, hoary fingernails and the spots of age running down his limbs. Blood leaked slowly from the body, sinking into the snow.

"The Pict chief?" Lancelot asked. He was wearing armour, and I wondered if he ever took it off. Arthur's dearest Knight. The one we should all aspire to be. God knows I had tried.

"Yes, Sir Lancelot. This is terrible," I said, my voice thin in the air. I heard a few gasps and mutters from the crowd behind us.

"Most dreadful," Lancelot agreed. I knew he was thinking that the concordance talks might not be salvaged after this, and not about the death of an old man.

We looked at each other. Him, the paragon of Knights, the most dangerous man in the country, and me, his former comrade, now reduced to a clerk who assigned beds. I realised after a few seconds that he wanted me to deal with this. Another problem to solve. I sighed.

"Sir Lancelot, please fetch me a shield to transport the body on. We're going to take it to the icehouse. Sir Hector, please disperse the crowd as best you can. If the Pict's second man is amongst them, tell him I will come to him directly." It was rather a thrill to give orders to one of the greatest men in the land and his brother, I just wish it had been under different circumstances.

Sir Hector and the Camelot stewards eventually got the crowd heading back to their camps, although God alone knows what rumours they would start when they got there. I had to find the truth of the matter before warfare broke out over breakfast.

When I was alone with the body, I finally risked flipping back the layers of rags and confirming that the body was indeed that of the Pictish chief, Nechtan. The rags were the remains of a hide cloak that looked like it had been shredded by a knife. However, I could see no stab wounds on the corpse. Instead the blood, which had rapidly stopped pooling out of the body, seemed to come from Nechtan's chest. It looked as if someone had stoved him in with a hammer or a mace, and broken ribs stuck out like a broken cage protecting his crushed heart. His arms and legs were shattered, and pointed out at queer angles, as if he had been thrown about like a doll. And yet there had only been one scream, I recalled. This looked like the handiwork of at least three men and the work of far more than a minute. How could somebody be killed so quickly and yet so brutally?

When Lancelot returned with the shield, we carefully bundled up the body and placed it on the long, flat, surface. No matter the care we took, we could still not avoid the loose rolling of broken limbs flopping and grinding about, and the sound reminded me of nothing more than tearing a roasted capon apart with my hands. I could tell Lancelot thought this work beneath him. Added to that, when he had returned with the shield, his expression seemed faintly disappointed that I had not already caught the villain who had done this and beheaded him in the courtyard. Arthur's best and bravest didn't work in the dark, carting bodies around like carrion after a battle. Leave that to the Knight of Ashes.

Chapter Nine

Merlin was waiting for me in the icehouse, sitting on a block of ice with densely packed straw around it. Like eating and drinking, Merlin never seemed to feel the cold like normal men either. When I greeted him, vapour plumed from my mouth, but he seemed as comfortable as a man sitting by a river's bank on a Summer's day.

"Wizard," Lancelot snarled at him as we pushed our way in. There was always a rivalry between the two men for Arthur's attentions, although courtly manners and love of the King kept in check.

"Good Sir Lancelot. A pretty pile of rags you've brought me here," Merlin said, gesturing to another block of ice at waist height where we could leave the body.

"Aye, pretty enough," Lancelot said, already backing out of the door with a bow, "and here I must leave you. The King must be informed immediately. May I tell his Highness this dreadful business will be concluded swiftly?"

Merlin looked at me, his eyebrow raised. He too, apparently, thought this was a knot for me to unwind.

"Tell His Highness that the matter is in hand. I shall have news for him in the morning." I hoped I sounded more confident than I felt. Lancelot must have thought so, because he smiled briefly and left quickly. I called after him to send his brother to me. I would need all the help I could muster.

Merlin ignored all this talk of Kings and concordances collapsing, and was already prodding the corpse with a long, thin dagger. He cut away the remains of the cloak, which were stiff with ice, far more so than I would have expected from the amount of time I thought the body had lain there.

"You heard the scream?" Merlin asked me. He was starting to probe the large wound on the Nechtan's chest, which as the rags were removed I could see ran the length of his body. No hammer or mace could be that large and do that much damage with one blow.

"Aye. I couldn't sleep. Tell me, Merlin, how could all this have been done in the time we heard the scream and then found his body?" I asked. Merlin looked up briefly from the gaping wound. He was measuring the width of it with a piece of string.

"A fine question. I suspect these injuries, as well as the death of this Pict, were done all at once, in no more than a second."

"Foolishness. We've both seen battle, Merlin. We both know that the body of a man can take plenty of damage before it departs its life. Even an old man like Necthan would have been able to put up a bit of a fight."

Merlin had moved on to measuring the cracked ribs with a tiny pair of callipers. "No weapon held by a man could damage the body so completely, and in one blow, as would have done for him. Go back to the beginning, Knight of Ashes, and use your eyes and any other senses you deem appropriate."

"The beginning?"

"The place where the body was found. I have no doubt he died there. If he had been killed elsewhere and moved, the trail would still be in the snow."

"A fair point." I wanted an excuse to leave the icehouse before those callipers probed deeper into Nechtan's wounds.

"And another thing," Merlin said as I was leaving. "He was holding something. There is an impression in his hand of a circular object, perhaps a medallion. He was clutching it so tightly I can still see the marks on his palms. He must have let it go in the spasms of death. Be a good fellow and see if he dropped it anywhere?"

Outside the icehouse I took in deep, lungfuls of the crisp night air. I breathed until it hurt, just so I would have something to take my mind away from the sight of Nechtan's corpse. Waiting for me was Sir Hector De Maris, looking pleased that he hadn't needed to come into the icehouse to fetch me. At some point he had found the time to strap armour on, and he looked strangely ghostlike in the moonlight.

We made our way back to the courtyard, finding the spot where Nechtan had been found easily. There was still blood everywhere, now starting to freeze. I prodded around the snow a little, thinking over what Merlin had said. Nechtan hadn't been killed elsewhere, that much was obvious. If the crowd hadn't gathered around I might have even been able to trace footsteps back to where they came from, and maybe found out how many men had brought him out here to kill him. Like tracking boar in the snow, I thought. Instead, the snow was a mess of footprints and blood.

"What do we do now?" Sir Hector said. I sighed, why ask me?

"Merlin seems to know how Nechtan was killed, but he won't tell me. He's also looking for a medallion he thinks the old man dropped. Try and find it please?"

Sir Hector smiled and began to look around the perimeter of the blood, glad to have a task. I focused back on the patch of ground where the old man had fallen. The more I stared, the more I thought something was amiss.

"Sir Hector, will you indulge me for a moment?" I was about to ask something a little silly, maybe even embarrassing. His brother would have cut my head off for suggesting it, but Sir Hector still had a lot of the boy in him, he might consider it a lark.

"Anything you require, Sir Ascamore."

"Fall backwards," I said.

"You jest."

"No, good Sir Knight. I know it's foolishness, but please fall backwards. Don't try and break your fall."

"My lord…"

"Pretend you've been struck with a Welshman's axe, if it makes it feel more noble. Make it seem like a military exercise." I smiled. Sir Hector still looked uncertain, as if the rest of his brother Knights were waiting around the cloisters that surrounded the courtyard, ready to jump out and laugh at him for his foolishness.

"Well, if it is your wish, and it aids the King…" Sir Hector said.

"It is and it does, Sir Hector."

Taking the time to adjust his armour and make himself look as noble as possible, Sir Hector stood straight, with his arms crossed over his chest like a saint's statue. When ready, he let himself fall backwards, keeping his legs as straight as tree trunks. When he landed, the snow puffed up from all over with a soft, almost pleasant sound. Showing solidarity, I crouched down next to him.

"Nothing broken, Sir Hector?" I asked. We smiled. If we were fools, at least we were fools together.

"Nothing but snowfall, Sir Ascamore," Sir Hector replied. I pondered that.

"Exactly," I said at length. "You, a young fellow in heavy armour, takes a fall in a snowy courtyard, and maybe sinks a finger's length into the snow. Nechtan takes a fall, and yet he sinks almost the way through to the flagstones of the courtyard. Through at least four finger's length of snow. He's not wearing armour—he's as skinny as a feather. Why does he sink deeper?"

"Maybe he was pushed down. There must have been a struggle," Sir Hector said. His teeth were beginning to chatter, but the cold seemed to be good for our brains.

"Maybe." To test the theory I stood a little away from Sir Hector and threw myself down onto the ground with as much force as I could muster. I sank maybe two finger's worth into the packed snow.

"Perhaps Nechtan was lying there for longer, and the snow piled up around him?" Sir Hector asked.

"Unlikely," I said, staring up at the sky. The Winter winds were strong, but there was not a cloud for them to throw around. I could see only the bright, full moon and what seemed to be thousands of stars. "We heard the scream, and he died almost immediately after. Not even the swiftest man on the scene said he had been alive when they arrived. Plus he was an old man. I don't give a curse how strong the Picts are, he couldn't have stood there for hours in a cleared patch of ground waiting for the snow to cover him. And why? And then why wait that long just to be killed?"

"I do not know." Sir Hector sounded regretful, and I was touched. Arthur would never say as much, but the death of an envoy was in my sphere of responsibility. My eyes wandered back to the skies, and a shooting star passed over us. I

52

pictured the rock, for that is what Merlin had once told me they were, on its long journey through the heavens, finally trailing down to earth. Something else Merlin had said, too. About how the rock would land with such force as to bury itself back into the earth. I closed my eyes again, and suddenly I could see how Nechtan could have almost hit the flagstones—he had been dropped from a great height, and the combination of the falling speed and the man's flailing arms had caused his injuries. His chest had been hit with one, large weapon very fast and very hard—the ground.

I explained this all to Sir Hector, who listened intently, with growing comprehension in his eyes. When I had done so, I leaped out of the snow, ready to find out from which window or rooftop Nechtan had met his fall.

"One more question, Sir Ascamore, since you are blessed with such wisdom this night?" Sir Hector asked. I walked over to where he lay, snowflakes already starting to burnish the polished armour of his chestplate.

"Yes, Sir Hector the Frosted?" I asked.

"How in the Lord's name do I stand up?" Sir Hector asked. I realised that he must weigh as much as a horse in all that armour, and that a fallen Knight would have a team of squires to help him up. At the look on my face, Hector began to laugh. After a moment, I did too.

We were still laughing like madmen a minute later, when a steward brought me a message—the Picts were leaving, and not even waiting for first light to do so.

Chapter Ten

Between a steward and I, we managed to lever Sir Hector off the ground and back on his feet. I told Sir Hector to check which of the nearest tower windows Nechtan could have fallen from, and I would meet up with him as soon as I had calmed the Picts. I followed the steward to the tournament grounds, where the Pict tents were already being dismantled. I stopped one of them, a skinny wretch who towered a head's height over me.

"Who gave the order to leave? Who's the chief now?" I

asked. He looked scared, perhaps thinking that killing Nechtan was part of a greater plan to kill all the Pict people.

"No chiefs, not anymore," he said.

"Where's the wife then, where's Modwenna?" I asked, almost shaking the man. He gestured towards the centre of activities, where the largest tent was lodged. I could see flurries of torchlight and movement within.

Modwenna met me at the flaps leading in, through which I could see men packing up furs and weapons into bundles. I could smell panic in the air, like the blood in the icehouse.

"I know you must blame us for the death of your husband, but I have sworn an oath to uncover what happened to him, please believe that, Modwenna," I said.

"My husband was not the best of chieftains, Knight of Arthur," Modwenna said. I was shocked. tThese were a cold people.

"No man deserves to die in that manner, though," I said. "He was thrown from a great height. Your people must be furious, but I beg of you to stay."

"Maybe my husband was thrown, Knight of Arthur. Maybe my husband walked into the air himself." Modwenna smiled a little at that, showing the tips of her filed teeth on her chapped lips. "He often made the worst choices for good reasons."

"Who's the new chief now?" I asked.

"Nechtan's brother. He only has a few more years on him, but he is a good man. Maybe…" She trailed off.

"Is he here? Can I speak to him?" I asked. Modwenna just shook her head.

"Please don't go. You'll appear weak in front of the Welsh. And the Gaul," I said.

This woman saw right through my appeal to vanity. "No. Maybe they stay, maybe they make peace. Not us," Modwenna said. Suddenly a Pict ran to her, whispered something in her ear and tried to pull her away.

"Please, we're not finished here. You must listen!" I said. I could hear the desperation in my voice.

"We must leave." Modwenna let herself be led away from the camp by the messenger.

Hoping to plead the case for concordance, I followed them. Modwenna was still being led by the young Pict, who would turn occasionally and whisper to her. He seemed scared, and his hand shook as he spoke. I kept a distance behind, hoping that being away from the camp, and Nechtan's tribe, might help her to see reason.

We progressed further away from the tournament grounds, and Camelot, the messenger lighting the way by the torch. I was quickly losing my sense of direction; the snow and the wind were picking up considerably. Maybe the Picts wouldn't even be able to leave if this carried on, the roads were going to become impassable eventually. I shivered in the light leather tunic I wore, and my boots began to soak and cling to my weary feet. What was I even doing following these Picts? I should be back at Camelot trying to find Nechtan's murderers. Trying to save the concordance.

Finally I saw a grey wall of ice in the distance, and I realised we had made it to the church. The pathway had been covered with snow, and a walk that would normally take ten minutes on a pleasant Summer's day had taken three times that. I walked up to the church wall and rested my hand against it, which immediately slid off and toppled me over. Again, I was lying in the snow, looking up. Seeing as how I seemed to have all my revelations from this angle, I stayed there, waiting for wisdom to descend. While nothing came to me but snowflakes, I did notice two odd things. Firstly, my hand had not slid off a patch of ice on the grey stone wall of the church, but instead a large sheet of ice that covered the entire side of the building. Icicles dangled down from the gargoyles that lined the roof, and the stained-glass windows were dull and opaque behind a layer of thick ice. The whole building appeared to be encased in ice, and as I got up and wandered around I could see that every entrance and exit had been sealed off. I wondered if any of the Brothers had been trapped within, and whether they could even breathe in that icy tomb.

The second thing I noticed was that the snow was still falling and yet there was not a cloud in the sky. The icy church was perfectly lit by a non-occluded moon and stars. Everything was still and white, as if the land was holding its breath, waiting for life to come back into it. The only thing with any life in it were Modwenna and the messenger, who I could see wandering around the other side of the Church.

"Have you seen this?" I asked Modwenna, pointing at the ice block that had been Arthur's new church.

"We have no time for your church, Knight." Modwenna scanned the treeline that separated the church from the fields beyond it that marked the beginning of Arthur's kingdom. "We have lost men."

"Men?" I said, "You mean it is not only Nechtan who has died this night?"

"Three of the tribe, all of whom fought alongside Nechtan in his youth, havevanished. This messenger came to tell me that one had been found by your church. Dead. Killed as my Nechtan was."

I was interrupted in replying by the shouts of the messenger, who summoned us over to a clearing just before the treeline. He was waving the torch over his head frantically.

"He is here!" The messenger screamed, and as Modwenna and I ran over to him we could see the cause of his frantic behaviour.

The corpse was a man's, and one not as old as Nechtan's but neither in the first blush of youth either. His arms and legs were twisted and broken, and I could see by the fallen branches that he had struck a tree on his descent. This may have been what had cracked his head open like an egg, but I guessed it was the fall that had killed him. His face looked shocked, as if he had been taken by surprise and died before he could even think about fighting back.

"He fell," I said to Modwenna. "He was taken to the top of those trees and thrown down. Why would someone do that?"

Modwenna turned to me, her eyes not full of anger or grief but pity. It was as if she desperately wanted to tell me something but knew I wouldn't understand.

"I must speak to Ryrid of the Welsh. There has been bad

56

blood between your tribes for centuries. If he had a hand in this, then we shall see him punished."

Modwenna flicked her pitying gaze from me, and focused on something over my shoulder, back towards the church, back towards Camelot. "He climbed to the tops of those trees? An old man with a foot cut off years ago to stop a rot?"

"He may have been dragged up there. Or hoisted, and then left to fall," I said, hearing how feeble my reasons were. My mind was desperately trying to find a middle ground through what was likely, what was possible, and what was rational. It was concordance as weak as the one that would be forged in Camelot after all this bloodshed.

"Perhaps, Knight, but what about him?" Modwenna said, pointing over my shoulder back to the ice-covered church.

I turned around, struck again by how eerie the church looked in its icy armour. Shards and needles covered every eave and doorframe, giving it a dangerous appearance. It was not until I saw a faint flutter of material in the breeze that I realised we had found another missing Pict. On top of the spire, a form was spread out, like a target pierced through the centre of a lance. That the man was dead there could be no doubt, the spire had pierced him through the middle of chest, and the force of the fall had caused such damage that I could see the hands and legs holding on to the trunk through a few tatters of flesh and rags. He had landed facedown. There were no trees or buildings he could have been thrown from anywhere near the church. It was as if he had fallen from the sky itself. The fact that death would have visited him in an instant was of no comfort.

"Lady Modwenna, what is killing your tribe?"

Chapter Eleven

Modwenna whispered a few words to the messenger, who ran back to Camelot. He kept on looking over his shoulder at the man skewered on the spire of the church. I assumed Modwenna had given him instructions to the rest of the tribe to continue preparations for leaving. This had all gone horribly wrong.

"Your King's peace is a fine thing, but we do not understand fine things," Modwenna said. She walked back to the corpse by the treeline and pried something from his fingers. She handed it to me; a crudely carved circular medallion. One side was blank, and felt as smooth ice, on the other side was a landscape, barren except for a few trees. The stars had been carved into the sky above it, except for a figure that looked like the silhouette of man. This silhouette towered over the trees and had no features at all except two large eyes, much bigger than would be suggested by the size of the figure. The eyes had been bored into and were dark no matter how much I turned the medallion to the light. It was an ugly thing. I recognised the size and shape of it matched whatever had been in Nechtan's hand when he died.

"If we want something, we take it. We are not crude people, not even cruel as you would understand the term, but we take. If we are hungry, we take. If we want a ship or a wagon, we take. This breeds hard people, yes? Breeds fighters?"

"Of course." I knew that only a couple of generations back the Britons had been no different. Arthur had given them something new, but peace and justice were still fragile, new ideas that were greeted with suspicion by most.

"Nechtan, he was the strongest of them all. Like your King, he gathered up other strong men, took them from their villages and made them help him take. If Nechtan took, everyone could take, you see? Stronger together, take more."

"No—" I began.

"I know, that is not what King Arthur teaches, he says the stronger you are, the more you must give. Strange idea. I doubt the Welsh will ever understand. The Gaul will do whatever he can to save his tribe. We will carry on taking."

"Who killed your husband?" I asked. The fear of the Picts was infecting me, and I kept on casting my eyes around, increasingly looking at that horrible clear sky from which snow was somehow following.

"His is the snow. His is the wind. His is the cold that kills."

"Who, damn you!"

"You already know. The men from the land of ice told you in their play. I enjoyed it more than Nechtan, but we always prefer it when the jokes are on other people, don't we Knight?"

"The play was about Nebuchadnezzar sacking the Temple of Solomon, not your husband," I shouted. The wind was picking up now, and shook the remains skewered on the steeple like a dog would throw a rag around.

"Did you ever see the Temple of Solomon? It must have been incredible, maybe even more than your Camelot. The temples of the Cold One, the one who the men from the land of ice worship aren't so impressive. Just rocks in a pile, maybe a shelter for a fire. When Nechtan saw it on the raid, he said it reminded him of nothing more than a hermit's hut, no place for a God. That's probably why he did what he did..."

"What did he do?" I shouted.

"Took it, of course, that is our faith. They took the food and drink that they left the Cold One, and then they took the lives of the priests guarding the temple. It was easy, my husband told me. They lined them up on their knees before the altar and took off their heads one by one. Maybe Nechtan thought their god would appear before each strike and stop him, I suppose the priests thought that too. Either way, Nechtan and his men made it home with rich plunder. Over the years the Cold One ignored them, perhaps, or simply time moves slower when you're a god. Either way, Nechtan thought he had outrun any retribution for the sacking of the shrine. So did Galam," here she gestured at the wreck of a man who had been found by the treeline, "and so did Talorc," Modwenna said, gesturing towards the man on the church spire. "After the play, each man found these stones hidden in his possessions, all with the mark of the Cold One on them."

"The medallions?"

"Yes, each man who had destroyed the shrine found one. As soon as they picked it up, they were unable to put them down. This is how the Cold One marks his prey. This is how he finds the ones he will sweep up into the sky and drop back to the earth," Modwenna said.

"You say this is vengeance for the desecration of a shrine? The shrine of the men of the land of ice? The actors, yes?" I shouted. The wind whistled around us but did not shake a leaf nor a branch in the forest behind us.

"Yes, but the fairness your King lives for will never let him punish them. How could they be punished? How could they show how these men were killed by other men? Impossible. To accuse the actor and his troupe is to admit that the Old Gods are still strong enough to reach out and affect the lands of men. I expect that's why he has frozen your church. His church is the cold, the Winter, the biting wind, and you can't keep that in a building, and you can't make it sign a concordance," Modwenna said. Again, she was looking at me with pity, and I felt the sudden urge to seize her. To tell her that Arthur's way was the only way out of the fighting, and that the One God would inevitably displace the old, bloodthirsty gods. I wanted to shout this to her, for I knew it was true, but I also knew there was the other truth—that not everybody could come with Arthur into the future, that some people could not sacrifice or escape their pasts and be born anew. Merlin would be lost eventually, the last of an old breed, then, I suppose me, the Knight of Ashes. The one-eyed Knight who couldn't hit the sky if he fired an arrow into it and could hit the training dummy with the point of a sword three times out of ten on a good day. We would be gone too, like the ice around the church when the sun comes out, like a dream dies at the beginning of the day.

Chapter Twelve

When we arrived back at Camelot, the Picts had already finished packing up their wagons, and only waited for Modwenna to join them. As I watched her talk to a few of her tribe and secure a few ropes, I hoped that Nechtan's brother would see the sense in letting her lead. She was a fighter, sure enough, but she knew better than to desecrate shrines and that may lead on to greater wisdom. Sir Hector buzzed around me on my return, disappointed that no window or roof could be found that Nechtan could conceivably have jumped from to land where he had in the courtyard.

"They're leaving then? You won't stop them?" he asked. From the main gate of Camelot, I could see Hector's brother Lancelot staring at me. I had let him down. A lot of other people too.

"How can I? We brought them here to learn peace, we can't do that at sword point. Let them go home and mourn their dead. Maybe they won't harass any more of our monks this time, eh?"

Sir Hector smiled wanly; he believed this was a defeat of sorts, and any defeat contained no honour. But he didn't leave my side whilst we watched the Pict wagons roll past, so maybe there is hope for the future yet. We saluted Modwenna as she drove away into the night, the snowflakes falling gently now, and the wind no more than a whistle. She smiled at us, showing those sharp little teeth again. Unusual woman.

After the Picts, another train of wagons departed, this time with the brightly painted canvases of a stage lashed to their sides. Bulvak wandered over to me as his troupe trundled by.

"We will leave now," Bulvak said. I hoped it would be a promise, an oath, but a smile touched his thin lips.

"You won't stay and entertain our envoys another night?" I said. I was angry with this man, this acolyte for sacrificing a potential peace for petty revenge.

"Ha, no. Our audience is very specific. What is it your god says? 'Whoever has an ear to hear, let him hear'?"

"And your god? What does he say?" I snarled at Bulvak, resisting the temptation to push him into snow and pummel him.

"Great Ithaqua will always be with us, Sir Knight. All of the cold, empty spaces are his. Places where even your god may be afraid to shine a light," Bulvak said.

"Not Camelot," I said, "Not here."

"Even here men's hearts may be the coldest, darkest places of all," Bulvak said. He nodded back to the castle gate, where Lancelot was glaring at the departing actors. He smiled again, that damned cold smile, and leapt up onto his wagon. As he left, the last remaining snow flurries followed him, and the wind died down to nothing.

I left the gate and made my way back up to the chambers, too tired to sleep, but knowing I should. Tomorrow would be a busy day. The Welsh would leave, thinking the Picts left so they could still continue their fight. The Gauls would leave, although we would spare them a garrison of our troops to defend themselves. I would ask the garrison commander to kill any seagulls he would see while traveling through Dungeness, revenge for my eye. I should sleep, I thought— tomorrow will be a long day and I would have to give bad news to a King; never an enviable position to be in.

One last thing, I thought, fishing the medallion out of my pocket and rubbing my fingers along its icy sides. I threw it into the blazing fire where it immediately caught with a flash that seemed to leave two, large orbs burned onto my vision, staring at me, warning me.

SOOThES ThE FIRE

Josh Reynolds

Three days after Bedivere's death, I took the saddle from my horse and set him free. For all that he was loyal to me, the animal was obviously glad of it. He galloped north, away from Mongibel and the horrors that awaited me. I watched him go, and felt some regret. The horse had been the last of my companions, ever since Sagramore had gone mad.

It had happened just before we reached the foothills. He'd begun screaming in the night, when something he saw in our campfire had called out his name. Whatever it was had unmanned the young knight so utterly that he had gouged out his own eyes in an effort to erase it from his sight, despite my best efforts to stop him.

I do not know what it was that he saw, nor do I wish to know. Blind and witless, he could no longer even be trusted to ride a horse. Certainly he could not wield a sword, or couch a lance. I left him in the care of a local friar, and continued on alone, though I was no longer certain as to why, or what I hoped to accomplish.

There had been twenty of us at the start, led by battle-diademed Bedivere. All that remained of the company of the Round Table, after Camlann and Mordred's uprising. Young Safir had fallen in Vosges, bewitched by fae-lights and drawn into a bog. In the Alps, Priamus had been snatched from his horse by a hag-wind, and as we watched helplessly, he was drawn up into the starless skies until he vanished from mortal ken. The others had fallen in their turn, lured by enchantments or slain by sorcerous means.

By the time we reached Sicily, only three of us remained—myself, Bedivere and young Sagramore. Bedivere was the best of us, and Sagramore, the hope of our future. And then…there was me. Neither the best, nor the worst. Not kind or pure of heart. My heart and soul were heavy with fetters of my own forging, and I was not even sure I was still a knight—for that matter, I was not sure I had ever been a knight.

Bedivere had perished near the City of the Elephant, slain by a strange knight with a surcoat the colour of ash. I recognized him, though he did not speak. Ziliante, a knight of Florence, sworn forever to the service of his lady, Morgan le Fay. Even death would not sway him from her command, no matter how he might wish for it.

The knight had departed with nary a word as Bedivere gasped his last. We buried him in a grove of citrus trees, and pressed on—we had sworn an oath, and though I might have turned back then, Sagramore convinced me to go on.

But now Sagramore too had fallen, and only I remained.

Sir Marrok, the Cursed Knight. Sir Marrok, seven years a wolf. That is the song the troubadours sing, and like all such songs there is some truth to it. I closed my eyes, as red images filled my mind. Of hunting beneath the moon. Of clawing corpses from the cold earth when I could not find enough flesh to satiate me.

I forced the memories back into their cages and turned to study the cruel shape of the mountain rising above me. Mongibel, the demesne of Morgan le Fay. It loomed over the surrounding lands, a pall of smoke rising from its summit.

My hand tightened about the hilt of my sword. I glanced once more in the direction my horse had fled, wanting to follow, but knowing that I could not. I had made my decision the moment I set out with Bedivere and the others. I would follow the road wherever it led, whatever the cost. I had sworn an oath, and would see it through. For Arthur, and the fading dream of Camelot, I could do no less.

The climb was not an easy one, or short. The higher I went, the harder it became. The sky was the colour of blood by the time I neared the summit, and I was exhausted. The air was hot and dry. Smoke intermittently cascaded down from the summit, enveloping me like a poisonous shroud. I endured it, where other men might have succumbed. My experiences had toughened me inside and out.

Sweat beaded beneath my mail, and my gambeson stank of my exertions. My tabard was stained and torn by travel. I carried only my sword and shield, and a single skin of water, slung across my chest. Everything else, I had been forced to abandon in the foothills. I did not expect to need it, for the likelihood of my survival was not great.

I did not fear death. Indeed, I welcomed it. I yearned for the soothing fires of Hell, where I could be exculpated of my sins, one lash at a time. How many had died by my teeth and claws? Worse, how many had I damned by my callousness, my myriad cruelties? I had been a wolf in spirit long before my wife, my dear Heledd, had cursed me—I knew it, though I often wished to forget it. Now she lingered in a cloister, praying for forgiveness and I was here, seeking my own penance. And if not penance, then at least an ending.

As I climbed, the mountain trembled and at times threatened to give way beneath my very feet. I could barely breathe and I could not see—yet I persisted. Despite these obstacles, despite the fatigue that threatened my steps, I reached the top. At its summit, the mountain boasted a great, fuming crater, filled with the clamour of Hell.

A field of stakes spread before me, along the crater's smoke-shrouded rim. On them were mounted the skulls of a hundred men or more, not all of them Christian. I saw the horsehair plumes of Romans, and the spired helms of Saracens. The dead of centuries, left to rot beneath the indifferent sky. Bones littered the rocky soil and carrion birds danced among them. The birds hurtled skyward at my arrival, croaking *'tekeli-li'* in voices too much like those of men.

Merlin had told me of this place, and its history. He'd told me why Morgan had set her keep here, and what lay sleeping within the fiery heart of the mountain. She'd always been one too keen to interfere with things best left buried.

There was a smell on the air, drifting beneath the sulphur stink of the mountain. A sour odor that I had smelled before. The stink of dark magics, of old magics, the kind that sit like stagnant pools in forgotten places. Whatever Morgan intended, it would end poorly for all of us if she were allowed to see it through.

Bedivere and the others had been of similar mind, that day on the bloody field of Camlann. Barely hours after the last echo of battle had faded, and Arthur's sword had vanished beneath the water, Morgan had appeared to escort the mortally wounded Arthur to Avalon. But it was not to Avalon she had spirited him; rather she had brought him here, half a world away from Camelot. For what purpose, none of us knew. We'd known only that we must follow, and return Arthur to his resting place.

My memory of that day was still hazy—I had fought until my limbs were leaden, and my pulse pounded in my ears. I had slain men I had once fought beside, all in the name of the only man not to look at me with fear—with disgust. Arthur alone of all men had seen the wolf that was Marrok, and known no fear. It was Arthur who had reinvested me with my lands and tithes when I shed my wolf's skin. Arthur, who had made me a man once more, where once there had only been a beast.

It was for Arthur that I pressed on, and for Arthur I would see this thing to its end.

When I reached the summit, Ziliante was waiting for me, as I had known he would be. He sat on an outcropping, his sword thrust into the soil at his feet, and his helm discarded carelessly nearby. The dead man's armor was stained with ash, and his tabard was the colour of dried blood. He seemed weary, for which I could not fault him—eternity was a tiresome thing, even to the strongest of men. Thin hair whipped in the wind, and his rictus smile greeted me. "Marrok."

"Yes." I threw off my own helm, hoping for a taste of clean air, but only the stink of sulphur met my nose. "You slew Bedivere."

"It was you my blade was meant for."

I did not know what to say to this, so I said nothing at all. Instead, I peered upwards. Something wavered in the sky above—a vast edifice of incomprehensible angles and impossible beauty, its turrets pointing downwards. It stretched as far as the eye could see, but was only visible to one standing directly in its shadow, as we were now.

Many knights had laid siege to its enchanted walls, but none save Lancelot had ever breached its gates—and even then, only at the whim of its mistress. I was no Lancelot, and Morgan le Fay held no love for me, but I was determined to try.

"Is she up there?" I asked.

"That is not for me to say." Ziliante stood and retrieved his helm. Up close, I could see his bones through the frayed parchment of his flesh. "I have but one task, and it is not one I welcome." He pulled on his helm, and wrenched his sword free of the ground.

I raised my hand. "I am tired from the climb, Ziliante—I would beg a moment's grace of you. At least let me have a swallow of water."

He paused. Whatever else, Ziliante was a knight—or had been. I drank gratefully, clearing dust and sulphur from my mouth. "You know what she has done," I said, dropping my waterskin to the ground. "Arthur is dead, and she has taken his body. I would see it returned to its people."

Ziliante nodded. "I know." He gave a sudden rattling laugh. "Do you fear she will make him like me, then?"

"I do not know what mischief she intends. I know only that I cannot allow it."

"Who are you to deny her, Marrok? After all that she has done for you?"

I stiffened. "I am a knight of the Round Table. The last knight of the Round Table."

"Yes. Have at you, Sir Marrok."

I barely had time to draw my own blade as he attacked. I parried his first blow, and caught his second on my shield. He fought lazily—what did a dead man have to fear, after all?

Ziliante had always been skilled, and death had not dulled him. He had slain Bedivere handily enough, and I knew a moment's doubt as we traded blows. Was my quest to end here, on the slopes of Mongibel? Would my skull join the others on a stake?

A part of me hoped so. There was relief in such an end. I had tried and failed. Perhaps God would see, and know and forgive. But a greater part of me knew better. There was no forgiveness in defeat, and precious little in victory.

So I fought. And as I fought, I grew wilder. Something in me snarled in fury and battered at the walls of my heart, driving me to greater lengths. Suddenly, I was once more on the field of Camlann, watching my king fall. I had felt it, in my bones. I had howled my grief to the sky, and in that instant wanted nothing more than to become again what I once was. To shed this frail flesh, and leave the world of men and all its madness behind.

But I could not. Not while my oath held. Arthur had made me a man, and I must remain so for a while yet, at least. With a sudden burst of strength, I shoved him back. Surprised, he staggered and I struck him on the hip. He sank down to one knee, and I hit him again, nearly cleaving his head from his shoulders. He fell in a heap, sighing. I made ready to bury my sword in his withered heart, when I heard a voice call out, "Stop."

I turned. Morgan le Fay stood behind me, wreathed in smoke, raven-haired and black-eyed. She was as beautiful as I remembered, but it was not a human beauty. She had always been other—alien and unpredictable. It was said Merlin had taught her, or perhaps she had taught him. Regardless, she was a power in the world unlike any other.

I swept my sword out, and made my voice firm. "I have come for the King."

"The King is dead," Morgana said. "And the world is poorer for it." She was clad in green, with a cloak of fur and feathers. A bejewelled slughorn hung from her belt, and something in me curdled at the sight of it.

"You stole his body away."

She stared at me a moment. Then she gestured, and the infernal smoke of the mountain thinned, revealing a crystalline bier situated at the edge of the great crater. Within the bier lay a familiar form, still clad in his battle-torn mail, hands folded over his unmoving chest. Arthur, King of the Britons, ruler of Camelot. I saw that his features were peaceful in death as they had never been in life, and felt a flicker of envy that I quickly quashed.

"Is this what you wished to see?" she asked, as she turned to face me. "I have not harmed him. He is beyond harm. Beyond everything."

"He would not want this." I took a step towards her, closing the distance. Behind me, I heard Ziliante pick himself up, seemingly none the worse for wear. I wondered if he would strike me down, as I spoke to his mistress. But I did not turn. Could not. "Whatever it is you are planning, he would not wish it…"

She glared at me. "Who are you to say what he would want?"

"I was a knight of the Round Table." The words felt as hollow now as when I had said them to Ziliante earlier. They were empty of meaning, without Arthur to give them power.

Morgan must have felt the same for she laughed bitterly. "There is no more Round Table. There is no more Camelot. The world burns and now is the hour of wolves and ravens." She gestured to me as she spoke, and I almost bared my teeth at her.

"And whose fault is that?" I said, stung by her laughter. "Your sorceries were very effective. If you care, the others are dead, or mad, or worse."

She sighed. "I would have had it differently, but I could not allow you to stop me." She looked at me. "Ziliante was meant to kill you."

"So he said." I paused. "Do you still bear me a grudge, then?"

"You were cursed fairly, Marrok, whatever lies you tell yourself. In undoing your curse, I condemned your wife, and erased the memory of those who you slew."

"I forgave her," I said, softly.

"And yet she withers in her isolation, while you went on to serve at Arthur's hand. Your past indelicacies forgotten, or forgiven."

"Arthur made enemies into friends, when he could," I said.

"Even when he should have known better."

I frowned. "Which of us do you mean, Morgan?"

She sneered, but I spied the flicker of old hurts in her eyes. "Does it matter now?" She turned to the bier and that which lay within. "He is dead, and his dreams with him." Her expression softened. "But I can turn back time. I can make him live again."

"How?" The word left my lips before I could stop myself. I wanted it to be true, I realized. Maybe Bedivere had been wrong; maybe we all had.

She looked out over the crater. "The Greeks believed that this mountain was a prison, that it held a beast called Typhon—the father of all monsters. They were right and wrong, as is often the way with these things. Mongibel is not a prison, but a gate—a threshold."

"And what is on the other side?"

"My mother claimed that it was the realm of my father, though whether or not that is true, I cannot say." Her smile was cruel and cold as she turned to me. "That is why I set my banner here in this place of fire, so that I might learn the secrets of those who wait on the other side, be they my kin or no."

"Annwn," I said, with a sudden chill. "You are speaking of the Otherworld." Suddenly it seemed as if the smoke around me were populated by unseen gargoyle shapes. Lurking, waiting, watching—I could sense them now, and my hackles stiffened.

"Perhaps. Or maybe it is a different place altogether." She stroked the slughorn on her hip. "This horn comes from there—one of many gifts they have bestowed upon me over the years. When I sound it, it will stir those who wait at the threshold. I will call my father's name, then, and he will answer and give me that which I desire."

"You have not yet blown the horn," I said. Another step, two, and I would be on her. I did not desire her death, despite all she had done, for I owed her something. Even so, I knew she had to be stopped.

"But I will. You are too late." She looked up at the darkening sky. "The stars have aligned and the grand conjunction is under way. The veil grows thin." She hesitated, looking again at Arthur, and then at the slughorn. "If the deed is to be done, now is the time." She turned. "I did not expect you."

"Would you have preferred one of the others?" I let a hint of bitterness creep into my voice. "Lancelot, perhaps?"

Her gaze hardened and she turned back to the bier. "If you truly loved Arthur, and what he stood for, you would lay down your sword, Marrok."

"It is only for love of him that I stand against you."

She went on, as if I had not spoken. "Logres—Camelot— was a foundation stone of the world." She ran her hands over the facets of the crystal bier. "It has fallen, and so too shall Rome, Jerusalem, and all the rest, in their turn. Unless something takes up the weight."

"I do not understand."

She laughed. "I will do what Merlin could not—would not—do, and I will bring him back. I will make him strong again, and I—not Merlin, not Nimue—will be at his left hand. A new Logres will be born here, on the fiery slopes of Mongibel." She lifted the slughorn from her belt and held it up, as if it were a sword. "When I blow this horn, a door will open, and our sleeping king will wake." She smiled then, but there was no joy in it. "He will have Arthur's face—his mind…"

"What about his soul?"

Morgan fell silent. "What is a man without his soul?" I asked. "You would make a damned thing of him, like me, or poor Ziliante."

"Not like you," she snapped. "You were a beast, and Ziliante is a husk. I will make an emperor of a king."

"Then why do you hesitate?" I took a step towards her, my

71

sword low. "Why did you wait? You speak of stars and conjunctions—but is that the truth, or mummery?"

"I thought it would be Bedivere," she said, after a moment. "I thought he would be the one to match me. Not you. That is the way of these things." She looked at me, and her eyes blazed with a revulsion I knew all too well. The same fires burned in me—the fires of hatred, not for the world, but for oneself. It hurt, that fire, but it was soothing as well. When the flames had you, there was nothing more to fear.

Finally, she spat, "I should never have saved you, Marrok."

"No. You should have left me a monster. It is what I deserved."

"Arthur thought different," she said.

"As he thought of you. Consign him to his rest, and do not make a nightmare of his dream." I took another step towards her, and another after that. "Do not do this, Morgan. Let him fade, if that is God's will…"

"God? Which god?" she demanded. "Your god? Or mine?"

"His," I said, not retreating. "The god he worshipped. The god he loved."

She stared at me, her eyes wild but her face composed and still, like marble. She glanced down at the slughorn in her hand. I stretched out my own hand—I thought perhaps to snatch it from her, before she could blow it.

As if reading my thoughts, Morgan stepped back, out of reach. "You speak of love, Marrok. But I do not think one such as you would understand it. If you did, your wife would not have cursed you, and you would not have done as you did. It would have been as the troubadours sang…instead of how it was."

I swallowed a sudden rush of bile. I remembered a peasant's hut, and screaming…red rushes of heat, and a sickening satisfaction. Seven years of huts and peasants, seven years of screaming. Tears beaded at the corners of my eyes. Morgan read the sorrow on my face and nodded. "He asked me to help you."

"I know."

"And now I ask you to help him. Let me help him, Marrok. Let me lend him the strength of the old ones, of they who came before man and will be here after. He will rise, and Camelot will rise with him. A new Camelot—a stronger one. A better one."

"All things pass," I said, softly. "Even kings and kingdoms. Do not taint his memory this way. Do not make a monster of him."

She looked back down at Arthur. "I would not. I would guide him. As I always should have done. Merlin was a fool, and in his foolishness he has damned the world to a slow death. Arthur might have saved it, had his strength not given out. Had he not been merely a man…"

"Had you not undermined him, and broken the fellowship of the Round Table," I said, growing weary of her justifications. She had always spoken so, blaming others for her crimes and mischiefs. "Had you not hated his queen, turned his friends against him, had you not—"

"Enough," she snarled, rounding on me. "Enough of your yelping. You should not even be here, Marrok. It should be one of the others—that is the way this story goes! My wickedness, matched against their courage. That is the way it has always been. Their humanity, against my inhumanity…against what will come."

Her eyes widened, and became less human. Her loveliness seemed but a mask for something great and terrible. Her form, once lithe and graceful, appeared crude now—as if it were not the form of a woman at all, but another creature entirely, one as alien to this world as any demon invoked by sorcery.

"All my life, I have matched myself against those who could check my desires. In my own way, I have kept the world safe. But now, those days are gone and I can feel those of the air—the ancient masters of this world—working their will upon me." She cast a glance over her shoulder, at something I could not perceive. I wondered then if she saw what Sagramore had seen. Indeed, perhaps she had always seen it.

I bristled at her words. "You will have to make do with

me."

Morgan turned, her eyes gleaming. "No. You are no man. No knight. You are nothing, save a beast." She gestured as she spoke, and I felt a tremor run through me. My stomach lurched and I fell. An old, familiar pain ran riot through me. "Ziliante—take his foul head. Let the company of the Round Table come to its inglorious end."

"I beg you no," Ziliante croaked in a harsh whisper. I felt his shadow cross me, and heard the creak of his armour. "I have already slain one knight—do not make me kill another, even one such as him."

Morgan's gaze flicked to her servant, startled perhaps by this hesitation, and I seized the moment with as much strength as I could muster. Limbs cramping, world blurring, I lunged to my feet, sword in hand, and spun. The edge of my blade bit into Ziliante's neck, where his mail was thinnest, and the force of my blow sent his head flying. His body staggered back a step, and for a moment, I feared he might fight on. But then he gave a great sigh and collapsed. Morgan screamed in fury and raised the slughorn to her lips.

I did not pause to apologize for my dishonourable act, but instead turned to lunge for Morgan, hoping to stop her. But I stumbled and fell, as a familiar pain ripsawed through me. My sword clattered away as her spell continued its fell work. I felt the old enchantments fraying and splitting, as something long asleep now hurled against the cage of my soul.

The sound of the slughorn was not as I had imagined it. It was not thunderous, or cacophonic. Rather, it had no sound at all—merely the memory of sound. An echo without a voice to cast it. And yet, I felt something pummel at me, and the mountain spat fire. Mongibel shuddered like a wounded animal, and the smoke grew thick and choking. Vague shapes moved within the pall, lean and a-thirst as they circled like hungry beasts.

Morgan paid them no mind. She had eyes only for the bier. The blast of the slughorn had shattered it, exposing Arthur's body to the elements. Cinders danced in his hair and beard, and ashes settled on his tarnished mail.

"It will be better this way," she said, though whether the words were meant for me, or for herself, I did not know.

The sky boiled overhead, as if some great entity were squirming behind the veil of smoke and clouds. The birds began to circle in a black, screaming whirlwind, so many and so fast as to form a single shape. Morgan raised her arms, threw back her head and screamed, "Y'AI' NG'NGAH, *YOG-SOTHOTH* H'EE—L'GEB F' AI THRODOG, UAAAH!"

There was a crack, as of thunder, followed by a dull and hideous whine. As the echoes faded, the birds flew down to peck and claw at what lay on the bier. I watched in horror as they squirmed into Arthur's mouth, and maggot-like through the wounds that had claimed his noble life. *Tekel-li-tekel-li-tekel-li,* they croaked, as they burrowed into him.

Silence followed. But only for a moment. For slowly, surely, Arthur sat up, his torn mail jangling, his limbs rustling.

Morgan sighed and cast the slughorn away. "It is done."

Arthur turned at the sound of her voice, and I saw that, as with her, there was nothing human in his gaze. Nothing of the man I had known and loved. Instead, I saw the eyes of a goat or a crow or something fouler still, bulging from bloody sockets. Arthur's mouth sagged open, vomiting spheres of sickly light. These spheres clung to him like an infernal halo as he spoke. It was Arthur's voice, but distorted and jagged— like the sound of a broken sword, striking bone. "*Morgan,*" it—he—rasped. Then, "*Marrok?*"

I screamed then—a scream that became a howl.

My body felt like a seedpod, newly split and disgorging itself. Something moved in me, and I frantically tore at my armor with unnatural strength. The world changed before my eyes, and my mouth filled with blood and bile. My skin tore like parchment, as stiff quills of hair pierced it, rising and spreading over limbs that broke themselves, lengthening and strengthening. Flensed and dripping, I howled again—a howl for all that I had lost.

Morgan spun as I scrambled to my feet. I saw myself in her eyes—spindle-limbed, hairy and bestial, clad in rags and torn mail—as I leapt forward with a cry of mingled hunger

75

and frustration. My vision was tinged with red, and I saw only her smooth flesh and frightened gaze. But she was not my prey.

Instead, I struck the thing even then rising from the bier. Clouded as my thoughts were, I knew that whatever it was—demon, spirit, or something else—it could not be allowed to rise and settle in its new shell. I had to kill it before it gathered its strength, even if it meant killing the man I had called king. And so I bore it backwards with a snarl.

It fumbled at me, uncertain of its own form, or perhaps surprised by the attack, and I struck quickly, my teeth fastening into its throat—Arthur's throat—as it tried to speak again. It squalled in an odd, tremulous fashion, and the glistening spheres burned my unnatural flesh, and seared my eyes. They burned me, but I hung on with fierce savagery, biting and tearing until my teeth met bone—or something like it—and I crunched it between my jaws.

Arthur—the thing wearing Arthur's body—fell back onto the bier. Iridescent smoke boiled from his wasted form, as whatever force had claimed him departed to unknown vales. I howled my bitter triumph to the blistered sky.

A vast convulsion seized Mongibel, and stone and ash began to fall from the sky. To my animal gaze, it seemed as if Morgan's citadel were aflame and coming undone. Perhaps it was. Perhaps those things she had bargained with now sought to levy a punishment for her failure. I do not know. I cannot say.

All I know is that when I turned from my gory repast, she was watching me. On her face was a look of utter desolation—but also, I think, relief. Or maybe that is merely what I wish to think. "Maybe this moment was yours after all," she said, in a hollow voice. "Another would not have had the courage—or the fury—to do what you have done."

I snarled at her, not understanding. She smiled then, but there was only sadness there. "The king is dead. Long live the king." She turned away, her eyes fixed on the fires above, as if seeking some answer in the smoke and flame.

I howled again, in sorrow this time. Neither of us had

gotten what we wanted, and we would both have to live with that, for as many days as were left to us.

I leapt from the bier and loped away from that place, leaving Morgan to what fate I did not know. Nor did I care. I was no longer a man. No more a knight. Only a beast.

Perhaps it was better that way.

ThE GILDED ShULLS

Edward M. Erdelac

Galloway was a hilly, decadent land of little more than backward peoples and stout, hornless black cattle, yet as a knight of Albion and lord of The Castle of Marvels, Sir Gawaine of Orkney was bound to protect it. He was new to the burden of rule, which, to his free, wandering spirit, felt more like servitude. He wondered at his uncle Arthur's affinity for it. Gawaine did not find governing to his liking; this seemingly endless, tiresome business of listening to the griping of peasants made him tug at his own red beard, and yet, Arthur showed infinite patience ruling a kingdom ten times the size of Gawaine's own modest knight's fee.

He could not deny that the matter before him was pressing, though.

Nor could the knight at his side, Sir Sillimac, master of the Castle On The Rock, which neighbored Gawaine's land.

They had both witnessed the inexplicable darkening of The Wild Forest from the windows of their respective keeps. The center of the thick emerald span of wildwood between their two castles had grown black overnight, as though ravaged by some invisible fire. The blackness seemed to grow outward with each passing day, like a spreading rot. The leaves there curled and dropped from the scorched branches, and the undergrowth withered and died.

Game that wandered dazed from the center of the woods onto Gawaine's land were wild-eyed and mangy. When taken into the pinfold, shot and butchered, the meat was found to be wriggling with bizarre maggots, black as dog snouts, the meat inedible, and noxious in the extreme when consigned to the burning heap.

So they had set out together with a contingent of two men-at-arms and two aspirants each to discover the cause of the strange phenomenon. Gawaine welcomed any excuse to leave the confines of his castle and its attendant duties to his steward. He wanted to ride forthwith into the wood itself, but Sillimac suggested another course. His superstitious tenants blamed the corruption on the desecration of nearby Cairnholy, the site of an old tomb of a mostly-forgotten Caledonian king named Galdus, which overlooked the firth. Gawaine had agreed to investigate the old cairn first.

Gawaine had his own theory, though.

Although he had been dedicated to the sun god Belenus by his mother Morgause as a babe, and revered the priestesses of Avalon, he held the power of the Crucified God in grudging respect. He wondered if perhaps some Christian relic had been disturbed. The growing corruption in the Wild Forest reminded him of stories he had heard in Camelot of late, about the kingdom of Lystenoyse, rendered a waste land after Sir Balin had upset and lost some sort of holy cup in that country.

Just why the desecration of a Christian artifact had such a detrimental effect, he did not know. Certainly nothing from the treasure house of Avalon would so despoil the land. Gawaine could only surmise that it was because unlike the gods of rock, tree and stream which the druids and the people of Avalon revered, the Crucified King was not native to these isles. The land itself rejected this strange, meek foreign faith, as a strong body fights an invasive sickness.

Yet, for good or ill, the new faith was on the rise, with Merlin gone and a High King who lent his ear to both The Lady of The Lake and the Archbishop Dubricius.

Gawaine knew there was some manner of hermitage on an assart along the Luce River on the edge of his land, and wondered if one of the doddering monks had tipped over some holy dinner plate and unleashed evil. The Christian god was certainly a stickler for table manners.

When they reached the upright stones of Cairnholy, penning in the windswept barrow of the old king like a henge of jagged teeth, they found the peasants had been right. The tomb was cracked open and the old king's bones lay scattered across the hill as though dogs had been at him.

"Do you see, Sir Gawaine?" said Sillimac, the wind off the firth flinging his cloak about him. He stooped near the open grave. "The skull is missing."

Gawaine nodded from his red-eared horse, Gringolet.

"Passing strange," he called down above the blow of the air off the sea. "Who could have done it? Grave robbers?"

"There is a rusted sword in the hole," reported one of the squires. "And some gold."

"Be sure you leave it where it lies," Sillimak ordered. "Gather the bones and re-seal the tomb."

"Not robbers then. But why take his head?" Gawaine wondered aloud.

Far down the hill, at the mouth of the river Nith where it emptied into the strath, Gawaine watched the fishers wading, dragging for salmon.

He scanned the ground intently as the squires picked up Galdus' bones and the men-at-arms bent to the heavy stone.

"I know not. Some ancient clan feud?" Sillimac said.

Gawaine dismounted, and knelt to inspect a portion of tamped grass. He discerned a trail, a few days' old, and, straightening, followed it with his eyes till it disappeared in the distance.

"Tracks," he announced, "headed for the Wild Forest."

"We follow them," said Sillimac.

After they had replaced the bones of Galdus, they rode along the course Gawaine followed. The horses balked at the border of the wood, whether at the faint odor of decay emanating from within or from some other undetected menace, they didn't know. They rode two more hours into the green, and the smell grew steadily more pungent. When at last the tracks led them within sight of the blackened edge of the spreading corruption, their steeds would go no further. They dismounted, and only after the squires bound the horses' muzzles in damp cloth to shut out the stench would they consent to be led.

The increasingly noxious fetor reminded Gawaine of a summer morning long ago in the Orkneys, after a particularly horrendous storm. He and his brothers and sister had been children then. The previous night, the howling wind and rain had pelted the roof and churned the dark sea, raising waves so high and terrible he had been afraid to look out at them. The lightning had lit the sky bright as daylight and thunder had crashed so loud it shook the house stones.

In the stillness of the morning, the sun had come up hot and vengeful, and they'd heard a peculiar droning sound, steady and unbroken in the distance. Curious, Gawaine and the other Orkney children had followed the noise to the seashore. The stones had been gilded silver with scores of dead fish rotting under a horde of crawling, buzzing black flies. His sister Clarissant had spotted a trio of capsized Pictish boats covered in the hides of black and white cattle, and they'd gone searching for survivors, thinking how they would be lauded if they found and nursed some hapless sailors back to health.

At Gawaine's approach however, the largest of the wrecks had suddenly shuddered and thrashed, kicking up a cloud of stinging midges, which whirled about impatiently before resettling. Gawaine had been terrified at first, but Clarissant had giggled.

"They're only whales, Gawaine," she'd said.

The bloated carcasses had been so alien looking, with their strange, stark, black and white patterns, apparently eyeless heads, rows of fist-sized teeth, and lolling pink tongues. The smell of those gigantic rotting corpses with their strong, fertile hint of the brine, recalled the stench that now pervaded this black part of the Wild Forest.

In the end, all of them covered their faces against the wretched smell.

Yet unlike that stinking shore so long ago, there came no insect drone. There was no sound at all; neither not the cry of birds nor the crashing of startled game. That was how they heard the trickle of the stream so clearly.

There was no moving water of note through the Wild Forest that either of them knew of, yet they came across a wide, slow-moving stream. Gawaine had assumed the grave robbers would obscure their trail in the stream, but he found their prints in the black mud that lined the near bank. They had turned and gone directly upstream.

What flowed in this foul smelling course could hardly be called water. It was leather-black and sludge-like, flowing thick as curdled milk. It burbled and slid through the forest, and along the edge, Gawaine noticed a number of animal carcasses. The horses made no move to dip their faces, and had to be reined in. They recoiled at the very sight of the stuff.

"What is it?" Gawaine gasped, horrified.

"No doubt it's what's poisoning the wood," said Sillimac. "It seems to be spreading."

"If this foulness spilled into the Nith, or any of its tributaries…," Gawaine ventured. "If it reached the firth…."

"Gods, look!" one of the squires exclaimed.

A number of small, oily creatures were slowly extricating themselves from the stream, putting out spindly limbs and dragging themselves twitching onto the bank.

Leaning down from his saddle to look, Gawaine wrinkled his nose in disgust.

They appeared to be trout, their lidless, boiled white eyes round and staring, fish mouths gulping, gills flaring on their flanks, yet rudimentary forelimbs ending in repulsive little fingers of some kind protruded from their bodies, just behind the gills.

Gawaine reached for his lance and neatly skewered one, raising it up curiously to eye level, where the other men at arms and Sir Sillimac grimaced at the sight.

It flopped and squirmed on the lance point, tiny arms waving miserably. Underdeveloped nubs back near the tail twitched, the start of hind legs. Black blood bubbled from its fatal wound, drizzling down the stock of the lance. It seemed to turn its body to regard him, and Gawaine saw, in its gaping mouth, rows of teeth that looked disconcertingly like a man's. They clicked as it worked its mouth. He flung the abomination back into the murky stream, where it bobbed once and sunk in silence.

The squire reached for the lance dutifully, but taking a second look at the black stuff now coating its end and threatening to run over the vamplate, Gawaine shook his head and discarded it too in the plague waters.

Sillimac was dumbstruck.

"What are they?" he murmured.

"This way," Gawaine said, and spurred Gringolet, not knowing what else to do. He could hardly slash or stab this putrid stuff, so he resolved to affix his purpose to something he could understand. If there was some connection between the desecrators of old King Galdus' tomb and this black stream, so much the better.

They rode upstream along the murky bank, leaving the remainder of the pitiful things to writhe in their black slime cradle.

It was nearing evening when the trail led them out of the Wild Forest. They need not worry about losing the track in the failing light. They had not deviated from the course of the black stream and there was no reason to believe their quarry did not follow it to its source, which revealed itself, stark and imposing on the edge of a long plain, sprouting from the base of the foothills, huddled in the shadow of the uplands.

It was a strange, black castle.

Gawaine had never seen the like, in all of Albion or Gaul. The wall was a cyclopean jumble of black stones, not cut from the red sandstone so common in the region, but imported; though from where, he could not guess. Behind the familiarity of the curtain wall rose a black keep of utterly bizarre construction. The cluster of twisting towers that rose from the bailey did not conform to Gawaine's admittedly limited understanding of architecture. They sprouted and leaned like something shaped according to a lunatic's whim rather than a builder's plan. It seemed impossible that the bartizans that bloomed outward like curling oak branches could remain standing in such a disordered jumble.

In the shadow of the sheer slope against which the fortress leaned like a wary, cornered combatant, it was difficult to discern the movement of sentries atop the walls. All was cast in an obscuring greenish haze of mist, for some two hundred feet above the highest point of the keep, a white fall of clear water tumbled from some icy loch nestled in the uplands above.

Gawaine marked the whiteness of that fall, for whatever it passed through in the bowels of that strange castle, the water emerged drastically changed via a kind of sewer gap beneath the wall. This was the black sludge that flowed into the Wild Forest.

"I do not know this castle," said Sir Sillimac. "Do you?"

"I've never seen its like," Gawaine whispered, and none in the party of arms could say they had either.

"Why is it so dark?" said Sillimac.

"It lies in the shade of the uplands," said Gawaine, surveying the approach.

"But look at the position of the sun," said Sillimac, pointing to the orb. "The shadows...they seem too deep for this time of day. And the towers...I don't think they're stone...."

"Look there!" said Gawaine, pointing to the long plain.

Between the forest and the black castle, moving slowly east toward the castle gates, Gawaine had spied a glint of gold. They heard the squeak of axles.

A gaudy, gilded cart pulled by a team of two white draft horses trundled along, driven by three monks in coarse blue robes, their bald pates stark in the growing gloom.

From within the belly of the castle, a deep horn groaned like a hunting call and the tall, banded gates swung open, disgorging a line of lancers in helms and dull black armor that drank the sinking light. They charged full force at the cart of monks, their course unmistakable.

Gawaine looked to Sillimac, but the man had already slapped down the visor of his helm and couched his lance. They had no hope of intercepting the body of riders in time, and were sorely outnumbered, but suddenly he found himself in the dust of his neighbor.

Not to be outdone, Gawaine tore his bossed shield from the arms of his squire and gave his spurs to Gringolet, his own soldiers falling in abreast of him.

They rode for the golden cart, but the black knights, twenty in all, swiftly surrounded the monks. The hapless priests were seized and dragged roughly down from their cart.

Closer, and now the gilded cart looked to be some kind of ostentatious carriage. The black warriors broke open the doors. Gawaine feared some august passenger would be pulled from it, but the knights instead seemed to reach in and remove a number of circular, golden and ivory objects.

Sillimac roared his battle cry in challenge. He and his men pulled ahead as Gawaine strained to see.

Now the black knights fitted whatever they had taken to the points of their lances and raised them sparkling in triumph. Gawaine saw that they were in fact sparkling gold and white skulls. They wheeled and made once more for the open gate. Apparently they had no regard at all for Sillimac's challenge.

Sillimac and his men gave chase.

"Sir Gawaine?" one of his men, Pardnum, asked.

Gawaine bit his lip. It looked as though the blackguards would retreat into the safety of their castle with their stolen goods before Sir Sillimac ever caught them. He hated to bow out of a fight, but he was sure there would be no fight. One of the monks seemed to be lying in the dust bleeding from the head, his two brothers attending to him.

"Support Sir Sillimac in case they turn and give fight!" Gawaine ordered. "I'll see to the monks!"

He slowed as they reached the ransacked cart, and his men went on without him, the two squires, eager to see a fight, brought up the rear.

Gawaine reined in Gringolet and called down to the monks as he approached.

"Are you priests badly hurt?"

They turned their pale faces up to him, and Gawaine nearly

tumbled backwards from his saddle in surprise.

They were not tonsured monks at all, but women; slender, fine featured, and entirely hairless from crown to brow. He saw that there were faint markings about their faces, blue woad paints perhaps, or fine, tangled tattoos.

He saw also that among their number was his own sister.

"Clarissant?" he faltered.

"Who are you?" she demanded, glaring up at him and rising to stand between him and her two companions.

He showed her his shield, but of course, the *Purpure, a two-headed eagle displayed or, beaked and membered azure* charge embossed there probably meant nothing to her.

He raised his visor.

"It's Gawaine!" he exclaimed. "Your brother."

"*Gawaine?*" Clarissant muttered, in equal shock.

The woman on the ground, bleeding from her bare scalp, rose and pushed aside all help. She lurched unsteadily toward the open carriage and thrust her head in.

"They've missed one!" she announced, breathlessly.

She reached inside the carriage and returned with a skull grasped in both hands. It was inlaid with gold and silver accents, the teeth spangled with gemstones.

To Gawaine's bemusement, she began to limp toward the castle, raising the skull high above her own head.

"Amplfise!" Clarissant called. "Wait!"

"Take the reliquary and go!" the tall, bleeding woman with the golden skull called back. She fastened her wild eyes on Gawaine. "Sir knight! I charge you! As a man of honor you are bound to protect these ladies! See them safe!" Then she turned back to her purpose.

But Gawaine's attention was past her.

As he had suspected, Sir Sillimac and the others had not caught up with the black knights before they reached the open gate. Yet four of the dark warriors at the tail end of the black train stopped in the entrance way and turned to regard their pursuers. Gawaine grimaced, thinking he would miss a clash of arms after all.

Then there came the whistling of arrows. Archers on the

walls let loose a merciless flight down on Sir Sillimac without warning and with no apparent discernment between warrior or squire. Even the two boys at the back cried out, sprouting bristling coats of black feathered shafts as they fell dead from their collapsing horses.

Gawaine stood aghast as Sillimac slumped bleeding in his saddle and crashed to the ground with the others, his armor pierced many times over.

One of the horned knights rode out then, and drawing his sword, swung down from his mount and took off the head of the master of the Castle On The Rock in two chops.

The woman, Ampflise, called out to them again, holding up the glittering skull like a prize.

Behind Gawaine, the gilded cart began to rumble away, and he found himself torn between avenging the base and unlawful murder of his comrades, protecting the strange woman with the skull, or honoring her request to cover the escape of the other two ladies, one of which was his own wayward sister.

As he stood, wheeling Gringolet about in indecision, another murderous flight from the bowmen on the wall felled the woman, Amplfise, and the gilded skull tumbled from her hand to the ground.

Now Gawaine kicked Gringolet in the flanks, raising his shield against the villainous archers.

But Gringolet's head jerked strongly right and the horse cried out in protest and nearly threw Gawaine over his red-tipped ears.

Clarissant stood holding his horse by the bridle with both hands.

"No, Gawaine! Wait!"

Gawaine glared at the black knight. The man's armor was of strange fashion and wickedly spiked from sabatons to gorget. Perhaps it was the dullness of the blackened steel, but Gawaine could see no visor or slits in the bell-shaped helmet, and precious few seams or joints in the extremities. The sole weak point seemed to be between the top of the gorget and the base of the helm, where a wispy beard on the end of a pale chin just peeked out. The knight leaned from his saddle and scooped up the golden skull without slowing, turned, and rode for the gate.

"I can't just let them go!" Gawaine cried behind his teeth, beside himself for want of action.

"You can and you must!" Clarissant snapped. She looked back at the gilded reliquary, rolling off toward the forest with the other woman at the reins. Then she looked back at the body of Ampflise. "Gawaine, help me up."

Gawaine reached down and hoisted her onto the back of Gringolet, then turned to follow the cart.

"No wait! Go to her. Ride to her body! Quick!"

Gawaine had never known his elder sister to be sentimental. She'd shed no tears at their father's funeral. He turned Gringolet back again towards the body of the woman and rode. He was already leaving five men and two boys to rot on the porch of this hellish castle. It wasn't right to leave the lady too.

He raised his shield as they got to within bow shot, expecting any minute to feel the thudding of arrows against his armor, to feel the pricks of a dozen deaths, but Clarissant slid boldly from the horse almost before it stopped, and to his shock, she dragged his own sword, Galatine, behind. She had whisked it from his scabbard in the same moment she had jumped from Gringolet's back.

"Clarissant, what…?" he began, peering anxiously over the lip of his shield up at those black, wet walls, expecting to hear the twang of bowstrings and the whistling doom any moment.

Instead, the edge of his own sword cut the air.

Clarissant clambered back onto Gringolet a moment later, ramming Galatine home into its scabbard and drawing her arms around him.

"Now ride, Gawaine! As if hell were at your back, for it is!"

He wheeled yet again and drove his poor, confused charger on after the dwindling cart. No arrows sang down from the walls, no knights rode up to cut them from the saddle.

He glanced down, and saw, held in place on the prow of

his saddle by his sister's hands, the head of the woman Ampflise, one bright blue eye staring up at him in death, the other pierced by a single glistening black arrow. From around the killing wound, a lattice of inky black spread like webbing across her drawn face.

They were not pursued, and caught up with the lady and the cart. Clarissant would not make camp until they were out of sight of the castle and it was well dark.

Gawaine considered his sister as she spread out a white linen cloth on the grass and laid the sack in which she had placed the head of the woman Ampflise upon it, as though it were the centerpiece of a table setting.

She had always been strange, very much their aloof mother's daughter, bold tongued and frank-eyed to a fault; the only one of Lot's children their sorcerous Aunt Morgan had ever taken a liking to. Clarissant had preferred her secret fairy games to the war play of Gawaine and his brothers. The few times they had tried to include her she would never deign to be rescued. She had once thrashed their brother Gaheris soundly for trying to force her to comply.

When they had gone off to Camelot and knighthood, Clarissant, dissatisfied with the role of a lady of the court, had struck out on her own. He knew she had apprenticed with their Aunt Morgan for a time, and he had heard rumors of her strange career; everything from her walling herself up in a Christian anchorhold to being inducted as a lady of Avalon. He had unhorsed more than a few wagging tongues over her numerous reputed amorous adventures as well. She seemed to change beds as often as she changed religions.

"What brought you to Caer Delex?" Clarissant asked him, while the other woman built the fire.

He looked at her blankly.

"The castle," she reiterated, slowly, as if he were an idiot. "Caer Delex."

"I didn't know its name," Gawaine said. "The Wild Forest is blackening and dying outward. Sir Sillimac and I set out to find out why. We tracked a pair of vandals from the tomb of

King Galdus at Cairnholy. It led us to a poison stream which flowed from that castle."

"What did they do to Galdus' barrow?" asked Clarissant.

"Broke it open, scattered his bones. Took his skull."

She looked at the other woman and nodded.

"That makes sense."

"Does it?"

"Betimes the heads of ancient kings are set to ward their lands against invasion," she said thoughtfully.

"Are they?" Gawaine asked, chuckling in exasperation. "What are you talking about Clarissant? What in the world were *you* doing there? What is all," and he gestured widely with his hand, to encompass the reliquary, her robes, and her shaven head, "*this*?"

"We," she said, indicating the other lady and the severed head on the linen in turn, "Floree and Ampflise and I were trying to infiltrate Caer Delex," she said. "You and your Sir Sillimac certainly ruined *that* plan."

The fire roared to life, and Gawaine caught his breath at the sight of Floree, her face illumined in the dark. It warmed him more than the fire itself, for despite her strange, smooth hairlessness, she was an exceedingly comely woman. Perhaps, he thought with a strange shiver, *because* of it.

Floree produced a hunk of bread and a jug of wine from a sack and held it out.

"Sir Gawaine?"

"Thank you," he said, taking the offered repast, and wondering when her large blue eyes met his.

"The Black Hermit rules in Caer Delex," Clarissant explained. "He is not a man. Not anymore. One of the nameless Architects of R'lyeh inhabits him. He grew that fell castle overnight."

"*Grew*?" Gawaine repeated.

She ignored him.

"The Black Hermit seeks to bring forth the other Architects to remake Galloway for Tulu The Dread, the Sleeping Leviathan, and to wake him that he may return and rule as he did in ancient days."

91

Floree, chewing quietly at her bread, met Gawaine's appreciative stare and smiled. Gawaine felt his blood bubble over and grinned back at her.

"Are you listening?" Clarissant snapped, shoving his head lightly as she had done when they were children.

He had heard most of it.

"So this Hermit, he's some kind of…what, demon? What about those men of his? Those black knights?"

"I don't know if they *are* men. Black metalcraft is the tool of the Hermit. He was once Tribüet, the master smith of old. Do you know his story?"

What knight did not? Tribüet had set out on an obsessive quest to become the greatest of metalworkers. He had forged various arms and armor by secret means in increasingly diverse and unearthly fires. The finest of his works, it was said, had been the last of three swords wrought in the furnaces of the gods; the most sinister, a cursed suit of armor fired in the flames of hell. It was said that the only thing that could break one of his masterworks was another weapon created by him.

Gawaine nodded.

"Tribüet found a secret way to R'lyeh and dived down into its depths. In its black forge, under the tutelage of the Architects, he forged the Mad Helm, his crowning achievement. But the Architects tricked him. The helm was a vehicle for one of their number, to take it beyond the twisted walls of R'lyeh. When Tribüet returned to Albion, he brought the Architect with him."

"What were you hoping to do?" Gawaine asked. "What was your plan?"

"We're sisters of the Order of the Elder Star," Clarissant said. "Dedicated to keeping the Old Ones from invading these lands. That reliquary," she said, pointing to the gilded carriage with its broken doors, "contained the skulls of thirteen of our departed masters and mistresses of old. The skull is the repository of all spirit and knowledge, Gawaine. I believe that is why The Black Hermit's knights claim the heads of their victims."

"What does he do with them?"

"Syphons their wisdom perhaps. Who can say? The gilded skulls were brimming with ancient knowing; knowledge that if accessed, could hold back the servants of Tulu."

She spat in the fire at the last.

"The stars told Ampflise the Black Hermit would seek them, so she conceived a plan to gain entrance to Caer Delex by bringing them in his reach. We had hoped to enter the castle with them, and use them to drive him back into the vastness."

"Well, it wasn't Sillimac and I that ruined your plans, then. Your Lady Amplfise was a poor tactician," Gawaine muttered.

"We were riding to present them as a gift. We assumed he would let us into his presence, where we'd be able to use the skulls to banish him."

"Surely he's destroyed them by now," said Gawaine.

"He cannot," said Clarissant. "The golden embellishments embossed within the braincases will bind any who attempt to do so with ancient logics."

Gawaine blinked, but she gave no further explanation.

Bolstered by the gaze of Floree, he drew himself up. "Well then what if I called this Black Hermit out?"

"Why do you suppose he would respond to a challenge from you?" Clarissant said. "Anyway, even if the archers didn't shoot you down, you'd never defeat him."

Gawaine bristled at that.

"I've a magic sword myself, remember," he said.

That was Galatine, his father's sword, which he had pried from the dead fingers of his father's slayer, King Pellinore. The golden quillions were adorned with etchings of Belenus' sacred plant, black henne-belle, whose seeds his father had taught him to chew before a hard fight. The pommel was emblazoned with the sunburst countenance of the god, and golden embellishments of his fiery chariot team twisted up the richly worked scabbard in gold filigree. The light of the sun fed its strength. At the zenith of noon, Gawaine was nearly unstoppable.

"No sword in Albion could hope to break The Mad Helm of Tribüet, except perhaps Excalibur itself," Clarissant said impatiently. "You would be defeated, Gawaine, and we would still be outside the castle."

"It's not a bad plan. We could disguise ourselves as Gawaine's squires," Floree said helpfully, "and so enter undetected."

"Again," Clarissant said, "if we're not pin-cushioned by black arrows without a word of warning before the gate. Was I the only one who saw what became of the others? The Black Hermit is no respecter of courtly manners. We can't shame him into a duel or appeal to his vanity."

Gawaine pulled his beard and rose, pacing, sullen at having his worth questioned in front of Floree by his own sister.

"What if we could appeal to Tribüet, who is within the Black Hermit?" Floree wondered aloud.

They waited for her to explain.

"Firstly, I know a knight who I feel sure would be able to defeat The Black Hermit," Floree said, her eyes darting apologetically to Gawaine.

"Who?" Clarissant said, as Gawaine turned his back and sulked, looking outward from the fire.

"Sir Percival de Galis."

"*Percival!*" Gawaine said, forgetting his churlishness in his surprise and turning to face Floree. "That wee *Christian whelp*?"

"My cousin," Floree said meekly, but quickly, before Gawaine could say more.

Gawaine bit back his words. Percival was brand new to the Round Table. Gawaine had never met him, but he had a reputation as something of an idiot who had practically stumbled into knighthood. Arthur's fool Sir Dagonet jokingly called him the only knight more perfect than himself. Yet, he had gained some renown. The Christian knights he knew said that his god was with him, while most others thought him exceedingly lucky.

"He might be the most skilled warrior in all Albion, but

what does that matter if he can't set foot within the walls of Caer Delex?" Clarissant asked.

"He bears the Last Sword of Tribüet," said Floree. "It was given to him by King Pellam of Lystenoyse."

This astounded Gawaine. How had Percival The Fool gotten a hold of a weapon like *that*? These Christian kings did not apparently distribute honors based on merit. But Pellam was Pellinore's brother, so Gawaine's opinion of the King of Lystenoyse could not be much lower.

Clarissant tapped her teeth with the end of her finger.

"Whatever this Percival's reputation, The Black Hermit, or rather, Tribüet, as you say, might not be able to resist reuniting that sword with the helm. It may stay the aim of the Hermit's archers, and it *is* the only thing that could break the Mad Helm. But where is he?"

"Alas, I don't know," said Floree.

"He quests for the Lost Grail," said Gawaine, "as do most of the Round Table. He could be anywhere. We might spend ages crawling over the hills and dales looking for him."

"Then we need the eye of one no longer bound by hills and dales," Clarissant said, and moved over to the sack containing the head of Ampflise. "Floree, bring me The Revelations."

Floree rose and went to the reliquary. She began to rummage inside.

"I thought you'd had your fill of Christianity when they bricked you up inside that chapel wall," Gawaine said teasingly.

"That was a misunderstanding on my part," she said. "And I didn't say which Revelations."

She removed a number of candles from a bindle, which she set around the corners of the linen cloth.

She undid the fastenings on the sack and reached in to take the head of Ampflise from within. Her eyes narrowed.

"Gawaine," she said, an edge of urgency to her voice. "Bring your sword over here."

"What's the matter?" Gawaine asked.

Clarissant stood and shook the sack from the head. When it fell away, Gawaine nearly pitched back on his culet.

95

The head of the Lady Ampflise twitched and shook in Clarissant's hands. The black webbing that had spread from the arrow in its eye just beneath the flesh, had sprouted a mass of similarly black tendrils from the neck. These snaky protuberances writhed and wound around Clarissant's wrists.

"If you're doing that, stop it," Gawaine said gravely.

"Of course I'm not doing it! Cut it, Gawaine! Use your sword! Cut it away!" she said, with an ever-increasing air of panic.

Gawaine drew Galatine and stepped toward his sister, unsure of precisely where to cut.

"Hurry, Gawaine! It's….tightening…."

Gingerly he reached out and gripped one of the black tubers encircling Clarissant's wrist with his gauntleted fingers. He was shocked to find them quite hard and unyielding. They were not roots or serpents at all, but a kind of animate metal, somehow hard as iron and yet pliant.

Floree came over with a thick, mottled book bearing strange markings, and a blue velvet bag which she dropped in surprise. The bag opened, spilling its contents; a mortar and pestle, a tinkling bell, a brush, and a set of iron tongs.

"Oh!" Floree exclaimed, putting her hand to her mouth.

Gawaine pulled at the coil of black metal around his sister's left wrist as much as he dared, and slid the blade of Galatine between it and her flesh, eliciting a sound of squealing metal against metal as he worked it down. He wasn't sure if he could cut the stuff, but to his surprise, the edge of Galatine parted it easily. The severed portion fell to the grass and whipped about, the cut end glowing a bright emerald color.

Gawaine kicked it into the fire, where it flared green and melted instantly away like candlewax.

"Floree, pass me the tongs!" Clarissant called, as Gawaine gingerly sawed the other tendril from her wrist and again, hastily toed the cut portion into the campfire.

Floree handed her the tongs.

Clarissant put her palm to the severed head and pinned it to the ground, avoiding the mass of snaking metal tubers groping beneath the neck. She pinched the shaft of the black arrow in the tongs and pulled it from the narrow opening of Ampflise's eye socket.

Gawaine watched in sickly fascination as the mass of tendrils were drawn up into the neck, the eye socket bulged, and the whole affair came bursting out of the wound, a disgusting, gleaming black mass caught like a squid in the pincers of Clarissant's tongs.

Immediately the arrow shaft lost its rigidity and began to writhe and whip about like a thing alive. It was as if it had only been masquerading as an arrow.

Gawaine raised his sword to slash at the thing, but Clarissant swiftly turned and held it in the fire.

Floree set the book down and took up the mortar.

The black thing curled and undulated like a ball of snakes in pain over the flames, then ignited as the cut halves had, in a strange, green flash, dissolving too quickly for any natural metal. It liquefied like emerald mercury, and Floree was there to catch the drippings in the mortar, where it cooled instantly into fine green shavings.

"What is that stuff?" Gawaine whispered.

"The raw material of R'lyeh. That in which the Architects work," said Clarissant. "Metal and stone, alive and dead."

She went to work pulverizing and mashing it down with the clinking pestle, muttering under her breath words Gawaine could not understand. They surely weren't the Latin spoken in the Christian masses.

Clarissant laid aside the tongs and took the mortar from Floree, who in turn, picked up the book with the mottled cover and knelt before Clarissant, holding it open, a human lectern.

Clarissant stirred the brush in the green stuff, reading in a loud voice some incantation from the strange book. She then turned and began to paint sharp, intricate green symbols on the severed head of Ampflise with the brush.

When she had inscribed the woman's entire face and scalp, she sat back on her heels and dumped the remaining pigment in the fire, where it flared an angry green before being consumed. She set the painted head of Ampflise in the center of the linen and lit a candle at each corner. Then she put her forehead to the ground, spoke more words, and rang the bell three times.

The slack face of Ampflise began to twitch, a horrid sight, around the gaping, ragged wound through which the black metal thing had been pulled.

Gawaine's neck hairs uncurled. Gooseflesh rose on his arms.

"What is..." he began, but Floree hushed him.

He stepped back and stared wild-eyed at the magic proceedings, gripping Galatine for all his worth and wishing it was morning. Every shadow around the edge of the fire seemed pregnant with all manner of horrors, demons worse than that in Caer Delex, manipulating the dead face of Ampflise with unseen hands, like puppeteers of indecorous humor.

Clarissant addressed the head, but the only words Gawaine understood was her name, Ampflise.

The unmarred blue eye, which had been drooping in the dead face, rolled and focused finally on his sister.

Gawaine put the edge of his hand in his mouth to keep his teeth from clicking together. He bit deep into the leather between the steel joints of his gauntlet when a low voice answered from the pale lips of Ampflise, echoing as though it came from somewhere far off.

Clarissant and the head conversed this way for a few moments, and the eye of Ampflise darted about as though searching for something. Then Clarissant rang the bell three times more and touched her head to the ground.

Floree shut the book. As soon as it closed, the animated face sagged lifeless once more.

Clarissant blew out the candles, carefully, reverently wrapped them up with the head in the linen cloth, and then stood and dropped the bundle in the fire.

"Sir Percival rests at the hermitage of Elyas on the River Luce," Clarissant announced. "Do you know it, Gawaine?"

Gawaine sighed.

"It's not far from here."

He absently rubbed the marks from his hand and turned from the fire, pursing his lips. It was where he'd intended to go in the first place. If he had spoken up, perhaps Sir Sillimac and the others would still be alive. But then, perhaps, Clarissant and Floree would now be with Amplfise, wherever she was.

"Then let's retire. We will ride forth in the morning," said his sister, with an air of self-satisfaction he found ill-suited to all that had just transpired.

The women huddled beneath the reliquary wagon. He slept away from the fire, one arm through the loop of Gringolet's reins, in case anything should come upon them in the night. The smell from the dwindling fire did not agree with him.

He dreamed fitfully of speaking skulls chattering away in foreign tongues on the bodies of bare, naked maidens, ankle deep in black metal grass that waved and curled up their legs like serpents.

Gawaine awoke to find Clarissant and Floree muttering prayers and scattering the campfire ashes to the four directions.

They breakfasted and set out over the countryside for the assart on the river, his sister driving the squeaking reliquary cart. Gawaine ranged ahead as was his habit, but fell back mid-journey beside the cart. In the light of full day the details of the carvings stood out. There were many symbols in the gilt-work he did not recognize. Prominent and recurring was a stylized, circled star with a kind of branch in the center, and a blazing eye. Mesmerizing whorls twisted like tentacles across the frame. These things did not interest him for long, and in the slender neck of the Lady Floree he found a more intriguing couch on which to rest his eyes.

Floree caught him looking at her.

"Is anything the matter, Sir Gawaine?" she asked, fighting a smile with mock innocence.

He did not look away. He was too old for such pretenses. She really was a lovely woman, with full lips and high cheeks, bright blue eyes and perfect, round ears, like fruit halves.

"I was just wondering what color your hair might have been, my lady."

She had no eyebrows even for him to guess.

She hid her smile with the back of her hand as beside her, Clarissant blew out her lips and cracked the reins, as though to pretend it was intended for the horses.

"Fair," she said. "The color of corn silk, like my mother's. I'm a sight now," she said, running a dainty hand self-consciously over her hairless head.

"You are at that," Gawaine agreed, appreciatively.

"Most men find it unseemly," Floree demurred.

"I am not most men," Gawaine said.

Floree smiled brightly and exchanged an amused look with Clarissant, who rolled her eyes.

"Why is a shorn skull required by your sisterhood?" Gawaine asked.

"Oh it's not! I lost it all in the strange wave that blew across Lystenoyse when Sir Balin struck King Pellam with the Holy Lance," Floree said. "Your sister too, and Lady Ampflise. We were all there at the christening of Pellam's daughter, Helizabel, when the Palace Adventurous fell. The waters dried up, the cattle fell dead, the crops shriveled. I fear our hair won't return until the Grail is restored."

Clarissant shrugged and scratched the top of her head absent-mindedly.

"I like it. Less of a bother in the morning, really. And no lugging around all those hairbrushes and combs and oils."

Floree laughed. It was a musical sound.

Gawaine shook his head.

"These Christians," he remarked. "They will be the doom of us."

"Why, do you think?" Floree asked.

"They are not of this land. The Crucified God is a god of the desert. Like this Black Hermit, he would make Albion a wasteland to suit his coming."

"Floree would not agree with you," Clarissant piped up in a singsong manner.

Gawaine looked from her to Floree. The latter had a pinched expression on her face, and lowered her head slightly.

Gawaine looked over at his sister, questioningly. She made a rapid, surreptitious cross sign with one hand, indicated Floree with her eyes and raised her eyebrows.

"My lady, your pardon," Gawaine said. "I didn't know. That is, after last night, I assumed…"

"That I was not Christian? The Order of The Elder Star welcomes pagans and Christians alike," Floree said tersely.

"The Templiese who guarded The Grail and the White Lady of Avalon, though opposed to each other, are the two great powers keeping the Old Ones out of Albion," Clarissant said. "When the Grail was lost, the Black Hermit saw an opportunity to encroach upon a weakened land. That is why the Order of The Elder Star moved to block him."

Gawaine tugged at his beard, wondering how to regain ground with Floree, but Clarissant widened the gap perniciously and said, "And you were doing so well, brother."

Gawaine went back to riding in front, the backs of his ears as red as his beard.

They sighted the stout wooden cross rising above the huts of the small hermitage on the far bank of the Luce, and found an elderly monk in plain sackcloth fishing there. He hailed them, and pointed out a safe place for them to ford upriver, gathering up his hook and line and a bucket of trout. He walked along to meet them at the crossing.

"God be with you, sir knight," the priest greeted him, and bobbed his head to the women. "Ladies. My name is Elyas."

"I'm Sir Gawaine, lord of the Castle of Marvels. This is my sister, Lady Clarissant, and this is the Lady Floree. We've ridden here seeking one of my companions of the Round Table, the Lady Floree's cousin."

"Sir Percival is here," said the old monk eyeing the bald women and the strange markings on the reliquary with growing suspicion. "He has been waiting for you."

Gawaine looked at Clarissant, but she did not seem surprised.

The monk led them back to the hermitage, and the other brothers paused in their various chores to stare at them as they passed. There was a rude chapel fashioned of the woven branches of the living wildwood. Inside, they found Sir Percival praying.

Gawaine almost laughed out loud at the sight of him. There was a running joke among the pagan knights of the Round Table about the great lengths to which their pharisaic Christian comrades went to demonstrate their piety. Sir Percival could not have arranged a more sanctimonious presentation for himself if he had donned a golden halo.

The young knight knelt at the altar, his bright blonde head bowed in humility before the great cross suspended from the ceiling. The many crisscrossing shafts of sunlight seeping through gaps in the leafed, lattice walls of the rustic chapel rendered his meticulously polished armor a blinding suit of pure light, so it was actually difficult to look directly at him. His shield leaned against the altar, bearing his attributed arms, *Purpure, semy of plain crosslets or.* There was something familiar about that charge, but Gawaine couldn't place it. Heraldry was not his strong suit.

The sword of Tribüet, the polished pommel and guard glinting in the rich scabbard woven with lines of thread-of-gold crosses, rested at his side.

Chattering crossbills and twittering little robins flitted back and forth from their nests in the ceiling, circling him like attendant cherubs, sometimes landing on the altar to peep at him. He was like an idealized Christian tapestry come to life. What was the warrior angel his uncle Arthur invoked in his knighting ceremonies? Michael. Percival looked like an illuminated page from a hagiography of St. Michael.

"How long will he be at prayer?" Gawaine whispered discreetly to the old hermit.

"He has been thus since his arrival, three days ago."

"Three days?" Gawaine exclaimed loudly. "We don't have time for this." He stepped into the chapel nave and cleared his throat. "Sir Percival! I am Sir Gawaine."

"I remember you, Sir Gawaine," said Percival, his voice

102

emerging in a lilting Welsh singsong. He rose and turned, and the sunlight crested behind his head, lighting his blonde hair gold. Gawaine realized wryly that the boy had no need of a halo. He nodded to them, peering with his huge blue eyes through a curtain of mussed yellow hair.

Gawaine frowned. Had they met in Camelot? He didn't think they had.

"Hello, cousin," Percival said to Lady Floree. "And you are, Milady?"

Gawaine furrowed his brow and looked at his sister when she did not answer immediately. He found her lips parted as if in wonder.

"This is my sister, Lady Clarissant," Gawaine said.

"Clarissant!" She blurted at the same time.

"I dreamed of you, Milady."

Gawaine thought she would crumble to the floor, but she caught sight of her brother's apparent amusement and regained her composure, although she could not stop her blushing.

"We have come...."

"You have come to lead me to the end of a quest that has occupied my family since my grandfather's youth."

"We have?" Clarissant asked.

He bent to retrieve his arms and spoke as he belted on his sword.

"There was a maiden, pure and innocent, the daughter of a king named Hipomenes. She had a brother, Hocelice, who by night dabbled in unholy sciences. He conceived in his dreams a wondrous little copper trephine, and bored a tiny hole through which he could peek into the depths of Hell. He wiled his days peering through the burr hole at Hell's sights and writing down all he saw. By this means, a demon wriggled into his eye, and he saw his own sister through the haze of the demon's lust, and ravaged her. Her father found him in the act, and set dogs upon him, and tore him to pieces. An abomination was born of the maiden, Galtisant by name, which slew its mother and all the attendant midwives. The king's brother, my great grandfather, vowed to destroy the beast and its sire. God told me last night that the Black Hermit you oppose is the same demon that fathered Galtisant, and that you would come to lead me to him."

Arthur had told them of this thing years ago. Galtisant was an immense hooved monster with a head like a serpent, and the body of a leopard. He had told them it made a sound like thirty hounds copulating.

Something made the bottom drop out of his guts.

"Did not King Pellinore hunt that beast? The Questing Beast?" Gawaine asked.

Percival came to stand before them now. Gawaine thought he smelled of that incense the priests burned in their services.

"He did," said Percival, looking frankly into Gawaine's eyes, "before he was slain. Now that task has passed onto Sir Palamedes. But the sire of Galtisant is mine to destroy."

Gawaine tensed. That was when he remembered the field of little crosslets on Percival's shield. Pellinore's charge had borne them too; as did the crests of all of his sons. He hadn't known Percival was one of them.

So had Percival been awaiting Clarissant's arrival, or his? Did the young knight mean to avenge his father? Surely he knew from his brothers who Gawaine was, and what he had done.

Percival looked past him to Clarissant.

"When will we start?"

"Why are you not out after The Grail?" Gawaine asked.

"I sought The Grail for a time," Percival answered. "But I am not the one who will win it. God told me so."

"You mean you gave up?" Gawaine said, probing.

"The Lord revealed my true destiny," said Percival, unaffected by Gawaine's purposeful jibe. "It is to slay the demon sire of The Questing Beast. With this," he said, drawing out the sword at his side with a ring.

Gawaine nearly drew Galatine in answer, but Percival made no move to attack.

The Last Sword of Tribüet caught the light, and as his sister had been enamored by its handsome young wielder, Gawaine caught his breath at the fineness of the blade. It was plain of marking, not even gold-chased. To the untrained eye, it was quite plain. But Gawaine recognized its exquisite craft. It appeared flawless. There was the legendary maker's mark; the small red 't' of 'Tribüet' worked into the design of the blood groove. He supposed King Pellam had thought it was a cross.

"The Last Sword of Tribüet!" Gawaine whispered appreciatively.

Gawaine reached out impulsively and gripped Percival's sword hand. He turned the blade to the light to better see it.

The young knight looked aghast at Gawaine's impertinence, and tried to pull the sword away, but Gawaine, testing the boy's strength, found he was stronger. He didn't let go until he had inspected the sword to his content, and noticed the infinitesimal lightning sliver running from the foot of the maker's mark down the blade's ricasso, to the crossguard.

"Be careful, lad. It's ready to break," Gawaine said, releasing Percival's hand.

"It saw many battles before ever it came to me. God revealed to me that it has but one blow left," said Percival, easing it back into its sheath. He looked meaningfully at Gawaine. "That will be enough."

"A fine thing, to go into a fight with a sword ready to break," Gawaine scoffed. "Miss your one blow and you may break in its place."

"I don't believe it's God's will that I miss," said Percival, and then looked once more to Clarissant. "When?"

"After supper, I think," Gawaine said, stretching and looking to the monk. "If we haven't caught you during a fast, Father?"

The monk shook his head. "You are our guests."

"You look a little underfed, Percival," Gawaine remarked, and rapped the younger man's breastplate once soundly with the back of his gauntlet. "We've a saying here in Galloway. He who has contempt for food is a fool. Tuck in. You'll need your strength."

"As will you, I think," Percival retorted, almost under his breath.

Floree stepped between them and embraced her cousin, kissing his cheek.

"Tell me of my uncle and my cousins," she said. "How is Aglovale?"

They walked off arm in arm with the monk, toward the hermitage proper, chatting away.

"Try not to chivvy the lad into a fight before we return to Caer Delex," Clarissant whispered, putting her hand on his arm as they walked behind. "Why did you bully him?"

"He's one of Pellinore's sons. Pellinore killed our father."

"And you killed Pellinore," said Clarissant. "And there it should end."

"There is what should be and what inevitably will be," said Gawaine.

"He was a boy when all that bad blood began," Clarissant said. "I beseech you. Don't ruin our quest before it's begun, brother. There's more at stake than you can believe. More than some petty feud."

Gawaine fought down his ire and managed a smile for his sister.

"I'll spare him awhile." He laughed and patted her hand. "For you."

"There's no such stuff in my thoughts," Clarissant said gruffly.

"Hah, you forgot to breathe when he showed his pretty face."

"It wasn't that," she said. "Didn't you see it?"

"What?"

"The blessing of Belenus. It was shining all about him."

After they had enjoyed the hospitality of the hermitage, the monks offered to let them stay the evening. It was a few hours from sunset but Gawaine, sleepy with beer and roast swan, was wont to take them up on the offer. Percival was eager to be on his way though, and with Clarissant and Floree in agreement, he was outvoted.

His annoyance at departing so late in the day combined with the sight of the handsome, clean young knight riding with his lance high in the saddle of his muscled black destrier taxed Gawaine. This was the youngest son of his hated enemy, and he knew the youth was plotting his death, just as he had done for Pellinore. He knew badgering the boy would only hinder their quest and likely swing him from the favor of the Lady Floree, and that vexed him all the more.

There was an otherworldly detachment to the boy he usually found prevalent in Christian priests. Such aloof self-assurance in one so young and inexperienced naturally annoyed him. It was as if he thought himself too good for this world; certainly too good for Gawaine's company. Gawaine was determined that the fight to come should be in the open. He didn't want this Christian passing a dagger under his chin while he slept, and he didn't want to issue the challenge himself. He decided he would force the would-be avenger's hand.

When he caught Percival muttering a prayer into his mailed fist on the trail, he rode up alongside him. He had found the easiest way to rile a Christian to fight was to call into question his inane faith.

"You seem to speak an awful lot to your god for a living man."

"My God is a living god," Percival answered with a shrug.

"I thought you only got to see him when you died."

"Who do you pray to, Sir Gawaine?"

Gawaine pointed to the sun in the sky.

"There's *my* god. Belenus. Every day he rides his chariot across the sky, so I know he's there."

"Where does he go every night?" Percival asked.

"To shine his blessings on other lands. Other peoples." As a child he had assumed Belenus retired to his stables at night, but now he knew the god's ride was endless around the earth. Merlin had once told him it was so.

"So he exists in some place you cannot see," Percival said.

"Of course!"

"Then one does not need to see to know. That is faith, sir."

Gawaine frowned, but quickly forced a laugh.

"Ah, but you just now admitted Belenus existed," Gawaine

said. "Isn't that a grave sin in your faith? Isn't your god jealous of other gods?"

"God makes himself known to many peoples in ways in which they may best understand Him," Percival said. "God cannot be jealous of Himself. It is the burden of men to learn truth or cleave to lesser perceptions."

An answer for everything. And Gawaine hadn't even understood it. It was like arguing with a damned priest.

Ahead of them, the reliquary came to a stop, and they drew up the reins of their horses.

"The only truth is," called Clarissant, leaning from the cart, "whatever gods there may be, it would be better for men not to pray to them. It's grave misfortune to attract the attention of a god."

"Why'd you stop?" Gawaine asked.

"There is something up ahead," said Floree.

Gawaine and Percival looked at each other, both embarrassed at having their female charges alert them to anything amiss. They trotted their horses up in front of the cart.

They had come to the outer edge of the Wild Forest, very near the long plain and the foothills of the uplands where the castle crouched. They could not see it yet, but Gawaine did make out the dark shimmer of the malignant black stream in the far distance.

Floree pointed to the tree line. After a few moments of staring, something disturbed the bushes there.

"Just game, foraging for food," Percival suggested.

"Perhaps," said Gawaine. "Or an ambush." He nodded to Floree. "Your eyes are as sharp as they are beautiful, milady. Don't stand there like a quintain, boy!" he barked at Percival.

He spurred Gringolet into a gallop toward the trees, and Percival had to urge his horse to keep up. When he fell in, Gawaine slowed to allow him to ride alongside. He didn't want the Christian accidentally piercing his back.

"If it is an ambush should we ride into it in this way?" Percival asked, fumbling to fasten on his helmet. "We don't know their number."

"We certainly don't play the fools and let the women ride into it. If they are hostile, they already know we've spotted them. Best to get the fight out of the way."

He was not one for clever maneuvering or subterfuge. If it was only animals, or brigands, they would break and run. If archers from Caer Delex, well, they would know in a minute. Whatever their number, as he drew Galatine and the high sun caught the bare blade, Gawaine felt the strength of Belenus in his arms and hollered a wordless challenge.

Percival leveled his lance.

What the bushes concealed did not break and retreat deeper into the wood. What instead rushed out to meet them seemed too nightmarish to even exist under the light of the day. There were six of them, hideous, akin to men in size and little else. They bounded out low to the ground like hounds on four wiry, clawed limbs, yet they were hairless, and rippling, black and orange-spotted hides of dull brass scales covered their bizarre bodies. Their oblong torsos began in blunt, neck-less heads of white bulging eyes set on either side of their narrow faces and tapered into whipping tails with flared, sharp looking fins like those of overgrown finnocks. They sported overlong, protruding lower jaws and wide, thick-lipped mouths of broad teeth that clicked as they came. A putrid, but all-too familiar smell of sea-rot preceded them.

Gringolet reared in surprise at the sight of them coming low through the grass, and Gawaine slipped from the saddle and crashed on his back.

Percival's horse, whether steadier or simply too committed to stop its charge, stayed its course. The knight's lance shot straight down the open maw of one of the low things, going so deep Percival was forced to leave it there. The thing shuddered and collapsed, its great, crooked, square teeth chipped and broken, its yawning jaw propped open by the flaring handle of the lance protruding from its mouth.

Gawaine rolled to his feet as the other three came slashing wildly toward him. Galatine sang and flashed silver. Scales scattered across the blue sky like dull coins with twisting, clawed hands amid whips of murky black blood.

The things made no outcry in pain or rage, only hissed like serpents or ground their teeth. One leapt at him like a lion and he brought up his shield. Its claws gripped and slashed around it, and its tail battered against him. It brought its full weight up on his shield arm, forcing him to let it go or be dragged down. As the thing writhed to get out from underneath the discarded shield, Gawaine drove the point of Galatine under its chin.

The others swarmed over him, slashing and nipping. He struck and flung them bodily away, but without room to swing his sword, they only regained their feet and returned. As he was driven down by the sheer weight of them, he felt part of his beard rip painfully away, and wished he had donned his helm. Their claws raked his face, seeking his eyes, his throat. He wondered if this would be Percival's revenge; to stand idly by while he was dismembered by this pack of oily horrors.

Then Percival, having rounded his horse, returned. He leapt from the saddle with his shield in one hand and a javelin from the quiver on his horse in the other. He brought the tapered base down onto the back of one and it hissed and shook, allowing Gawaine to shove it off.

Above him, Percival struck left and right, alternating between his battering shield and stabbing javelin, stoving in skulls and transfixing bodies with neat precision. Gawaine had to admit the young man was an able fighter.

Gawaine found his sword and hewed all about him, fighting his way to his feet again, hacking until his face was spattered in the foul smelling blood. Percival bashed with his shield, and, having lost his light javelin, jabbed his armored thumb and forefinger into the eyes of one of the creatures and jerked it by its skull to the ground. He pushed the edge of his shield down through its belly and cut it in two. Its stinking innards spilled around his mailed sabatons as its upper half scrambled away from its thrashing lower portion.

The last of the legged finnock-things crawled away headless. Gawaine leaned on his blood-blackened sword and watched its bug-eyed head lying a few feet away gulp air for its lost lungs and finally surrender.

He wheeled on Percival, who had already gone to one knee, bowed his head, and begun uttering a prayer of thanksgiving.

"A shield and a pig sticker? You've a sword at your side!"

"A sword with only one blow left," Percival said, straightening. He wrinkled his nose at the stench the weird carcasses gave off.

But who was that one blow meant for? The Black Hermit, or the knight who had slain his father? Gawaine wondered.

When they returned to the reliquary, Clarissant and Floree raised their hands at the smell they brought with them.

"What were they?" Floree asked.

"Sillimac and I found creatures like these along the banks of the black stream that's running through the Wild Forest. They were pulling themselves from the muck. But they were smaller. Just whelps."

"They were like great trout with legs," said Percival in amazement.

"Beasts fit for the kennels of R'lyeh," said Clarissant. "Likely they *were* fish at one time, as the black knights were once men."

"It was like fighting a pack of wolves. If they can leave the streams and grow so quickly, they could raid the farms and villages," Gawaine said.

"All the more reason for us to be on our way," said Clarissant.

"We should stow the cart here," said Floree.

They pulled the golden reliquary to the shade of some trees. As Percival unhitched the horses from their traces, the women produced a set of tunics and hoods taken from the hermitage and went behind the cart to change.

Gawaine drove Galatine into the earth to clean the blade of the black blood, and stooped to hastily braid a pair of bridles for the draft horses. As he worked, he spied the long white legs of Floree under the wagon.

"What are your designs on my cousin, sir?" Percival asked in a low voice.

Gawaine couldn't stop a surprised laugh.

"Nothing worse than your father had on your mother, lad."

"She is a Christian woman, sir," said Percival. "If you would dishonor her, then we shall be at odds."

He came around the rear of the horse with one hand on his sword hilt.

Gawaine stared soberly. Was this fool's understanding of men and women so naïve, or did he simply assume he was a lusting barbarian because of his gods? Or, was this the moment at last? Was this the excuse Percival intended to use to challenge him?

"*That* is why we shall be at odds?" said Gawaine. "We've just faced monsters, and we'll face still more before the sun rises on us again. Your only hope is to deal one blow and one blow only to a demon from hell. But you intend to break your sword on me, don't you?"

Gawaine finished the bridles and stood.

Percival knitted his pale eyebrows, but did not back down, though Gawaine loomed over him.

"You don't remember me," said Percival, and there seemed to be a hint of disappointment in his tone.

"What makes you think you're so memorable?" Gawaine scoffed, turning his back on him and going to fit the bridles on the horses.

Percival didn't move.

"I bear you no ill will for my father, Sir Gawaine," said Percival, quietly.

Gawaine looked at him, surprised and a bit flustered.

"My mother told me how my father killed King Lot at Carhaix," Percival went on.

"Did she tell you it was after he surrendered to your father?" Gawaine growled, balling his fists.

"Yes," said Percival.

Gawaine had been ready to roar and fight. The simple affirmation stopped him cold.

"My father did your family a great sin," said Percival, thoughtfully, "and my brothers have perpetuated that sin in fostering their grief and anger. When you challenged my father and slew him, it was under the eyes of God. No knight who is false may stand against one who is true. So know, Sir Gawaine, I do not seek vengeance for my father. But I ask again; what is your intention with my cousin Floree?"

Gawaine stared long at Percival. Shamed by the youth's admirable forbearance, he immediately covered it with bluster.

"By the gods, you've pluck, lad," said Gawaine. "I can't say I like you, and I'm not sure as I respect you yet, but you've pluck. I don't know what you've heard of pagans, but I've no intent whatsoever of ravaging any lady, least of all your fair cousin."

"What word can you give?" Percival pressed.

"Are you really serious? What word would you take? You Christians don't respect any oath not taken on some bit of your god; his blood, his toenails, slivers from his deathbed...."

"Swear by your father's name," said Percival. He gestured to Galatine. "On that sword. That you will protect and honor her, even in my absence."

Then Gawaine understood the trueness of this young knight's heart. Percival was not a fool at all; he had no illusions about the outcome of their quest.

Gawaine pulled Galatine free of the earth and considered it. He held it up, put the cool blade to his forehead, and stared into Percival's eyes.

"By this sword, Galatine. And by King Lot of Orkney, my father. I will protect and honor your cousin in your absence as I would my own life. I swear it."

"What do you swear?" Lady Floree asked as she and Clarissant came around the side of the wagon in their squire's disguises; ill-fitting tunics, worn breeches, and drooping hoods.

"I would swear you were squires if I didn't know better," Gawaine said coolly, sheathing his sword.

He shot a wink at Percival, who nodded in silent acceptance.

113

The women mounted on the white draft horses. The knights handed them their shields, and they rode for the black stream. The sun was down behind the uplands when they saw the carrion birds wheeling about the exposed bodies of Lady Ampflise, Sir Sillimac, and the others well before they saw Caer Delex. They marked Lady Ampflise as the outer range of the archers on the wall, and so stopped a few feet from her headless body.

Gawaine had his hunting horn, and sounded it. The carpet of black crows converged on the bodies of the dead before the gate stirred and fluttered, then settled back down to their grisly repast.

They received no reply.

Percival drew his sword and held it up, so it caught the fading sunlight.

"I am Sir Percival de Galis!" he yelled in a surprisingly commanding voice. "And this is my witness, Sir Gawaine of Orkney! I would challenge the master of this castle, who calls himself The Black Hermit! He must answer for the deaths of Prince Hocelice and the Princess Marche, and for the rampages of the creature called Galtisant, and he must answer for these goodly men and this lady lying dead at his doorstep."

There was still no response.

Clarissant hissed behind him;

"Mention the Last Sword of Tribüet. Tell them you have it!"

"I bear The Last Sword of Tribüet!" Percival added, a little unsure. "May it, with God's help, bring you swift justice!"

Gawaine braced for a flight of arrows, and wondered if they truly were out of range. He could see the ravens worrying the headless corpse of Ampflise like black demons rooting for the morsel of her soul within. Could the archers see clearly to shoot in the gloaming?

There was no sound but the cawing of the ravens.

Then the great doors groaned slowly open, setting the black birds flapping into the air. No knights poured forth. No one at all emerged from the deep darkness to meet them.

Percival and Gawaine urged their mounts forward. Clarissant and Floree pulled their hoods low.

The clopping of the horses joined the intermittent cries of the resettling birds, and as they passed among the picked over corpses of the men and boys, they heard the bubbling of the black stream coursing under the wall nearby.

Gawaine feared he would sprout a headdress of arrows at any moment. Searching for any thought that would break the tension, he remembered something Percival had said.

"Sir Percival," he said.

"Yes?"

"You said I did not remember you," Gawaine said. "Where have we met? At Camelot?"

"No, sir," said Percival as they passed under the arch of the front gate. "I will remind you, by and by."

A pair of the black armored men in visor-less helmets pulled the gates shut behind them. They clanged with resounding finality in the still courtyard.

"You must ensure there will be a by and by, then," said Gawaine.

"With your help, there surely will be," said Percival.

They became aware of another sound, a low, persistent hum they could not place. It reminded Gawaine of the drone of insects to which he had awakened in the Orkneys all those years ago.

They crossed the barren, black stone courtyard to the base of the strange, windowless keep, where another faceless man in black spiked armor stood aside and opened the door for them.

They dismounted. Clarissant and Floree took the helms and shields from their horses and walked behind Gawaine and Percival like dutiful squires, but the armored man put out his hand in front of the women and stopped them from proceeding.

"These are our squires," said Percival. "They go where we go."

The black armored man kept his arm out, but then slowly lowered it and stepped back.

115

Gringolet shone pale as a ghost horse in the darkening courtyard, and Gawaine wondered if he would see his faithful mount again.

They had expected the flickering of torch fire in the sunless keep, but there was only a steady, if dim glow, emanating from where, they could not tell. They found themselves, not in the foyer of some multi-leveled fortress, but in the bottom of an immense, shadowed well. The entire central tower of the keep was hollow, to accommodate a breathtaking pillar of burnished, apparently seamless copper, which stretched near to the ceiling and glowed dully in the ambient light.

Numerous passages, spiraling, concentric balconies and oddly angled stairways were set high into the walls, no doubt leading to the crazily branching towers they had spied from the outside, though they could not see a way to reach the lowest landings.

No tapestries, no banners hung in that dreadful space. The Black Hermit employed but one decoration; bones, piled in tall, disorderly ricks on the floor against the wall.

"No skulls," said Floree.

"What?" said Gawaine.

"Bones, but no skulls," Clarissant affirmed. "Where are the reliquary skulls? They could be anywhere."

The well echoed with sound. They discerned that the source of the steady hum they had detected in the courtyard originated from somewhere within the copper pillar. It pounded and churned and burred repetitively, like the predictable, mechanical turning of a watermill, or, many watermills made of metal. There was a distant roaring above too, of water falling. They realized that the clear water that spilled from the uplands overhanging the castle poured directly into the open, funnel top of this copper pillar hundreds of feet above their heads. It passed through the guts of this thing, which meant it was the source of the blackening, noxious muck that flowed from Caer Delex across the plain and into the Wild Forest.

Walking further into the grand chamber, they perceived the

faint, familiar stench of the black stream, and Gawaine saw a ring of seepage staining the base of the copper pillar, or machine, whatever it was.

"This is the source," said Gawaine.

"He's pumping the stuff of the Architects into our world through that," Clarissant said.

"Like the trephine," Floree said.

They turned to look at her for an explanation.

"Hocelice's trephine to Hell," she explained. "But larger."

"Not Hell," Clarissant whispered. "R'lyeh."

At her utterance of the name, there was a loud, ear-piercing cry from above, somewhere between the hoarse shriek of a vulture and the yowl of a panther in the night. Something stirred at the top of the copper pillar, something shiny and black, which began to slither slowly down, wending around the structure like a serpent descending a tree. There came the tromping of many steel shod feet, and they turned every which way to discern the approach, but could not, for it came from all around.

From every honeycomb passage in the walls of the well, down every steep stair and out onto every balcony, lines of bell-headed blind warriors assembled in spiny black armor. Their marching out was a rhythmic thrumming that beat in time to the internal hammering of the pillar, so loud in the cavernous well tower that Gawaine and Percival, Clarissant and Floree pressed their palms to their ears to dull it.

When it finally stopped, men stood silently surrounding them, arranged like a coliseum of faceless spectators. The steady noise of the copper pillar seemed relatively quiet in the aftermath.

Meanwhile, the immense, oily black creature descending the copper column curled about the base. It possessed a bulbous body indistinguishable from its head, in which a number of shining black eyes, each the size of a round shield, bulged and moved independently. Its bulk was borne by the cooperation of an uncountable number of segmented millipedal limbs, each one tapering into a slithering tentacular extremity, like feet dragging stretched-out hosiery. If the

117

finnock-things were of R'lyeh's kennels, then, Gawaine thought, this must be a beast from that fell city's stables.

Atop it, or perhaps emerging from it somehow, for they could see no legs astride it, was a figure they took to be The Black Hermit himself. He was a gaunt shape in spiked black armor, but his drawn, elderly face could be seen beneath the visor of a magnificent, gleaming black sallet meticulously embossed with strange, curling golden designs. His eyes glittered in the darkness.

When he spoke, his teeth were black, and the corners of his lips were pitch-stained, as though he had drunk from whatever font discharged the black liquid. Gawaine noticed too that the web of dark veins he had seen spread across Ampflise's head from the malignant arrow covered The Black Hermit's face too.

"Who bears the Last Sword of Tribüet?" he croaked. His voice seemed a long way off, and again Gawaine was reminded of the voice of Amplfise as it came from her severed head.

Percival drew the sword and held it up.

"Give it to me," said The Black Hermit, holding out his black armored hand with its long, pointed fingers.

"There is only one way you may claim it," Percival said.

"Gawaine," whispered Clarissant, tugging his arm. "Look."

He looked where she indicated, and saw, standing among the stoic, uniformly armored onlookers, a hint of gold and a glint of jewels beneath the rim of one of the bell-shaped helms.

"There are seven of them," she whispered, pointing out the others.

"What does it mean?" Gawaine wondered distractedly, more interested in how Percival's challenge would unfold. He looked back at The Black Hermit, and saw him plunge his hand into his mount's back and draw forth a long black flamberge. He didn't understand if the weapon was stored there, or somehow formed from the creature itself.

Clarissant slapped him upside the head.

"Gawaine there are seven, you lummox! Our seven skulls!"

Gawaine furrowed his brow.

"Then fight and die!" The Black Hermit called down.

The creature released its grip on the copper column and drooped heavily to the floor with a wet sound.

Gawaine drew Clarissant and Floree aside as Percival took up his shield and slapped down the visor of his helm.

The thing wended toward him with surprising speed, and with equally remarkable grace, the young knight dodged aside and raked the flank of The Black Hermit's mount with the pointed end of his shield as it slithered by.

"Gawaine!" Clarissant called. "Their heads! You must take off their heads! Remember Ampflise? These metal bodies grow out from the heads. The skulls are inside the helmets!"

Gawaine looked around at the multitude of armored men standing witness.

"If I attack they'll all attack," Gawaine said.

"If you do not attack, there is no hope!" Floree said.

Gawaine picked at the chord around the back of his neck and drew out the sacket of henne-bore seeds he kept there behind his breastplate.

"What are you doing?" Clarissant asked as he tore the sacket open with his teeth.

"If you can manage to get a hold of our horses in the courtyard, you can make your escape," Gawaine said.

"There is no escape without the skulls!" Clarissant insisted.

"Oh hell, then let no one escape!" Gawaine said, and dumped the seeds down his throat.

He threw down his shield and drew Galatine two-handed, felt the blood in his face boiling as the blessed seeds of Belenus did their work, injecting sun fire into his veins.

He rushed at the wall of knights. They didn't react, even when he drew back the sword and swept it cleanly under the bell helm of one of their number; the one with the golden chin and the jeweled teeth.

The helmet clanged to the ground and the gilded skull

rolled out glittering, black tentacles such as he had seen sprouting from the neck of Ampflise spilling out, glowing green where they had been severed, then flaking away to filaments.

His sister had apparently run behind him. She scooped up the skull and put her own forehead to it muttering something that caused the jeweled eyes to shine.

Then she glanced at her brother.

"Don't stop!"

He couldn't if he wanted to. He had never ingested so many henne-bore seeds at once, and as the black metal men belatedly raised their weapons, he cut down three more, knocking their heads spinning from their spiked shoulders, whether they were golden or not. He tore the arm off another with a mighty swipe, but noticed the thing hardly reacted. Black metal tendrils writhed from the empty stump. Only the heads mattered. Well, he had had some experience with severing heads, when the Green Knight had come to Camelot all those years ago.

He heard his sister calling out instructions, but whether they were to him or to Floree he hardly knew or cared. He gave himself up to the will of Belenus, letting the god fight for him.

As his mind clouded and swam in a scarlet haze, like a drowning man, he held one thought above the rising red depths: *take their heads.*

They came at him in bristling black streams and he mowed them like a farmer at harvest time, sending them tumbling opposite their rolling helms. They leapt from the heights of the balconies, somehow landing on their feet with tremendous impacts, and he beheaded them before they straightened, rushing back and forth to catch and kill them as they came down.

He stumbled over armored bodies, pricked his legs on the sharp spikes protruding from the fallen, who became like siege obstacles on the floor, at least providing some use in death. Some struck him. He was aware of blows, but dimly, as one half-asleep is aware of a conversation in another room.

Blood splashed his face now and then, and he knew it must be his because no blood poured from his enemies. They cut at him with their swords, and when he lopped their weapon arms away they crowded him *en masse* with their spiked pauldrons, bodily forcing him back in a heaving tide, dinting his armor, ringing his helm, steel and evil iron squealing as they met.

He shoved back and struck, heaved and kicked out, clearing them away like a whirling silver wind till a knee high wall of headless dead ringed him and the black metal knights had to scramble over a berm of their fallen to tackle him. Still he put his feet apart and stood. When he had no room to swing Galatine, he thrust his fingers under the helms of the warriors pressing him and grabbing fistfuls of the black metal tendrils he knew to be there. He yanked them out bodily and ripped the heads free, throwing them over his shoulder. He twisted them around and off. He wrenched them clear of their shoulders and battered them loose with his blood-soaked gauntlets.

Still they came at him, scaling spider-like head-first down the very walls of the well like black steel vermin.

Exhausted, soon he was only held up by the dead and those about to die pressing close all about him, thrusting at him with their weapons and their wicked armor. He tasted his own blood. Smelled it. Blinked it from his eyes. As his lids fluttered, he cast his gaze about wonderingly over the hedge of black iron thorns and saw the slight bald form of his sister arranging something on the floor. He saw the white form of Floree dart for the door and flinched as it wrenched open and the light of the outside spilled across the floor. Light? What light? It was surely black dark outside.

Then something else bright caught his eye. He spied the rearing bulk of the thing that was The Black Hermit, or his steed. He saw a small, glittering silver form clinging to it, scaling it; Percival, his armor hanging from him in broken pieces, bleeding from a dozen wounds. The Black Hermit raised his long sword and brought the wavy blade crashing down on his helm before he could raise his sundered shield. At first Gawaine feared the youth's head had come off, but

121

the blonde hair caught the light, blood running freely from his scalp, painting half his face red like some savage warrior Pict.

But what light glanced off his broken armor and golden head? It seemed like a sunbeam flowed across Percival as he watched, and the Black Hermit's mount reared. Gawaine looked again to the open door. Was that sunlight? Had the morning come? It didn't seem possible.

But with Belenus, it was.

Gringolet galloped in, with Percival's black steed behind, and Floree waving her hands and shouting from behind, as if the two loyal warhorses needed encouragement.

Gawaine, drowning now in blood and iron thorns, felt the sun fall warm on his face, warmer than the blood running there, and with surge of effort, he burst halfway from the tangle of metal men, lunged, and caught Gringolet's stirrup as the horse charged close by. The destrier jerked him free of the tumult and dragged him across the chamber, his bloodied armor scraping along the flagstones, Galatine sending up a trail of sparks behind.

Percival let go of the black beast and dropped onto his horse's back as it passed, galloping alongside Gringolet. The two horses stopped when they reached the opposite end of the chamber, and Clarissant was there to catch their muzzles and stop them from ploughing into her work. She had arranged the seven golden skulls Gawaine had freed from their black metal hosts, and set them in an oddly shaped pyramid. Her arms were dripping with blood from deliberate slashes on her forearms, rendering odd patterns.

"I'm almost ready," she said, it seemed, more to herself than to them, for she turned back to the pile of skulls and flailed her arms one after the other, flecking the gilded bones deliberately with blood and chanting in that unknown tongue.

The eyes of the skulls glowed with a gold and blue light.

Across the room, the horde of black metal men clattered toward them, the writhing beast with the Black Hermit falling back against the copper column, the vile rider directing them with his flamberge, shouting commands in a language not dissimilar to whatever spell Clarissant was working.

"His beast is too strong," Percival gasped, laying against the neck of his horse. "I can't even reach him." He hadn't even drawn the sword and his harness was hanging off him in pieces.

"Leave the beast to me," said Gawaine, picking himself off the floor.

"You can barely stand!" Percival said, sliding off the back of his mount to help Gawaine up.

"I don't need to stand," Gawaine gasped. He felt little pain. His whole body was growing numb from the legs up. He feared he had not long before his arms would not heed his commands. "Help me into the saddle."

Percival was exhausted himself, and it took both him and Clarissant to heave Gawaine up on Gringolet's back.

"Mount, Percival!" Gawaine urged, as the host closed on them. "Draw your sword. One blow!"

"One blow," Percival nodded tiredly, unfastening his armor and letting it clatter to the floor. He pulled himself back on his horse with a groan.

"Follow my lead!" Gawaine roared, and spurred Gringolet directly at the black metal men.

"For God and Albion!" Percival called behind him.

"For Belenus," Gawaine muttered.

Gringolet lowered his head and crashed headlong into the host, shrieking as the spikes of their armor tore his hide. Still it leapt and kicked and forced its way slowly through, like a beast thrashing in a field of brambles. Men fell; others took their places and so fell, still others slashed at him, tried to pull him from the saddle. He only hoped Percival was directly behind.

They pushed through toward the great black beast and the Hermit astride it. Then he felt Gringolet shudder between his knees. He grieved. Long he had ridden the magnificent charger, and who knew how many battles it had seen under Clarion, the Saxon king whom Gawaine had won the horse from at the siege of Carhaix. As its mighty heart gave out and it stumbled headlong, Gawaine leapt from the saddle over the remaining warriors and plunged the point of Galatine into the

123

side of the Black Hermit's mount, sinking it in to the crossguard and riding it down, tearing a broad gash that spilled a murky grey mass of coiling innards over him. He fell spluttering on his back, drowning in the stuff, but rolled to avoid the massive body falling and the flailing Black Hermit pitching with it.

Gawaine saw Percival's black charger leap overhead, and the Last Sword gleam in the light from the doorway as he brought it down in a silver arc on the head of The Black Hermit. It split the Mad Helm in two pieces, revealing the wide eyes of the old knight beneath. The blade seemed to shatter like crystal into glittering shards, but there was enough of the edge left to cleave The Black Hermit's skull down to the lower jaw. As the head came apart in a spray of red and black blood and white teeth, Percival fell from the saddle and Gawaine lost sight of him in the tangle of metal warriors rushing from all sides.

He knew any moment he would be pinned to the flags by dozens of sword points or trampled by spiked sabatons, but suddenly there was a brilliant flash of light that lit the chamber so that it was as though the sun had tumbled down the well and landed in their midst.

The blue-gold light he had seen in the eyes of the gilded skulls seemed to be everywhere. It cast the enemy in gray and lit the copper column like a brand of white fire. There was a terrific sound of rending metal, and the column wavered and began to melt down like a candle. The fire from the column was intense, and Gawaine looked away. The warriors raised their gauntlets as thought to shield nonexistent eyes, and their metal helms glowed green and flowed like water, revealing the heads of men and women beneath. He recognized one of his own men-at-arms, Pardnum, just before the flesh of his face flowed from his white skull and fell.

Gawaine put his face to the floor, for the guts of the great beast were cool compared to the conflagration. His armor began to sear him so he hastened to pull it off and push his way deeper into the grey muck. He put his hands to his ears as a deafening tone filled the air, shaking him like the thunder of his boyhood.

When at last that tone ceased, he heard a new sound, as of the wind rushing on the sea, and he dared to open his eyes.

The column was gone. Where it had stood there was a black pool of the kind of sludge that had been destroying the Wild Forest. Yet he could see a sickly green light shining far at the bottom of that pool, and in that light he saw the silhouette of a vast layout of strange make and oddly angled towers, an entire city of leaning structures more fantastic than Caer Delex. Things moved in the avenues of that sunken city. It seemed even that the towers themselves walked and bowed toward some great central point, where a massive form shifted and one slit of an eye that seemed the length of the firth itself appeared in the dark.

Gawaine trembled and thrust his face back into the muck and would not move or look again.

"Sir Gawaine?"

It was Floree who spoke, and only her touch made him dare to pull himself out of the slime and look.

Her head was cut, and one arm hung limp, but she knelt by him and wiped the blood and filth from his face with the sleeve of her tunic.

She smiled. It was not enough to drive what he had seen from behind his eyes, but he held to it, wondering at that great eye he had seen and the head in which it rode, and what such an immeasurable brain thought, and why any man could call himself a king when somewhere there lay a kingdom with a master of such proportions. He could barely move. He feared if he looked again he would see that grand king rising to come up through the hole in the floor and lose all hope and reason.

But there was no hole; just a puddle of molten copper.

The henne-bore seeds. Perhaps the battle madness they induced had somehow saved his mind as it had saved his body. The blessing of Belenus.

He heard the steady step of a horse, and closed his eyes.

When he could see and reason again, it was in a monk's cot in the hermitage on the River Luce again, and Floree was holding his hand, reading a bible quietly.

"I will get your sister," she said, when she saw that he was awake.

"Where is Sir Percival?" he asked.

She smiled.

"I'll get him too."

Clarissant came first alone, and explained that the gilded skulls had done their job, the combined wisdom of the seven masters of the Order of the Elder Star had destroyed the Hermit's trephine. Cut off from its source, the gods of tree and water and stone would soon strangle the black corruption.

"I took a skull for your Cairnholy," she said, pointing to a grinning white head sitting on a table across the room. "It's probably not King Galdus, but you can tell the peasants it is. Maybe if they believe you it will still serve its purpose. Belief is the most important part."

"You look older," Gawaine murmured.

There were rings under her eyes, and there would be strange scars beneath her bandaged arms.

"I opened myself to things long forgotten, and what the masters of old knew I know too, now," she said. "One day my skull will be set in the reliquary."

Gawaine shuddered.

"That's a cheery thought. Don't expect me to visit."

"I expect you to deliver it. There's silver among your red now," she observed, scratching at his beard.

He slapped her hand away.

"What of Caer Delex?"

"We saw the towers crumbling as we rode away," Clarissant said. "The mortar that held it together is no more in this world."

"How did the sun come so soon?"

"Sun?" Clarissant repeated, screwing up her face. "It was night when we left the castle."

"When Floree came through the door with the horses, I saw a beam of sunlight."

"I saw no such thing," she said.

Gawaine nodded to himself and said a prayer of thanks to

Belenus. Perhaps the god himself had come to his aide. Percival would call it a miracle if it had been his god's doing.

"Here is my cousin," Floree announced from the doorway.

Percival entered, in the robes of a monk.

"Don't tell me you're taking your vows," Gawaine said.

Percival smiled thinly down at his attire.

"My armor is gone. Yours too. But here is Galatine," he said, holding out the sword. "I oiled it for you. I am now as you first met me, Sir Gawaine, without armor or sword. Just a poor fool once again, with my javelins."

Gawaine started, and grimaced in striving for a memory, peering at the knight, suddenly finding a familiar face within; older, cleaner, but could it be?

"A poor fool with....Peredur?" he exclaimed. "Peredur, can that be you?"

Percival could not hide a delighted grin.

"That was the name my mother called me, when she raised me in the forest," he said. "She had taken me from Pellinore, my father, so that I would have no knowing of knights or kings or war. But one day out hunting with my javelins I saw you and your brothers riding in the forest in your armor."

Gawaine laughed out loud.

"The ruddy little lad who asked if we were angels!"

"And you told me you were men," Percival said. "You told me of King Arthur and Camelot, and of the Round Table, and all it took to be a knight. Truthfulness. Honor. Bravery. With all my heart, I wanted nothing more than to ride at your side," Percival said.

"And so you have," said Gawaine, clutching his hand, and seeing the wide-eyed boy who had idolized him all those years ago, whom he had set on the path to knighthood. His smile faltered a little.

They had been riding to confront King Pellinore that day in the wood. He had never known the boy they had happened upon was Pellinore's son. Gawaine had slain his father shortly after.

"You clean up well, boy," he said lamely, and was pained to see the adulatory flash in the Christian knight's eyes, as though it were his own father and not his father's slayer who had expressed pride in him.

"Glory to God," said Percival, heedless of Gawaine's discomfort. "This is a great day. The Black Hermit is slain, and the way to Hell is closed."

"Don't let down your guard," said Clarissant quietly. "As the heavens wheel, the stars will come around wrong once more."

"Between our Order and knights both Christian and pagan," said Floree, "surely we may make them right again."

"Perhaps," said Clarissant. She turned from them toward the window and the stars, which held no more joy for her now than moonlight on tombstones. "But for how long?"

Gawaine stared into the black holes of the skull sitting on the table.

A MADMAN AMONG MUMMERS

Simon Bucher-Jones

"A great king and his wise man bring harmonious days, but two great kings and two wise men must strife and terror raise
As certain as this dreadful verse engraves these prophesies
Only one vision can descend through Earth's eternities."

"When there is a great and puissant King, and when the King is advised by a Great prophet and Magician, there will be a time of peace and glory, but when there is more than one King and more than one prophet woe to the land wherein two Kings and two prophets contend for the souls of the people."

As with the Book of Revelation, there are three views we can take about the Prophecies of Merlin reported by Geoffrey of Monmouth (c. 1135), and revised and expanded in John of Cornwall's twelfth century poem of 143 hexameters[1], of which the last 4 are translated above, colloquially (in bold from the Welsh) and from the latin version (in italics). One view is that prophesies are written later from whole cloth: they refer to events contemporary with or just before their writing providing political commentary hidden beneath a veil of antiquity—in which case the conflict of lines 140-143 could refer to the battles of Stephen of Bois and the Empress Matilda, just as the abomination in the temple in Revelation may refer to its destruction by the Romans in 70 AD rather

---

[1] Vatican City, Biblioteca Apostolica Vaticana, MS Ott. lat. 1474

129

than a still future eschatological event. The second naïve view: that they represent a genuine prediction of future battles from mystics preceding them, we may as scholars set aside, but the third possibility remains: that they genuinely retain coded political and historical data concerning their mythic time of origin is, and must be, our special focus of study.

In examining the so-called Lancelot Testament[2], which contains much suggestive of a later origin, including an account that tallies with John of Cornwall, we may still find clues to the Historical Arthur, preserved from the sources that we may posit as available both orally and in earlier texts to its twelfth or thirteenth-century originator.

> —Doctor Theodore Blaise: *The Lancelot Testament—Interpreted*, Camulodunum Press, Colchester, 1983, Introduction, p1.

The seasons were famously clement in Camelot, but no one would have known it in the depth of that winter, when the well in the great Keep froze, and water for drinking was taken from snow-melt and the harvesting of icicles.

I use the Norman word now, but the King's Castle was not a Keep of the kind that they would know centuries hence, neither in design nor in the main construction, though it had cunning stone in its building as well as wood and daub. It was, though, greater than any lesser King's hall or long house, and it served the same function. It was the central point of the city, and of the habitations of men, and over the lives of men and women it cast a shadow that was not one of terror or fear, but of strong and upright justice, and of the protection of a power that knew responsibility as well as might. King Arthur's court was so new then, and the shields of its knights so brightly painted with heraldries, that the dark of the winter was held back by them—but no amount of polished armour and good will could hold back the cold. Banked fires, and warm furs, and strong ale and good company fought as hard in winter for man's good as ever Knights on horseback had

---

[2] Vatican City, Biblioteca Apostolica Vaticana, MS Du Lac. late c. 1390-1400

done in summer.

In attending to this story, you must look with both eyes and hear with both ears, for I will tell you of the Camelot that was, and of that which was not—and as to which was truest, I—Lancelot du Lac—can no longer judge. Though I was there and saw both the Camelot of this world and that of the spirit, and I saw them both in madness and in health, now I do not know which to commend to you, for the fourfold vision of the real and unreal, of the mad, and of the sensible is combined in my memory. My recollections are disturbed, and run sometimes as Merlin's were said to always, into futurity. How else can I set down in this night before I go to pay a debt, thoughts which include the Castles of Normans not yet come and things as yet unwritten?

Whatever was true about us—the Knights of Arthur—though, there was a thing less true and—praise God it always be so—a lie that came on the wind of that cold winter and would have torn and clawed and broken all Camelots, and made the world both emptier, and fuller. Emptier of joy and love and compassion; fuller of something other, sear as yellow leaves in autumn, icy as winter, tattered as flesh on the battlefield. It came first that winter...

Act One

There is a great fire in the long hall that lies aside the Roman Fort, between Deva Vitrix and Eboracum, and the logs burst and pop as the heat finds pockets of resin. For the wood is pine from the north, sweet scented trees from the forests of the King of Din Eidyn, not given as tax or tribute but as a yule gift, in honest friendship and fealty. King Arthur inspires this open-handedness in others by his own free giving, and his own careful and thoughtful friendship. Even this early in his reign he is loved.

I am not. Oh, I am respected. I am the mightiest Knight of the round table (it was indeed round, although it was not the great painted wheel which I dimly see will one day be pictured), but I have as yet no name and few friends. I am the White Knight, my own kindred unknown to me, raised as an orphan. I feel a double bond with Arthur for his ideals and for his own childhood—as I hear Dame Rumour prate that he too was raised without knowing his high birth. I nurse a hope that mine could be as high, even as I strive in my heart to reject vanity. All I know then, is that I was raised on the shore of a distant lake by a woman in samite, who made no claim to be my mother, and who was kind only in otherworldly, mostly unnerving ways. I owed her love, but found it sluggish in my heart, and the warmth of friends and hearth-fires was a new thing to me for which I gave thanks unto God.

I am mighty then, even so, and I can say so now without pride. Of the Knights, none can withstand me in combat save Arthur and he only by virtue of his sword. I bear one like to it, given me by the woman who raised me—but if the swords are brothers—the King's is the elder and the master-blade, though he might be my younger brother in age and stature. My sword Secace, is also sometimes called Caliburn, in echo of Excalibar.

I remember the defeat of giants in Holy Combat, and I remember the striving through mud on foot, and the death of a horse under me in the fighting with the village burners and pillagers. And I remember what came in that winter for the first time, and how it came. It came first playfully, with the mummers.

They are a ragged group of ragged men and women, clad in a motley tradition that everyone remembered although no one could recall clearly seeing before. They dance in the market square, and perform tricks of little magic. They play out scenes and pose in tableaus for a coin. There is no harm in them, and yet harm comes. It sneaks in like a smell or a sense of unease. Are we so shallow then, we men of Camelot, that we are disturbed by strangers? Not so! Arthur's court is a crossroads and many come and go, from the Emissaries of the Patrician Odoacer (Who some call the King of the Goths) seeking support for a war against Dalmatia (which support Arthur refuses deeming it a foolish, evil squabble) to the Monks of Maucteus bearing gifts of snakes for Merlin, that Maucteus' old master St. Patrick had cast from the shore of their Isle. Merlin welcomes such things and their scales are said to be of use in his magic. The snakes are turned curiously to rock, circled in spirals; the scales flecks like mica or fool's gold.

We claim we do not fear the different or the other, that we are a welcoming Kingdom, and yet there is something that is not welcome. It is not the players themselves for they seem, at least at first, honest men and women—but there is something, unclear as a haze over a moor, that blows through Camelot. There is a shiver at the back of the neck, and for a moment there are towers that seem to pass behind the moon. New words are whispered by drunken men: and strange signs are passed from hand to hand. in the heavens a conjunction of the Planets appears un-seasonally as if repeating July in December.[3]

Merlin squats like a toad in his narrow high room, as he casts the rock-flake scales of snakes that never were into a brazier that burns with a green light that ought to be healthy but which now shines sick. He and I are not friends. I wonder if he sees in me a threat to his hold (his mentorship, rather; *hold* is an unkind word that I repent me of) on the young King. I am growing close to Arthur. I am his right hand. Merlin is perhaps his left. The two hands of the King should not fight. Never the less, although we are not friends, the Magician has sent for me.

I remember him too in four ways, or more. Did he wear a high and pointed hat, as they draw him in later years, or a metal skull-cap close on a shaved skull? Was his voice Welsh, or British? I can only remember his eyes were tired, and his voice shook with fear. Tired or not though, those eyes pierce me.

"Camelot is a dream," he says, and I wait for him to explain because it is not a dream to me, but a fact. A town and

---

[3] This may date events to 591 when the Great Conjunction of Saturn and Jupiter would have occurred in July. December conjunctions (6 BCE for instance) are of course traditionally connected to the birth of powerful spiritual forces, and the identification of the conjunction with 'The Star of Bethlehem' is proverbial in some astrological traditions. Blaise, p23.

a hall, a meeting place and a holy place—a good place but still a real one. The only home I have ever had, save for the lakeside.

"Oh, it is real as well," he adds quickly as if answering my unspoken thoughts. "But the good it does in this world is only a shadow of the good it casts into the world beyond. Camelot casts its image into the hearts of men, and down the ages that image persists, further than you might guess: an aspiration and a dream. If everything we build here were burned to ash and spread upon the land and that land salted, still a tree would grow and bear a golden fruit, and that fruit would feed a new Arthur in a new age."

"With its own new Merlin, or still beneath your eye?" I ask, pointedly, and sigh inwardly for my lack of charity in the implication. I must pray about that.

"Mayhap a new Lancelot," he replies, failing to answer me. He spreads his hands out in the green light. They tremble, and he seems older.

A voice—not Merlin's—cries out from the Cauldron.

"Nid yw'n marw,
Pa tragwyddol yn gorwedd,
A chyda oedran rhyfedd
Gall hyd yn oed marwolaeth yn
    marw[4]."

It is neither a man's voice nor that of a woman. It sounds like the voice Iron might have, or blood. My Welsh is poor. If I understand the words a-right they speak of Old Powers sleeping, to waken only if Death itself passes.

"There is a strangeness in the air and in this winter," Merlin says, "the old hermit is abroad in the land, the one they call the mad man of Enas Wyrrt: Chwyfleian—the wanderer of the pallid countenance. These mummers are his play things, though they know it not. He has been seen standing at the

---

[4] Trans. "It does not die, that which eternal lies, and with a strange age even death may die." Blaise, p30

back of their performances like a shadow, or a prompter."

"Who is this…Chwyfleian?" My tongue stumbles over the old welsh.

"A prophet, so men say."

"Really, Lord Merlin—are you not the Prophet of Logres, and the foreteller of the King?"

"The future he sees is not the one, I see—not in its secret heart." The Magician hesitated and I could almost see his mind working as he sought to put into words, ideas he did not expect me to understand. It was easy to remember then that some called him the devil's child, in the white tufts of his beard (was it long or short?) there were still hairs red as rust.

"Long ages hence from this, there will come a thing—no, an idea—into this world, an idea that will be written down and once written, it will try and bend the world to its accommodation."

I considered this and could not grasp it. "How can an idea have requirements that can be met or thwarted?"

"It wants to be thought on. To dwell in the minds of men, and in so doing it will if permitted to persist remake the world around it, until it is the only thought that men can have—and thus the souls of all will be unmade. As our Camelot is the Good Dream that makes more things possible—it is the Nightmare that renders the daylight black, under the darkling stars."

"But this is, as you say, a future bane—no problem for these times, when Camelot is strong?"

"I see only in fragments, but as our dream persists forward through all its re-tellings as part of the strength and sinew in the good, so this future drama has reached back to Chwyfleian's mind. It casts its false echoes ever thus back into preceding time—as it is attributed to earlier and earlier writers…I have a vision of a man in Parisii, and one other centuries before him, though still after our time, shaking a spear on a great stage with words that will outlast a pyramid of stone. Oh, if only you were a poet and not a Knight you might understand. Suppose I take two famous lays, and make from them a third thing. Then if it be greater than both—more beautiful, or more dreadful in awe, soon *they* will be remembered only as *its* 'faint first stirrings,' intimations of a greater yet to be. We are a story that faces the menace of a later tale. If we permit it will make us a footnote to its mutterings, until the only 'shining city on a hill' shines with rot and fox-fire."

"What would you have me do? Shall I confront this Chwyfleian? Drag him before Arthur?"

"No. You are the strongest Knight of the Table, but this cannot be fought by force—at least not force of swords and armour. But you are also a man of faith, and though the God you worship is from the hot deserts of the East, and not one of the ancient Lords of Albion, still His is a Power in its rising. Trust your heart in this, Lancelot, and you will do what must be done." He scowled and looked at me much as a soldier regards a mis-forged knife that might turn in his hand. I wondered if the advice he gave me was such that he foresaw it might bring troubles in time to come. One day perhaps his brand of pagan lawless magic would have to be broken on the Cross. Ah, I was a zealot in my youth, to think of standing against Merlin. Still he could not both invoke faith and avoid its contemplation. I dared, then, to challenge him.

"If by my faith in Jesu, I prevail, Magician, will you acknowledge His Lordship in your heart, and take the sacrament?"

"Make my peace with God? A wise man ages hence will be asked that on his death bed, and reply that he and God, 'have never quarrelled.' I do not seek to deny any God who brings in more light, only those powers that rise with the dark stars, and would set the very sky in error. Argue your faith with Chwyfleian, man of Christ, and if you triumph, why I will affirm that the Moon is cheese, or that I am a stag of seven tines, or that Jesu be Lord, if you so will."

He looked sad and honest as he continued, almost contrite—I thought.

"But it is the curse, since Cassandra was a child, of prophets and magicians to be doubted. If I spoke only the truth, still men would spit behind my back and make the signs

136

against the Horned One. How will you or God know I speak the truth hmm? No matter. I do what I must, and that must be accounted good, lest the sky fall."

I left him, confused as to the state of his soul, but willing to set my faith to the task. I had no description of Chwyfleian, save for his pale face, but I realised now I had indeed seen him myself standing at the back of the mummers as if raised up on a dais. His thin hands had directed their actions or echoed them. Not so much a prompter I thought, as a puppeteer. I would find him again, I was sure, when they performed next.

It took me a week to find them, tracing the circular course that would bring them back to Camelot by Twelfth Night. They played to groups of villagers, and left behind them—in divers places—a child whose weeping brought ugly yellow tears, an old man whose voice had departed save for the word "Y'htill" which he trilled like a white bird, and many another besides who were shaken or touched in lesser ways.

I found them to the south-west, on the borderland, performing to a crowd half-welsh, at a crossroads in the shelter of dripping trees. There was nothing unwholesome in their antics, and yet, there was fear in the air, as if attendance were less a treat than a compulsion. I saw children being led away crying as I approached, their mothers crooning nonsense syllables to quiet them. "Chwid, chwid, chwidogaith, cer o'ma ymaith[5]."

They have puppets on strings, and tell a tale of a princess beset by seven unsuitable suitors. A stranger brings her a wish from a hidden King, and she wishes to be free of their demands for her hand in marriage. That wish made, the Princes all drown under a lake that is great as a sea of stars. And a worse suitor—the Hideous King, comes forth to take her.

---

[5] The opening three words whose meaning is now lost may also be found in Stanza 87 in The Gododdin of Aneiron (sixth century) where it appears in a fragment of a lullaby seemingly preserved from an older work. The remaining words are intelligible and could be roughly translated as "Away! Outside(ness), away!" Blaise, p34

They have some way of suggesting the lake by lights moved in waves, by the motion of their hands. It reminds me of my childhood. The mummer who portrays the Princess Cassilda is very like to my mother in her stature and colouring. It disquiets me, as if I were a child who might still need comforting. He is there: Chwyfleian of the Pale Face, and his name is a true one for his skin is white as marble and his eyes are orbs of misty milk. Such eyes might well be blind, but his dart and glint like those of a seeing man. A far seeing one.

He bears a sign around his neck, a strange spiral—yellow on black—a small thing—but big with power as is a crucifix or a saint's bones. As he to the mummers, so it strikes me, is this thing to him. I have been told not to use force, but perhaps force will have its hour yet.

I watch from the crowd's back. Catching only a word here and there, narrated over the dumb show of the puppets by a dark man in tatters. Each line ending with a hollow drum beat.

> "Since that lost day when servile emperors fell
> The butterfly winged angels torn and frayed
> The dominations and the thrones dismayed
> …
> That time will come again
> Hear the first stirring of the sin, black stars
> That burn around the entrance to the pit
> Under the worlds, where myriad crawling things
> Have made their empires under the King's hand."

This is not harmless. I cannot idly let this blasphemy pass. They have performed at court, and there I know, a prancing shining Knight would come to bring release from this foul incantation—but here there is no mummer in bright metal biding his time behind a tree. There are no good puppets in this sodden wood. Here amid the border folk, they uplift the darkness, and the yellow sign that gleams about the neck of their strange prophet is like the eye of Lucifer.

I realise that, in this performance—as Merlin must have

intended—the shining knight is I.

It had rankled with me, may I be forgiven it, that Merlin had spoken of me as a fighter and not a poet but all men who bear sword under Arthur and hear his words, know the value of the latter outweighs the former tenfold. It is Arthur's tongue and speech that is the true Excalibar. A true Knight is also a man of words.

I try to match mine to the rhythm of the narrators, and plunge bright sword extended—into the performance.

"No empire built in dark will ever stand—"

(I clatter my sword on my shield for my drum beat.)

"For more light comes, with every dawning day
The son of man, the Sun of Morning's dawning
Reborn, made whole, to sit at God's right hand
In Christ's name cast away the evil thoughts
That come by night to darken and to mock
Roll them from off your soul, as in the night
Unfallen angels rolled away that rock
That hid the resurrection of our Lord
And birthed anew to wonder and the world
Salvation freely given, never earned."

I don't know what I expected. Laughter or a tussle I was prepared for. To draw my sword and break up the meeting by force, mayhap. But the long slow bow, I received from the pale faced man, as from one stately ambassador to another discomforted me. He stepped forward now, and his voice unlike the deep one of the narrator, was a thin thing brittle as a reed—and yet the forest held its breath or so it seemed and even the water dripping from the trees fell in silence so his words were heard.

"The Living God needs no creation

(No drumbeat now, only a pause that sounds louder than

any sound.)

> And thus, no world was made
> The black stars endless against the black night
> Burn out the dark majesty of unmaking
> But unlike the Demiurge, red in the blood of innocents
> The Yellow King wakes and interrupts his dreams and
> ends the…"

The tip of my sword took him in the throat, and silenced him. Tearing away the flesh and skin as if his face was a mere mask. Was I right to have done this? Merlin warned me against violence, and yet as the pale prophet spoke the lines I'd felt a fear that I'd never felt in mortal combat. As if the world were a single candle and his words would blow it out. The mummers and the border folk fled, and I was left alone in the falling dark, the murderer of an old man. Did I see the skull under his mask of skin? I saw something that I no longer remember. Perhaps I saw my sin. Perceiving that sin (may God forgive me), my mind broke.

This was the first of those periods of madness I would suffer, and perhaps the root of them all. In later life they would be triggered by many things: a doubt of a love which I then thought I could never claim, a blow to the head in a tourney, the rising of certain stars. Much trouble would come from them, though also much joy for the birth of my son depended finally upon the one in which mute and wild in the wilderness I was found and healed by his mother Elaine.

This first madness though, was deep and stained yellow— like a descent into a mist that ate my mind, or the falling of an infinitude of tainted veils whose sepia tint cut me off from truly perceiving the world. For a week, maybe more, I ranged the forest, forgetful of my name, my duty—even my humanity. Perhaps I seemed the Hermit of Enas Wyrrt myself, gaunt, armourless (for I had torn it from me) and raving.

My squire found my horse, Benc, a-wander—and by that means and perhaps Merlin's vision, I was found. Subdued in a fight I cannot recall but in which I am told I bested unarmed a dozen Knights, before the weight of many felled me, I was carried back to Camelot and nursed. The mummers had vanished nor was the body of the Hermit found. The stars moved correctly again in the heavens.

I am told I prophesied at that time, on my sick bed—in words like Merlin's prophesies—of great contentions of beasts. But mine were creatures no loremaster of the animal world wot of: a forest whose trees were a thousand hooved things, a dragon from the sea with a face of great worms, a thing that stood like a man in scarlet robes and held a hushing finger to a mouthless blank face. And beside them…or behind them…a puppeteer in yellow tatters.

Act Two

Three years passed. Years of glory, of high renown—of wrongs made right, of false Knights vanquished—of the slow messenger driven process of earthly diplomacy and guile. I remember both cloth of gold and silver, and cold mornings in muck watching borders. King Arthur married Gwenhwyfar, the daughter of Cywryd of Gwent, and she was the most beautiful woman I had ever seen save one. (I say of Cywryd, but I also remember her being the daughter of a demi-god or a giant, but her face remains clear to me though her name and her parentage varies in my mind.)

Gwenhwyfar was as fair as Cassilda was dark.

Over the years leading to Arthur's marriage, I had dreamed often of the unknown woman who had played the part of the Princess in the mummer's play. Her dark hair and green eyes had o'erthrown my memories of my step-mother's face until she had come to fill a warped part of my imagination that I caressed even as it revolted me. The dark Princess had sent her twining roots deep into my heart by her single look—and by her desperate need in the play to escape a destiny forced upon her. Though no poet (in Merlin's eyes) I wrote and destroyed verse after verse in her honour. Some of it may have shown promise, some was lust and vileness best forgotten. I prayed to be free of her, but it seemed to me I heard—not the still small voice of conscience or God—but another older whisper saying: "If you wish you may be free of Cassilida, you have but to ask this boon. It will be given as freely as her own wish was. For the King has an open hand."

Did I hear that truly, or dream it? It is impossible to say, but forgetting the horrors that followed from Cassilda's wish, I asked that her grip upon my heart should be broken.

So, it was to be, though not as I had wished—for instead of peaceful calm acceptance, a return to my faithful chastity of thought—gradually another guiltier vision superseded her— still as slim, as proud, but fair—the white lady, Gwenhwyfar—the wife of my lord Arthur. I strove to drive these new and evil thoughts from me—by feats of arms, by fasting, by prayer. Nothing, and no old whisper from the dark, offered me release from them. Neither God nor fiend it seemed would free me.

In the end, therefore I have no recourse but the devil's son. I have not required of him that he acknowledge God three years before, and did he not therefore owe me for my work? I who was sent by him as sacrifice into that awful performance in the forest.

In his tower, I beseeched him. "You know many things Merlin, do you know how love may be plucked from a man's heart and rendered painless?'

"Three things there are, Knight, that are beyond what man may fathom, what the mind imagineth, what the heart desireth, and what the sea breeze bringeth. Leave Camelot and ride to the sea shore, to a place and at a time my art divines and bring me what you find there, and we shall see what can be done."

The next day he set out his rede more fully. "Duke Tytila the father of young Raedwald, whom he has petitioned to be given a seat at the table with Oswain, has made camp in the eastern fenlands and sets spade to make there a city there that might in time become his capitol. Dommoc it will be called, or Dunwich in the modern tongue. Seek out the shore line there and find…" His eyes went blank for a second, and he recited…

142

"Where Death and Life strain in the billow, in aeons of
    desolate speech
Where sea wrack, as a king with his fellow, waketh
    waves black and strange on the beach
When the sky rises haggard and yellow, and the Clouds
    nigh as breakers make breach.
When Death's robe is torn as the tattered, pale sky
    when the dawn rises there—
Then although no mere mortal has mattered, to the Sky
    and the Sea as they tear
You must hope that the Deep may be flattered, and
    permit an appeal unto Her."[6]

I found this council as chilling as it was obscure, and it
went hard with me to obey it—for who was the 'Her' of
which he spoke? And what did the prophet expect me to bring
him from the sea-strand? It was futile to attempt to question
Merlin further for the wizard had (whether as a ploy or
because of the strain of his utterance) collapsed across the
table and was snoring like a plough horse snorts as it pulls a
heavy plough through clay.

I felt I was meddling in pagan ways, but having no respite
in prayer and no release from the heat of desire—I resolved to
make the attempt. Perhaps a piece of driftwood would float to
my hand, or some trinket of the Dane ships, be found on the
beach. Who could say what flotsam or jetsam might yet be
found along the coasts of Albion?

Raedwald greeted me, at the site his father had chosen for
the foundations of Dommoc—and was, I felt, disappointed
that I had not brought from Camelot word of a place at the
Table for him. But he spoke me courteously enough—and
told me of a place along the shore where the folk his people

---

[6] It is hard to see how this medieval verse could have influenced Swinburne's
Beside the Sea, but there are some resemblances. Is it possible the Vatican
manuscript may have been tampered with—perhaps to conceal something? The
removal as it might be of an incantation or evocation formerly thought to have
real power? Blaise, p60

had displaced had a legend of the Sea and the Sky being at war—a war which must in the long grind of time, they had said, "eat up the land."

Duke Tytila had mocked that—and vowed that his Dommoc would stand for an age—but as I left my horse in the scrub grass of the dunes and set out, down to the shore proper, I would not have bet the smallest shiny coin of Arthur's coinage or the most worn denarius for the land's chances.

I left my armour strapped to my horse—and my squire (to watch both it, and his donkey) and began to comb the shoreline for whatever might attract my eye. I had decided simply to bring Merlin the first oddity I found, for the guidance he had given me was so unclear as to the form of what I was seeking that it might be fish or toad or rock for all I knew.

What I found though was unmistakable.

It was a statue or an icon, a tiny one, the size of my thumb. It was carved in a stone green and flecked with gold that was unknown to me. It was of a merwoman or a sea-nymph: but its tail was split into a myriad strands or tentacles like the head of a hydra. Mother Hydra? The name seemed to rise up in my mind from no source I could remember. Something my step-mother had once said by the side of the Lake where I was raised? No matter this was clearly what Merlin wanted, unless he sought a rock or a piece of sea-weed.

"We stand at an odd angle of time," Merlin said, as he examined the statuette I had brought him. "The power that has groped back to our age, seeks to usurp our story—but it is itself threatened. The creation of art knows no stopping point. After the idea of the Yellow King, arises the Dreamer in the Deep, of which this is a first faint echo. The one idea may yet fall prey to another."

"Can you not speak more plainly?" I begged. "Is there in this figurine some spell or surcease from the evil desires that afflict me?"

"Plainly, yes and no. I can remove, I hope, the effects of the geas—let it be called magic—which the vengeance of the

144

Yellow King has laid on you. That was the first cause of your love for the White Lady, but our emotions are strange and difficult. We learn to love the sensation of love as much as we love the person loved, maybe even more. I see in my own future—or my past—the maiden Nimue and the endless refraction of desire seen in crystal. I have always seen that your heart may yet destroy you. I cannot change the story that is Camelot—I stand as its defender."

"What good then are *your* mummeries Merlin?"

"Does not your God proclaim that by His grace, He has made Mankind free of will? So that the multitudinous calamities of life are set upon our souls or on the Devil's? I will return your freedom to you—that it is what it is do not blame me. I have been called many things, but I am not Chwyfleian with his Puppets. Lancelot must do as Lancelot wills and Guinevere and Arthur must do as they will."

He pronounced Gwenhwyfar, oddly as if he had mumbled it in his sleep too many times—but that perhaps that was just my seeing my own obsession.

"What you can do, do then, old wizard. Let me be Lancelot, uncursed by any. I will bear my own fate."

As he had peeled scales from the stone snakes of Eire, he broke flakes off the sea-green stone of the statue. Merlin's thumbs alone were strong enough for that work, despite his age. He grasped the world as if it were clay. Next to Arthur I mourn, now, his loss the most. Arthur's was the soul of Camelot, but Merlin was the mind. I was ever only the arm.

He raised a staff, or his wand, or just his left hand with many rings, or empty. My memory is at least four-fold.

"Let the is, be is, hold back the is-to-be, let the evil from the chambers of the future be restrained by the love of craft. Let deep waters swallow the dry rags. Let Green devour Yellow. Is it not enough that we have already been struck by so many storms? Oh, Ocean of the mind in which all stories reside, whose portal is every lake and every rain-drop: Oceanus—Son of Sky and Earth: world river and returning serpent, Ouroboros yet unmade—nameless now—to be named hereafter by your Call. For the enmity of Old between the Sky and Sea, we ask this, Goddess and God in one—three thousand spawn[7] anoint you in the deeps. Ia! Ia!"

A vision swam into my mind. Of a primeval Camelot—of the first story, into whose flesh the barbs of later ages, the storms that Merlin spoke of, had fastened as arrows strike even an armoured man through any weak-points. Yes, maybe they were dangerous but did they not also test and hone the story, striking bright sparks on its mettle? Making its spirit shine. Without them would our example even last in men's and women's minds? Would Camelot still be a story of brutes striving with stone knives between great standing stones for the Kingship of a field?

I see Cassilida in the dark shadow, her white hand to her red lips. She beckons me, and I see a door in Merlin's tower that I have never seen before, that leads to a narrow stair climbing still higher. Merlin is unmoving his empty (ringed) hand raised, lightning frozen on his staff (his wand). I follow here.

From the battlements I see the lake. Cloud waves break upon it and across its silver and blue surface a distant city rises its towers falling behind the curve of the crescent moon.

"Do not permit the Merlin his spell," she says, in a voice like my mother's. "Do you imagine we are the first new stories to have woven in and out of the tellings of Arthur. We will be accepted in our turn, and as the oyster maketh the pearl, so from our presence the Logos of England will make new beauties, rich and strange. He resents new magicks and fears them, he would reject all the changing words if he could—even you Lancelot. You are yourself a child in these tellings; born of the romances of the French. Cycles and Cycles passed without the name Lancelot. Even now Merlin sees dimly a version of Camelot without you, without the danger you represent. He would not have mourned if Chwyfleian had made you a madman among mummers, or if the powers of the sea would sweep us both hence, the Court of

---

[7] The three thousand river gods, mentioned by Hesiod? Blaise p78 cf. Thesophony 364-368

Carcosa and the Knight of the Lake alike."

The word Carcosa buries in my brain like a worm, and I know it refers to the City that Lies Behind the Moon.

Her cool hands touch the sides of my face as her lips draw close to mine. "My King is more forgiving than Arthur, and into my hands He will give you if you ask it. Is it not a glorious thing to fall into the hands of the handmaiden of the Living God? Am I not, freely given, better than a rutting sin, or an evil heartache? Only break the Merlin's staff." (Or snap his wand, or steal his rings, or pluck his beard, I cannot recall what she asked, although the kiss is on my lips).

I am a poor man. Not in the sense of worldly poverty— though I hold no vast estates. I learned my weaknesses in her kiss. Unable to decide or choose between Cassilida and Gwenhwyfar, between Arthur and Gwenhwyfar, between Merlin and Carcosa, between the old stories and the new—I embrace my madness and choose all.

Act Three

And now in penitence I write this account. Men know how I loved Gwenhwyfar, or how Mordred laid traps and lies to tar our blameless names. They know the evil wrought was mine alone. Or ours. Or yet a spell laid by Gwenhwyfach, her sister and sorceress-rival. That I killed Arthur, or Mordred did— though Arthur will live again, or mayhap never died. That Guinevere named, as in Merlin's mumbles, came to me at last and we dwelt in Joyous Gard for many years, or that she retired to convent and to Christ, repenting and austere. I have lived all these, in mad and shattered shards of memory and now, in my old age, across the sunrise path of light along the shores of this imagined lake, walk solemnly to the court of the Tattered King, to make whatever payment I may owe.

Of The Green Knight's Struggle Against The Black Goat

Ethan Sabatella

Merlin arrived on the borders of Bertilak the Green Knight's estate as warmth-sewn winds drew water out of the snow; grass stubble poked through the caul of winter upon the ground. The vassals working the fields recognized the wizard and sent word to their master, who rode out at once before the newcomer came too far in.

Merlin came halfway on the road to the gate of the Green Knight's castle when the master appeared to him alone upon a green-coated steed with another horse beside him. Presently, the Knight wore a soft tunic of green, a lighter shade than his skin, and loose trousers the color of tree bark. His verdant hair and beard were loose and fluttered in the temperate breeze. No weapon or tool hung off his supple leather girdle, strapped tightly round his narrow waist. One mighty hand held his own steed's reins and lifted his other open palm in a friendly sign.

Dismounting, the Green Knight hailed his guest. "Welcome, Merlin most wise! Your presence is unexpected but always welcome! Come rest your feet and ride next to me."

"Your hospitality is most generous, sir," said Merlin. "Your road is wonderful to walk upon, but I will accept this steed you have brought."

The pair rode side-by-side, the master entertaining his guest with anecdotes from the winter months the whole way to his lodgings. "I do hope I am not boring you, master seer?" Bertilak inquired as they rode with still some miles to go.

"Not at all," admitted Merlin. "Your words are most pleasing; they give me rest ere I must divulge the tidings I carry."

"They are grim tidings, then?"

"Grim beyond the ken of most mortals."

"Then it is my wish you save them 'til the best moments of your stay have passed."

Bertilak and Merlin came to the gate of the Green Knight's castle within the hills and woods of his estate; from a distance, its face merged with the wilderness, making it appear as a crag overtaken by vegetation. The mists of the melting snow hung over the wrought stone with creeping vines and budding flowers climbing upon the walls. At once, servants attended them, relieving them of the beasts and opening the ways for them.

Within the warmth of the castle walls, Bertilak threw his arms wide and proclaimed, "Welcome to my abode, Merlin! Its facilities and comforts are yours!"

Hearing her husband's voice, the small, fair wife of Bertilak emerged. She donned a dress woven with threads of gold within green fabrics; her hair was braided in many little knots and designs; makeup paled her cheeks and darkened her lips and eyes. The Lady of Hautdesert came beside her spouse and curtsied to Merlin.

"You do us honor with your visit, venerable druid," she said.

Merlin doffed his cowl in her presence. "The pleasure is all mine, noble Lord and fair Lady. Your kindness and hospitality I will recall ever more."

Servants were summoned to bring Merlin to his quarters and prepare the feast for that night. Once comfortable, the wizard sat before the hearth in his room and meditated until the flames waned. He remembered and dreamed of the knowledge and tidings he would share with Bertilak—in the shadows of his mind, the recollections whispered to him and chilled his marrow even though the fire blazed. The wizard walked a narrow path in his dreams, between shadow and light; things known and the unknowable; and details impossibly small and wildly cosmic. The warmth of the fire, the tapping of his fingers against his flesh, and the steady breath in his lungs all balanced his mind. He remained in such a trance until a servant stood at the threshold to his quarters, announcing the master and lady awaited their guest. Merlin rose and came to the great hall where a feast formed out of the last of the winter's store lay upon the oaken table. Bertilak resided at its head and his Lady sat to his left; he gestured to the seat at his right hand as his guest entered.

Merlin sat and supped with his hosts, speaking at length of his journeys while the Lord and Lady listened with rapt attention:

"Throughout the winter, I followed the traversal of the stars; I perceived a formation in the heavens, as if the twinkling princes of the night prepared for an occasion. It came to pass that I followed a trail of stones from Orkney all the way to the Caledonian Forest. Far older they were than the stones marked by the Picts. By the light of star and moon, and shade of cloud, a power resonated within them, holding all the way to the mighty pines of the weald."

During his report, Merlin spoke slowly and his eyelids fluttered open and shut, but not once did he nod off or halt his speech. "The woods of the world are realms ever-growing; things burst from the soil, rise and grow ere twilight takes them, and they stoop until their bodies rest in the ground as a feast for new things to follow. For ages uncounted, such a cycle has persisted in the great forest of Caledonia, tended and reaped by no mortal hand. At the threshold to the estate of darkness, I sat beneath a pine and slipped into a spell so I could walk through the woods using the legs of a wildcat and see through his eyes. Within those trees lay the stones I followed, overtaken and broken by roots and blanketed in mossy cauls. Overhead, the branches grew so dense over each other, the sun seldom found spots to shoot his beams through. Even in the dark and dampness, things grew; the trees' scaled mail darkened; the stench of fungus and fruit sprouting, growing, rotting, and reemerging in heaps filled the air. The stones I could find, which were not yet reclaimed by the earth, were painted over with dark substances formed into symbols of heathenry from the darkest days of the world."

With some wine upon his fingers, Merlin inscribed a symbol upon his platter: three circles, each not quite complete, clustered together. To Bertilak, it resembled some perversion of the Irish Trinity; his Lady shivered beside him as she beheld it. The wizard wiped away the mark before long and returned to his tale:

"True night soon ruled over the sky, sending spears of moonlight between the boughs. The eyes of the cat were even keener in such light, and the pads on his paws rendered him a ghost as my soul guided him through the trees. In the silence, down the path of the stones, a chanting pricked the knife-ears of the cat. I followed, weaving over the roots and around the trunks, slinking through the brush. Pressing forth, the trees and other plants of the weald did change, as though they were from no forest Man ever encountered—the trunks twisted upon themselves and bent upon each other in ghastly archways; their branches waved and twitched despite no breeze passing across them, and leaves spotted with putrid hues adorned them; fruits swollen and leaking with putrid sludge hung to the dirt, becoming feasts for hordes of insects; and the roots pulsed beneath my feet as if they were veins bulging from battle. Not once in this area of the forest did I feel alone, for shades flickered and shifted out of the corners of the cat's eyes and low, nervous whimpers caught in his throat.

"The number of stones increased, appearing in rings and thresholds and stairs, all overtaken with roots or moss or markings. A flight of mossy stairs led to a bowl in the wood, its edge lined with trees, whose branches formed a cathedral-like roof, through which peaked the eyes of the stars and shafts of the moon. Down there, the chanting grew louder, so I crept along the bowl's edge and peered down. Gathered within the curve of the bowl were naked forms of men and women, all painted with the same dark decorations from the stones; they danced and writhed upon each other, all calling out fell intonements to the trees:

"*'Iä! Iä! Shub-Niggurath!'*

"The trees above them twitched and leaned closer to their rite. Amid their cries, a grating susurrus emerged; many new, unseen tongues spoke words of maddening nonsense from the trees. And even more, between the branches and trunks, baleful eyes of yellow—with long, slanted pupils like goats' eyes—blinked with sights upon the wretched fanatics.

"Upon the edge of the bowl opposite the steps, a figure weaved out from the trees, stepping with even more silence than the cat could. It crouched at the lip, hidden from the direct light of moon and star; through the cat's eyes I could not perceive its exact features, save it looked mannish. A sudden bellow emitted from its throat—a harsh cry much like a goat pleading against its slaughter—and the fanatics ceased to behold its presence. They raised their hands and echoed the chant amongst themselves.

"Then, the figure spoke in a voice too alien for the speech it used for its listeners: *'The stars align...the moon grows full...the time comes to bring the woods She knows back to the world as it was on the night before its dawn. The blood of the forest's spouse will be the rain. Iä! Iä! Shub-Niggurath!'*"

Merlin's imitation of the creature brought fear to Bertilak's heart and his Lady trembled all the more, but he dared not interrupt his guest's trance and tale.

"The cat became too afraid," continued Merlin. "From the haze of my spell, the chant seemed to weave its way through to the beast's baser senses and gave it fright; his claws scratched upon stone and he caterwauled. I reclaimed control but the creature at the edge locked its eyes upon the cat—its irises like dimming fires hidden within a wood. Ere the thing could move, I bade the cat to run with all the speed and stealth it had. I looked straight on, affording not a single glance back; no sign of pursuers harried the cat's senses, but the susurrus continued and beneath it drummed the wild pattern of hoofbeats. Nothing came to catch the cat, but even when I brought it into the more familiar weald, I could not lose the feeling of being observed.

"The poor beast ran until morning when it reached my

empty body at the forest's edge. I returned to my own head and gave the cat his back in full, along with some morsels of meat so he could rest.

"Since then, I have meditated on the lore I gathered there, which has led me here: to the House of Bertilak." Merlin opened his eyes and looked upon his hosts with a somber masque.

Bertilak wrapped an arm around his Lady and asked Merlin, "What is it you have come to enquire of me in this matter?"

"The creature and its cult seek a spouse of the forest," answered Merlin. "You, dear Bertilak, possess an ancient soul in your verdant body, one of a creature revered in Britain before Christ. The winds in trees and hills were the holy ghosts once, and one such ghost out of the ancient weald haunts your head. Therefore, your Lady of Hautdesert is a spouse of the forest; her blood is what the creature seeks to spill, glistening in the light of the full moon as it will be a fortnight from now. With her essence, the other earthly trees of the Caledonian Forest will be changed into the weird plants from the festering share I entered—it will only spread over the years until all things are caught in its ever-growing cycle and dark wastes fester upon all lands. I have come to warn you, for the cult might seek this place out."

"Then I will not sleep or stray from my Lady's side 'til this wretched period has passed," swore Bertilak.

Merlin frowned. "Such a time as the one they wait for does not come often, for the stars too are in alignment to channel the enchantments they seek into the earth. Their efforts to steal the Lady of Hautdesert, should they find her, will be great. And if my suspicions of being watched hold true, then I fear my own path to your estate might show them the course."

"We will reside in the Green Chapel. Within its walls, I am the master, and nothing would dare defy my word there."

The Lady of Hautdesert turned to Merlin. "Dear seer, is it so? Will I be safe in that sanctuary?"

Merlin sighed. "I have looked where I can through the dreaming paths, but something clouds sight of what fate is to come upon you and beyond that. There are creatures and gods in this affair whose wills are unknowable, so the answers surrounding them are as tangible as mist in the night. If he believes the Chapel to be the safest place, I will not stop Master Bertilak."

Bertilak rose. "Then it will be so."

Bertilak brought his axe to the Green Chapel, the very same axe Gawain used to cut off Bertilak's head in their fateful first encounter that unusual Christmas Eve. He donned a shirt of his best mail and a heavy helm. He grasped his axe in one hand while his other rested in his Lady's. She slept on a small cot brought out by servants, set beneath the altar towards the far side opposite the barred door. The eldest, sturdiest oak composed the board between the occupants in the Chapel and the rest of the world. Upon entering, Merlin scribed a curious rune upon the planks—it appeared as a branch with five twigs splayed off the main stem.

Upon Bertilak's inquiry of the symbol, Merlin answered, "The Elder Sign provides some resistance against nameless creatures from the shades between the stars. It will not prevent entry if the door is destroyed by a powerful blow or spell, but it will keep certain things at bay."

Half of Bertilak's six men-at-arms faced towards the door, leaning on their spears; the other half, granted respite, bowed their heads in some of the pews. The wind rasped against the outside of the oak and howled further in the distance. A few wicks around the Chapel and altar burned with dim yellow flames, emitting wisps of smoke.

Merlin sat cross-legged beside the head of the Lady's cot. His hands were folded in his lap and his eyelids were shut, yet the orbs beneath them fluttered in another one of his trances. Hours into the night, Merlin opened them and turned to Bertilak.

"Seeing through the crows' eyes, nothing approaches the Chapel at present, Lord," explained Merlin. "I will keep looking as long as my strength will let me."

Bertilak stared at the door, positively glaring, as if trying to pierce through the grains in the wood with his sight. *I'd rather wish it meets us*, he thought, *whatever it is—has it no courage?*

He ground the butt of his axe-haft onto the stone floor, keeping his breath level. Bertilak remained there as his men-at-arms changed their shifts. In the silence, he sought birdsong as the signal of the dawn, but no such thing could he find. Though he refused rest, each time he blinked, it felt as if wide gulfs of time passed before him. Merlin reported nothing, and he said nothing as well. Lady of Hautdesert breathed softly, her sighs the single item of comfort to the Green Knight.

In an hour none within the Green Chapel could tell, there came a span of silence from within the holy place and without; the men were as stones in an empty field; the wind withered into faint threads. The Lady drew a breath in, as if drinking the final note of sound.

A knock sounded on the Chapel door.

Bertilak's stare grew harder; he rose and hefted the axe in both hands. His men-at-arms, those active and at rest, stirred and drew up their spears. All six gathered at the end of the aisle. Merlin's robes rustled as he broke from his meditation and stood.

Leaning on one of the pews, he looked to Bertilak. "I have used much of my strength to spy around this place. We must hope the Sign and the door holds."

"We will cut down whatever comes through," said Bertilak.

"Hiding and shrouding your mind and sight in ignorance provides more defense against these creatures," explained Merlin. "A blade might wound them, but to them it is only as if a fly were to nip at a man."

A man's voice came from the other side of the door: "Is there anyone within? We are a handful of pilgrims seeking rest and prayer."

"Speak nothing," hissed Merlin.

Bertilak echoed the wizard's words to his men at the same volume. They heeded, keeping their spear tips trained on the door.

"The winter's chill is not quite gone away," continued the alleged pilgrim. "We've been traversing the weald all night. Please let us in ere we freeze."

Silence trickled into the air.

"Then we'll show ourselves in!" After the pilgrim spoke a final time, the door jostled on its hinges; something battered it from the outside.

The men-at-arms grouped together and advanced to the door, leveling their spears to where the intruder's throats might appear. Bertilak walked down the aisle and loomed behind his men, resting his axe upon his shoulder; his arms and its haft were long enough for him to reach over the heads of his men to swipe at foes.

Lady of Hautdesert sat up, rubbing the sleep out of her eyes. "Lord? What is the matter?"

Bertilak looked at her over his shoulder. "Hide!"

She scrambled off the cot and darted behind the altar. Merlin shuffled before her, shielding her lovely form with his robes.

The invasive pilgrims continued to beat at the door. With each strike, the planks and the bar bowed; the wood cracked and the hinges whined. The men-at-arms advanced, training their spears over the edges between the door and the threshold as the gaps between them widened under each blow. Splinters formed in the planks of the door; the bar fractured at its center and either side slanted. After several more strikes, the bar shattered and the door burst open. Spears shot towards the shadows moving into the Chapel, catching the fervent cries in the throats of the false pilgrims. The first to be struck fell into the holy house and bled on the stones.

"Iä! Iä!" they chanted upon their entry, more surging in from behind.

They wore black, ragged skirts, filthy and torn around the hems dragging on the ground. Shaggy vests of goat-hide covered their otherwise naked torsos. The dark substance Merlin spoke of formed monstrous images on their faces and dribbled out of their mouths. The ones outside let a large tree trunk *thud* to the ground—their battering ram—and they drew their weapons: knives, clubs, one-handed axes, and a variety of foresters' tools. With their crude implements of raiding in hand they stormed the Chapel, screaming, *Iä! Iä!*

Bertilak wedged himself into the center point of his men's formation and swung his long-limbed axe down on the heads of the boldest intruders. His underlings held their shields tight and thrust their spears, slicing with ease through flesh and shoddy graith. The raiders fell, but more proceeded into the Chapel, newer arrivals learning to dodge the deadly leaves and grasped the rims of the shields. The Green Knight shattered the skulls of those closest to him with the butt of the axe, then turned its sharp beard onto the necks of those at a distance. His men wrestled with the raiders, kicking and shoving. One man-at arms on the far right of the formation let his spear clatter to the ground to draw his dagger. The point went through his opponent's throat easily enough, but a sudden burst of three raiders knocked him to the ground. One bearing naught but a stone straddled over him and bashed his helmed head in with it while his comrades' feet pinned the man.

"God's blood!" Bertilak swore. He slipped out from the center—his remaining men filling the gap—and he rushed to the compromised right end. He smote the raider closest to his still-living ally with the axe blade first, jamming it into the side of his head. With it stuck there, Bertilak rammed the butt into the murderer with the stone, knocking him into one of the pews; he fell forward onto the backrest, his neck crunching upon contact. The force of the battery tore the axe from the first victim. For the final one, Bertilak spun around and cleaved, aiming for the man's middle. He jumped back, clear of the axe's arc.

A dozen more pilgrims joined the fray and rushed to the gap made in the right side. Bertilak moved to fill it, but the raiders moved with such sudden speed they breached the wall of warriors before he could. From behind, they leapt onto the men-at-arms' backs, those with blades seeking exposed flesh, those with blunt objects bashing mail and bone. Two more men fell. The remaining three formed a triangle, their backs facing each other, and moved to reach their commander.

"Merlin!" Bertilak cried over his shoulder.

The wizard raised his hands shakily, shut his eyes, and spoke in a booming voice: *"Your presence is unwelcome in this place, children of black woods unknown. Your rot is to be cleansed with flame!"*

The wicks sputtered and sparked, their smoke growing heavier and thicker. Some raiders took heed and ceased fighting, while most of their kin swiped at the men-at-arms and the Green Knight. Merlin lifted his right hand in a claw-like position and the wicks on that side of the Chapel burned brighter. He waved it towards the raiders. By his magic, the flames flew off their wicks, coalesced into a glowing orb, and flew upon the greasy, matted hair of several raiders. They shrieked as their heads were caught alight. Bertilak and his men took advantage of the distraction and attacked the burning ones, ending their misery. Those spared from the flames for the moment retreated to the door. Merlin raised his left hand, and the wicks at hand surged.

The raiders halted at the door and called outside, *"Iä! Iä!"*

With the second fireball, Merlin only caught one; the other raiders sprinted out the door before they were burned. The final raider shrieked and collapsed, grinding his skull into the floor. Bertilak walked over to him and, like an executioner, brought his axe upon the wretch's neck. Once the head rolled smoldering on the floor, he removed his helm and sighed, resting it under his arm. He faced the darkness beyond the threshold. A sandy blue seeped into the sky, heralding the near-dawn.

"Never return here, cravens!" Bertilak called out. "Neither the Green Chapel nor the estate of Bertilak the Green Knight is to be sullied again!"

In response, something drummed in the shadows. The steady beat of hooves, it sounded like. The Green Knight was struck suddenly in the chest, his mail doing just enough to cushion the blow, but the force pushed him back into the Chapel. His bare head smacked against the stones, bringing darkness to his sight and mind. A heavy, musty stench pervaded his nostrils, further clouding his senses. Amid the haze, he heard the screams of his men and the incantations of Merlin. And he saw the tear-soaked face of his Lady.

"Arise, Bertilak," said Merlin in a stern tone.

Bertilak opened his eyes and did just that, his body aching all the way up. Merlin knelt beside him, a damp cloth in hand. He sat up in the aisle of the Green Chapel, a mass of bodies strewn within the entrance. Lying among the dead raiders were all six of his own men. Traces of the odor he sensed before he fell unconscious hung in the air; Bertilak detected the scents of a wet hairy animal, sweat, dung, and a sickly, fruity sweetness. He faced the altar; the wicks and artifacts upon it were extinguished and knocked over or upon the floor. The Lady's cot lay empty and she did not peer from behind the altar.

"Where is the Lady?" asked Bertilak.

Merlin submerged the cloth in a small bowl of water filled with herbs. "I failed to save her, Lord. She was taken."

Bertilak glared at Merlin, but took a long, heavy sigh. "Alive?"

Merlin nodded. "I tried to scribe the Elder Sign for her to use, but the creature had spells of its own. It moved with wolfish speed and leapt like the salmon. Your men were slain protecting you and your Lady. Its hideous stench made me ill and drowsy. Ere I could use what strength I had left, it took the Lady and fled."

"Why did it not kill us?"

"We posed no hindrance to it. Your men tried to strike it with their spears as wasps try to strike a wanderer. Like a wanderer in no mood to be halted by insects, the creature slew them, and the ones too weak to retaliate it ignored. To that creature and its ilk, we are but as insects are to men; we cannot know their goals and they do not care if we try to hinder them. Even such as you and I are like men to them."

Bertilak rose and wandered to the threshold, beholding the faces of his men as he passed. The raiders were a collection of Britons, Picts, Scots, Irish, and even a few Saxons—some bore features of multiple races.

The sun climbed towards its peak. The weald about the Chapel surged with the sounds of life.

"But even I have heard tell of insects hindering men," Bertilak said. "Can that not be done for these wicked creatures?"

Merlin followed him. "It can, for a time."

"Will you aid me, Merlin?" asked Bertilak.

"It will not put a rest to their eternal machinations…but I will. The powers of these beings are strong, and should any hope to withstand them, faith and courage are needed."

Bertilak's eyes scanned the horizon. "I know of a place and person to find such virtues."

Bertilak and Merlin set out to Camelot. The Green Knight rode his best and fastest steed. He donned his mail and helm. He bore an oaken shield painted green on his back. Strapped among the rest of his gear was his great axe.

Merlin wore only his robes and carried the simplest of gear on his smaller steed. Since a little less than a fortnight lay between them and the life of Lady of Hautdesert, he led the Green Knight on secret paths to reach Camelot with haste. From Bertilak's hidden home, it took four days to reach the borders of Arthur's famous estate. They rode in one dewy dawn when all the snow had melted away. Wardens of the realm recognized the wizard and his knightly ally, welcoming them with good faith and offering escort to the gates of Camelot.

"Go on with your duties," Merlin bade them. "We know and love the King's land well, and will bring ourselves there."

Merlin and Bertilak reached the hill upon which Camelot resided, and glorious it sat in the early morning. Not one strand of mist hung about its walls. The heraldry of Arthur showed proudly upon the stoic banners on the ramparts. The two travelers rode their horses to the iron-bound gates. They halted just before them as a helmed guard peered over the wall.

"Who goes there and what is your business?" he asked.

"It is I, Merlin," answered the wizard.

"And Bertilak the Green Knight," answered the green man. "We would speak with Sir Gawain about a quest."

"Your returned presence is most welcome in Camelot," said the guard. "The gates are open to you!"

Moments after the guard vanished, the mighty gates were opened. At once, servants and stable boys came to the needs of the guests; the former followed them into the castle with their excess gear in hand. Bertilak kept his shield on his back. He and Merlin crossed through the courtyard and into the threshold of the castle. The guards manning the halls said nothing and were like statues. Within the halls, the servants diverged and brought the gear to quarters elsewhere. Merlin and Bertilak found their way to the heart of Camelot and truly the heart of Logres: the room which held the Round Table. The great stone slab rested in the center of the hall with many unoccupied wooden chairs around it. The glow of sunlight struck against the windows and illuminated the hall.

Merlin strode to the Table and shut his eyes, smiling slightly. "Arthur and his Knights are on their way to their morning meeting."

Suddenly, a door on the other side of the hall, opposite the one Bertilak and Merlin entered, swung open. A young squire held it for the line of Knights entering the hall—each one wearing a green sash over his waist, the same hue as Bertilak's skin. They filed into the room but paused just before the Round Table as each beheld the guests, whispering their names amongst themselves.

"What is this?" asked a stern, yet good-natured voice. "We've much to discuss, men! Come sit—"

Maneuvering his way to the front came a tall, broad man in regal garments. His grey eyes held the weight of years beyond what his body showed, and were equally strong and kind—with them, he gazed at his guests.

"Dear Merlin! My teacher and friend!" said Arthur. He came up to the wizard who met him beside the Table.

"It is good to see you again, Arthur," said Merlin. "Do you recall my companion?"

Arthur turned as Merlin gestured to Bertilak.

"Good health to you, dear King," said the Green Knight.

"Of course I do!" answered Arthur. "Whosoever could forget that Christmas? Gawain, come forth!"

Out of the crowd of Knights emerged a young man with a proud face. He came beside his liege and smiled to the guests. However, his eyes wandered away from Bertilak's.

Bertilak laughed. "I haven't my axe for you today."

"It is good to see you both again," Gawain said. "To what do we owe the pleasure?"

"There is little pleasure in the quest we are on," admitted Merlin. "We come beseeching your help, Sir Gawain."

"Mine?" asked Gawain. "For how long? I am to campaign with my King very soon."

Arthur's smile fell away, but not his courtesy. "Yes, that is what we were to discuss this morning. What quest calls to you and requires Gawain?"

"My Lady has been taken," said Bertilak. "We come asking for Gawain because it is he who I know to be one of the strongest of his faith in Christ, his King, and his friends. Merlin said it is that and courage needed to survive this quest, which Gawain also has in bounds. It is with haste we must go to the Caledonian Forest ere the moon is full, but if Sir Gawain is occupied with the duties of his overlord, we will not withdraw him."

Arthur raised a hand. "This we may discuss. Have either of you taken breakfast yet?"

"Just a few mean rations eaten on horseback," answered Bertilak.

"Please, sit with us and sup, good sirs." Arthur gestured to the Round Table. "After we have finished and the talk of our campaign is done, Gawain and I will speak with you on the matter of this quest."

Bertilak bowed low. "Your hospitality hasn't wavered, Sire."

Merlin bowed his head as he and Bertilak took seats amongst the other Knights. Servants arrived with platters of breakfast—meats, eggs, cheese, bread with butter, and light wine. After the morning's feast ended, and the platters were taken away, Arthur initiated talk of his campaign. Saxons were arriving on the southeastern shores of Britain. Some were even spoken of landing in Scotland. Merlin gave his wisdom as the greatest adviser of the King, but Bertilak had little to speak of for the matter. Gawain as well, though most loyal of Arthur's Knights, gave scarce any words, eyeing Bertilak at times. The discussion of war drew on well into the late hours of the morning; they finished before he reached his seat above the center of the world.

"Your mouths have spoken long and well," said Arthur as the first meeting closed. "But now it is time to move those bodies; train and prepare as you need."

All, save the four ready for the second meeting, rose and bowed to their King. They left the hall in silence.

"Tell of your quest, Sir Bertilak," said Arthur once the last Knight left.

Bertilak reported on Merlin's arrival to his estate. The wizard repeated the news of his encounter in the Caledonian Forest and his warning to his host and his Lady. He included smatterings of strange elder lore, inducing tremors into the other occupants of the Table. With even temper, Bertilak recounted the raid upon the Green Chapel and the kidnapping of his Lady, thus how he and Merlin came to be on the quest.

Upon completion of his tale, Bertilak added, "I once challenged Sir Gawain's control over his self and his courage. He left my estate as a humbled friend. It is not merely his presence for the sake of ranks in our party that I desire him, but for his heart, which gives strength unparalleled to his skill."

Gawain nodded with a stern expression. "Your words and desires are kind to hear, Sir Bertilak, and I speak true when I say I would join you to save your Lady from this devilry most foul. But it is the word of the King that will allow me into your fold."

Arthur held his chin in his hand, grey eyes trained at the center of the Table. At last, he turned to his teacher and asked, "What can you see of Gawain's fate on this quest?"

Merlin sighed. "The matters of these eldritch beings are always shrouded. I am lucky to get a sliver of an image or a symbol if I look. But I can say it is my intention to make this quest brief; we would not dare to dwell in that share of horror overlong. There were many who attacked us at the Chapel, but I cannot say how many more fanatics might slither in the woods. No matter our own number, the will of what we face is unknown and unpredictable to us. I have faith that the skills of war in Bertilak and Gawain are strong in felling men, but to face the creature holding the Lady...I have no answer for the fate of either man."

Arthur turned to Gawain. "You will see to the safety of not only the Lady of Hautdesert, Bertilak himself, and Merlin, but your own as well."

"Of course." Gawain nodded.

King Arthur rose. "Then you may quest to the Caledonian Forest. A band of knights will accompany you. They have tasted combat before, but have time to show their faith and loyalty to the Kingdom. Once the Lady of Hautdesert is returned to her Lord, Gawain will be brought back to Camelot to prepare to join me in the southeast against the Saxons."

"We will see to it, Sire," said Bertilak.

Arthur gestured for Gawain to rise, and so the young knight did. "And there is one more thing: for this quest, Sir Gawain, I give you permission to wield my own blade Excalibur, for if Merlin and Bertilak claim these forces to be most dire, then the best of brands shall be in your grasp. You stand among the few who might brandish it. Be well, nephew."

As his King embraced him, Gawain said, "I will, uncle."

Bertilak, Merlin, Gawain, and a band of twelve knights departed Camelot the very evening of the day the Green Knight and the wizard proposed the quest. Due to Bertilak's desire for haste, they did not wait until the next dawn—less than ten days remained between them and the full moon. Once more, Merlin guided the party through secret paths to quicken their journey to the north, where the land swelled with hills and mountains. Mist coated their mornings and rain split through the grey wisps. Dotting the land were ruins of Rome where some refuge was found in the night. During those hours of respite, Merlin would seek lore within his memories, or wander ahead on the path; though he traveled with the knights to the same destination, other quests encircled his mind.

Sand blue light glowed within the clouds as they rose over the seventh day of their journey.

The party arrived in a Pictish village at dawn. It sat upon a low hill beside a river. Past it, on the northern horizon, the ranks of pines of the Caledonian Forest speared through the mists.

"We will seek respite and knowledge here for the day," said Merlin. "No doubt our horses will need rest too."

"Can we not continue to the forest?" Bertilak asked. "The pines are just on the horizon; I can smell their ancient breath on the wind."

"I did not find the place of horror coming from the south," said Merlin. "Woodsmen here may know of it or the path to it. There is no use in searching a great forest such as this with only three nights left and spending most of those hours lost."

The party proceeded to the village without argument. To their relief, the Picts were Christian and allowed them entry, but also recognized Merlin with some reverence. Their horses were tended and they were brought to the broch tower at the top of the hill. Within, the knights were fed and warmed by the central fire whilst Merlin spoke with Rou, the chieftain of the tribe.

"Ere Christ was brought to us, our ancestors did revere such dark things," said Rou after Merlin described the nature of their quest. "Shub-Niggurath was one such utterance we had for the thing which promoted growth and life, but of a consuming, overabundant sort where things would grow and rot and grow again in a horrid cycle. We have not engaged in dealings with it or the aberrations that serve it and would prefer to stay far from the dark gulfs of our past. However, you bring knights of Arthur with you, so the quest must be righteous."

Bertilak could not help but clarify, "The safety of my wife is the goal. I intend to enter the woods and leave with as little bloodshed on either side as God may will it."

"Your quest *is indeed* righteous," said Rou. "For her life saved means the roots of the Dark Tree Woman will not spread through yon forest, or indeed the forests of the world."

Merlin continued his business with the chieftain: "I have been to the cult's place of worship once before, but entered from a different way; have you any woodsmen who might know a path from the southerly entrance of the forest to the dim place we seek?"

"Two such men returned a few days ago with news of strange sights and sounds, perhaps they can show you," answered Rou. The chieftain sent for the woodsmen and a pair of Pictish men entered the broch. By the bidding of their lord, they agreed to show Merlin the way, though the discomforted expressions they wore betrayed their fear.

Before he left, Merlin came up to Bertilak. "I will return in a few hours' time—nightfall at the latest. Remain here with the rest."

Bertilak furrowed his brow. "Would we not make more haste going all together?"

"If we can afford a stealthy attack, I must plot a way for us to take," said Merlin. "Over a dozen armored men cannot do that quickly. What is more, I must know if we can expect to deal with trickery and how I might counter it. Remain here, sharpen your axe, and seek the north for a signal-fire."

Merlin went with the woodsmen from the broch, leaving the knights in the hospitality of Rou. Bertilak departed the warm, stony house and sat on the dewy brae it was upon, sharpening his axe and staring northward. He followed the black shapes of Merlin and the woodsmen trekking towards the forest until they vanished in the folds of the heath. Remaining there well into the day, when the clouds commanding the sky dimmed, Bertilak sharpened his axe until its edge could sever a blade of grass down its middle with the slightest effort.

"Bertilak!" Gawain hailed him from behind. He came

around the broch with a drinking horn in each hand. Excalibur slept in a fine sheathe upon his left hip; the gilded crossguard and pommel curved like the edges of the sun. A handle of wood wrapped in soft leather, etched with knotwork, conjoined them. The Green Knight set his axe down beside him and acknowledged his visitor.

"Might I join you?" Gawain asked.

Bertilak gestured to the ground. "Of course."

Gawain sat and offered one of the horns, which Bertilak accepted, though he sipped its honied contents sparingly.

"The knights grow restless," said Gawain. "The forest is in sight, but we must wait. I cannot pretend to believe to know what you must think."

Without looking at Gawain, Bertilak said, "There are times when patience is a wise skill, yet for this quest, it seems to me haste is better. For these fanatics surge like a tide, even when iron stands in their way, and only quiver when fantastic powers are shown to them; they bow and bend to the latter with scarce any hesitation. I fear they cannot be reasoned with; my wife's existence fuels their madness and dedication to their god—this Shub-Niggurath."

"Though this is a new foe, with no doubt the power of great fear, I believe our faith in each other should be the shield that wards it off."

"And the blade that cuts it." Bertilak thumbed the beard of his axe.

A soft breeze danced through the air, and with it came a familiar smell to Bertilak. The animal musk and sting of sweat, with stomach-churning notes of fruity sweetness. The Green Knight shot to his feet, spilling his mead as he bore his axe in both hands.

Gawain arose as well, eschewing his horn to grip on a dagger handle from his belt. "What news?"

"*It* is here!" said Bertilak, surveying the village below.

Suddenly, Gawain rushed past Bertilak, drawing his dagger and shouting, "Behind you!"

The Green Knight spun just as a nude Pictish man with black paint rounded the curve of the broch, a spear in hand.

Shaggy black fur coated his forearms and patches of his legs. Large, crooked teeth stuck out from between his lips. The stench grew stronger as he approached. Gawain met the assassin and thrust his blade's point through the Pict's eye. Before the first attacker collapsed, shouting sounded inside the broch; more commotion rang out from the village. The two knights rushed to the entrance of Rou's hall to find a battle spilling out from within; some of the lesser knights and Pictish warriors alike banded together against a mad horde of fanatics shrieking praises to Shub-Niggurath.

One armored soldier of Arthur's caught sight of Bertilak and Gawain amidst the struggle. "Go on, sirs! Go to Merlin! We'll hold them here and protect Rou's people!"

"Abandon you?" Gawain asked. "Nonsense! Come, Bertilak, to arms!"

"We'll find you!" shouted another knight. "Go forth, sirs! Into the black weald!"

Bertilak placed a hand on Gawain's shoulder. "To the horses, friend. The men have chosen their duty."

Gawain frowned but followed Bertilak as they turned from the combat and rushed down the hill, aiming for the stables. Keeping their weapons in hand, the knights struck down all fanatics in their way and aided innocent Picts in peril. Those they fought bore differing mutations: most sprouted dark hair on their bodies; additional eyes stared out from areas other than their faces; some stumbled about with feet split down the center, hardening and blackening like hooves. Each one of them carried the stink Bertilak first smelled in the Green Chapel.

At the stables, the keepers' bodies lay in a heap with gashes and blows upon them. The fanatics were letting the panicked horses loose. One small man mounted Bertilak's great steed and slapped it on the neck as it dashed out of the stable. Bertilak and Gawain followed the thief as he wrapped his limbs about the beast. Bertilak's horse bucked and screamed at its unwelcome rider.

Halting just short of his horse, Bertilak raised a hand to its face. "Calm! Calm!"

The horse answered its master by bringing down the height of its bucks. The fanatic upon its bare back looked to the Green Knight with three wide eyes—two on either side of his nose and one on his shoulder. Bertilak yanked the fanatic from his horse and drove his axe through the three-eyed man's neck.

More horses cried out and their hooves stamped through the dirt

Gawain spun back towards the stables. "My horse!"

Another fanatic mounted Gawain's beautiful steed and rode it out of the stable and through the village. Bertilak beckoned his friend to his own horse.

"There's no time!" the Green Knight said as he mounted his steed bareback. Reluctantly, Gawain sheathed his dagger and allowed the bigger man to swing him onto the horse; he sat between the beast's head and Bertilak. The true rider of the horse spurred it through the village, cleaving fanatics as they charged up to him. A crowd stood between the horse and the open gates to the village; it was hard to discern who among its members were pure and who were fanatics.

"Steer the steed, Gawain!" shouted Bertilak. Gawain leaned forward and wrapped his arms about the beast's neck. Behind him, the Green Knight hefted up his axe. They breached the crowd. The horse grunted and continued through, obeying Gawain's cues and spurring. Bertilak swept and chopped his axe upon the foes they passed, though he sought his targets carefully in the heat of battle. The fanatics tore savagely into the Picts who fought with more discipline and praises to their God issuing from their throats. Those who could cleared a way for the two knights on one horse. Bertilak's steed cried out as weapons nicked its hide and folk appeared in its way. Gawain urged it to leap over obstacles or run them down.

A Pictish warrior at the gates heaved and staggered amid a group of bodies, both Pictish and fanatic in origin. He hailed the knights as they passed, shouting, "For God and your King, good sirs! Bring down the spawn of the wretched whore!"

He spun around as they left, slashing at a sudden surge of

fanatics. Gawain and Bertilak did not discover his fate, riding away in haste. Their mounted forms blended with the twilit land. They rode with their eyes on the north. Both of them spurred on the horse, whose breathing became more ragged as the minutes flew by with the chilling wind. Their path wound across the heath, which dipped and rose; thick brush and flowers ran throughout the knee-high grass. Even with the sounds of battle faded behind them, they maintained the horse's speed.

It finally stumbled in a dense patch of heather growing in a divot. Gawain and Bertilak dismounted, both men heaving as much as the horse, and their sweat turned chill upon their skin and dampened the clothes beneath their mail.

Bertilak laid his hand on his horse's neck, glancing over his shoulder at the settlement. "Not much smoke rises, perhaps they have won out."

"Shall we wait for them?" asked Gawain.

"One of two kinds might come if we wait: our knight-friends or the fanatics. We should follow Merlin to the forest and use what hunting skills we have to track him. Our search might be difficult, for it is two woodsmen and a wizard we follow."

"What of your steed?" Gawain patted the horse's face. "He seems too worn to go on."

Bertilak frowned. "I suppose that is right. I am unafraid to let him wander the heath; he is loyal and will return if we emerge."

"If," echoed Gawain. "Nay, *when*, my friend." He gave a smile to his companion.

"When," Bertilak agreed, but in a dour voice. With a swift slap on the horse's haunch, he sent the beast cantering off towards a rocky hill, far from the forest. Turning, he beckoned Gawain to follow; the knights sprinted to the forest. No signal fire burned amid the trees. Though harried from their escape, Bertilak and Gawain were hardy and sped through the wild grass and plants, and against the winds of the oncoming night. The clouds overhead dimmed to a near-black with a faint glow of blue about them. Any rests they took were scant—a mere jog and a couple of deep gulps of air. Their water and rations were left behind in the chaos, so they prayed somewhat for a drizzle of rain to wet their throats.

They reached the Caledonian Forest under the cowl of night. Roots of a pair of trees served as seats for them to gain respite. While they took breath and eased their limbs, Bertilak gazed into the woods.

"With the moon concealed, only a torch would aid us this night," he said.

"And what of Merlin and his woodsmen?" inquired Gawain between breaths. "Perhaps for them we should wait."

"I would rather not risk biding our time 'til danger finds us. Though there must be some spell or place-lore the wizard uses to keep from going astray." As Bertilak spoke, he reached above his head to stretch. His fingers fell upon the trunk against him, and felt a carving in the bark. He traced the curious pattern and at once recalled the Elder Sign Merlin scribed upon the door to the Green Chapel. He felt about him, grasping sticks and kindling—dead leaves and such.

"Find a branch or two," he bade Gawain. Bertilak's companion rustled through the dark. He found a pair of broken but hard limbs, each as long as an arm.

Once the pair reconvened, Gawain drew a dagger from his belt; Bertilak gathered the sticks and kindling into a small lodge in a patch of dry dirt. With a careful hand, Bertilak guided Gawain's dagger to the beard of his axe and the latter knight ran his own blade across the Green Knight's. After several attempts, a burst of sparks caught and stuck onto the kindling. The knights fed it until it steadily blazed. Then, Bertilak took the tree limbs and tore off strips of cloth from the hem of his surcoat—Gawain did as well. With the cloth wrapped around the limbs, Bertilak ignited the makeshift torches.

"We'll find Merlin ourselves," decreed Bertilak. "Seek this Sign…"

He showed Gawain the Elder Sign upon the tree, which Gawain beheld in awe. "Of what faith is this symbol of?" he asked.

Bertilak shrugged. "An old one…a faith older than the druids I'd reckon, and perhaps even older than the race who erected the stones about Britain. Enough of lore; onwards!"

The knights entered the forest, torches borne in their left hands while their weapons occupied their rightmost grips. Even in the pitiful torchlit half-darkness, the blade of Excalibur glimmered with brilliance, as if the sun cast beams upon it forever. The canopy of trees brought even more darkness, shrinking the light to the surfaces of nearby trees, barely weaving through the spaces between them. With each turn, each step deeper in, the knights felt some invisible wall rise behind them, casting a shadow over their hearts and souls as both stirred within them, wild with questions and fears. Beneath his breath and the rasp of tree branches, Gawain recited prayers in Latin, but not ones begging forgiveness from his Almighty Lord—he beseeched his Holy Overlord for courage. Even when animals stirred in nearby brush, eliciting jolted turns from the knights, Gawain kept his prayers upon his breath.

Signs of previous travelers were evident on the ground and in parts of the trees—disturbed dirt and leaves, notches in the branches and trunks, and even a few cairns amid the roots. However, nothing guaranteed it as Merlin's path.

The torches burned low as they entered a clearing. At once, they sought the trunks about them whilst tearing off more of their surcoats for fuel.

"Lo!" said Gawain, thrusting his torch towards the northwest. An Elder Sign was carved into the trunk of a thin pine. He approached it and gazed into the weald beyond. A weariness came over him.

"Ah, Bertilak," he said, "though it goes against your desires, I feel I must rest; we traveled far and fast today."

Bertilak stomped to a halt. "What? Can you go no further, man? No horrors hinder us yet, and we might face them head on ere they come to us!"

Gawain leaned against a tree. "My limbs ache and my chest heaves. I am sorry, but I must rest. I do not have your fury to endure much longer."

"Find that fury!"

Gawain staggered back as the Green Knight stormed up to him. He recalled the strength and speed with which Bertilak swung his axe; he did not desire more than a nick from that iron beard. But he stood tall, stiffening his spine.

"I will rest, good sir," Gawain said. "And I will follow you with as much fury threefold when I am ready."

Bertilak sighed. "If that is what you wish. But we will sleep with our backs together upright, weapons in hand."

Gawain agreed and they came to the center of the clearing, sat against each other, and let their torches burn out, easing in what little night vision they could gain. Gawain drifted off first, leaning his chin into his chest; Bertilak remained awake, but his alertness dulled as fatigue crept in. He let a little fear into his heart and eyes to keep them alert and keen; shapes flitted and slunk in the black between the trees, but nothing emerged into the clearing. He also took deep breaths, seeking any sign of that wretched smell within the traces of pine and earth in the air.

Hours Bertilak could not count by numbers or light passed; he and Gawain might have stepped into a trap of endless night, he feared. Suddenly, a series of footsteps and steady rustle sounded from beyond the part of the clearing the knights entered from. Low, murmuring voices accompanied the disturbance.

Bertilak leapt to his feet, bringing up his axe. "Arise, Gawain!"

Struck from sleep, Gawain scrambled to his feet and gripped his sword, turning with Bertilak. They faced the edge of the clearing, towards the sounds; orange light danced upon the trunks. The footsteps hurried into the clearing and a friendly band revealed itself: three of the knights who set out with Bertilak, Gawain, and Merlin led the way like a spearhead; behind them came three Pictish warriors. Each man bore a torch alongside his weapon. The three knights also toted some additional gear. Once both sides were revealed, weapons were lowered and smiles came upon mouths—albeit reserved ones.

"What news from Rou's tribe?" asked Bertilak.

The leading knight, with the name of Dafyd, frowned. "The fanatics were quelled but many of the chieftain's people were slain. And we, save Sir Gawain, are all who remain from Camelot. These bold fellows agreed to join us, for they hate the fanatics and their dark god as much as we are beginning to."

Gawain stepped forward, arms wide. "Pictish friends! You are welcome into our fold. My sword will swing alongside your blades, and my shield would ward your flesh, were it with me."

The two other knights, named Aled and Maxen, removed some gear from their persons: Gawain and Bertilak's shields, as well as a small pack of rations and several waterskins. The party gathered at the center of the clearing and spoke to each other of what transpired thus far. From the mouths of the three knights and three Picts, Bertilak and Gawain learned of the unwavering stalwarts who that fell, nine in all, who stood between women, children, and the swarms of fanatics. For each knight felled, the men of Arthur in turn cut down around a dozen shrieking wild-things themselves each.

Gawain laid a hand over his heart. "May God keep them and grant them deserved rest forevermore! Amen!"

"Amen!" shouted the rest of the party in chorus.

From the Picts themselves, all the knights learned how the fanatics might have slunk in:

"Some amongst our village must have still heard the callings of the black daemon," said one warrior. "Once this quest was set forth, they must have guessed a party would come into Rou's fold, and an ambush would have at least hindered you all. More must have been allowed in by the traitors among us as night fell. Even when a king as great as Arthur rules, there are shadows that remain lurking in the hearts of men."

"Many looked like devils," said Gawain. "What of that?"

The warrior answered, "By fell magicks most likely, for in old tales it is said curses would be laid upon those who follow dark gods. For they who attacked us, however, it must be a blessing to them."

Bertilak took charge of the conversation before silence seeped in: "Merlin has left his Signs about the forest. However, there is a chance he will return. We shall take our rest here 'til he reveals himself or when we can track him in the dawn."

The party agreed and soon went to sleep afterwards. Even in half-slumber, Bertilak sought the edges of the clearing for shadows, and the air for the smell.

A three-syllable croak from a raven raked Bertilak's ears just as blue light emanated from the clouds beyond the branches overhead. The limbs of the trees shook as feathers flapped about. Shooting upright, Bertilak sought the air for the bird; its call sounded unlike other ravens', for when it came again and again, it sounded like it spoke:

Ber-ta-lak! Ber-ta-lak!

The Green Knight stood and followed a small, dark shape as it flapped down from the branches and perched upon a stone in the clearing. The other knights and the warriors took heed of the noise, arising from sleep. The raven cocked its head at Bertilak who beheld it with a puzzled expression.

"Merlin?" he asked.

The bird bobbed its head and croaked.

Gawain came up beside Bertilak. "What is this?" he wondered.

"One of Merlin's spells. Though why he comes to us in the guise of a bird, I do not know. Unless something has befallen him."

The bird croaked again, bobbing its head as well, and this time spreading its wings.

"Haste, then!" said Bertilak. "Break your fasts on the trail. Though it isn't dawn, we'll follow the raven to our course."

The party gathered and equipped themselves. While they did, the raven circled the clearing. Once they were set, the raven took off on the path marked by the Elder Sign; the party pursued the bird as though it were a game falcon. They twisted through the trail-less way, leapt over stones and logs, and tore away hindering brush and branches. Though they departed the clearing at the coming of day, the glow from above did not increase; the canopy thickened, the needled branches weaving together so only shards of blue-black showed through. The croak of the raven was enough for the party to follow. They ran without pause, but their path became no clearer as they went.

Some ways into their pursuit—not one of them could say how long, for it felt both brief and lengthy—a pungent odor wafted into the faces of the party. Though it elicited no memories from Bertilak, the Green Knight did not enter this part of the forest easily. Rotting plants seemed to be the source of the smell, though something else meshed into it: the sweeter scent of growth. The stink overall hung wet and heavy in the air, as on the eve of a rainstorm. Its feeling clung to the flesh and clothes of the party members.

Furthermore, the canopy blocked even more light, leaving the party to stumble as the raven flew and croaked. The roots were large, some even felt as if they slithered just below the earth.

"Someone," Bertilak called out, "light a torch if you have it."

One of the Picts ignited a tallow-torch. The light of it revealed only the immediate area; everything beyond waited in black.

The party resumed at a quicker pace once the raven croaked again. Its calls became more frequent and its movement hastened. The winged shadow flitted at the edge of the torch's glow overhead. It took a sudden turn to the right and the party followed. Several stone plinths emerged from between the trees. Black paint drawn in hideous symbols covered their faces—one being the perverted trinity. The raven finally perched on the branch of a large tree nearby and pointed its beak downwards, croaking. The roots were large and half-twisted out of the ground, leaving a dark space between the earth and the bottom of the tree.

The party ceased their pursuit and heeded the raven's direction. The torchbearer brought his light closer to the bottom of the tree; two feet in familiar travel-worn turnshoes lay beneath the cage of roots.

Gawain leapt forward and hacked the roots away. A dark sap trickled out of them. He reached in, once his path lay clear, and withdrew Merlin by the ankle. At once, the raven flew away. The wizard's eyes snapped open in the torchlight; he bore a grim expression as he came out of his trance.

"Put it out!" he hissed. "The Dark Young wander!"

The torchbearer hesitated, but lowered his beacon. A sudden noise caused him to lift it up again—something whistled nearby. The party bore their blades and wards, gathering in a circle about the prone Merlin. Again, a noise came, but this one a harsher, grating sound on a strong blast of wind. A soft note, like a woman's cry, resonated from Excalibur's edge. All eyes flicked about, but the torchlight did not allow them to search far. The forms of trees were evident; their branches twisted and loomed like claws reaching for hapless victims.

Several heavy thuds sounded beyond the stones. Hooves upon earth—a sound unmistakable to knights. A shape emerged at the edge of the torchlight; the party believed it at first to be a tree with thick branches. The horrid noise, which now included ear-biting whispers, grew louder in the direction of the tree. Along with the noise came a sudden surge from the smell in the air; even the hardiest man in the party gagged at the stench of rotting corpses. The party, from their circle, looked to it. In the torchlight, sets of teeth glinted within the boles of the tree. Its branches swayed, then writhed. Its trunk split apart, revealing not wood, but three-hooved goat-like legs. A shriek from the hideous mouths tore through the air, splitting the ears of the party.

Merlin shot to his feet and cried, "Away! Away! The terror of the Dark Young is mighty!"

The party divided as the creature—the Dark Young— charged. Its branches, really tentacles, flailed as it came within range of the darting forms. The torchbearer, Dafyd, and Gawain were grabbed. The torch fell to the ground, its diminished light revealing little else of the Dark Young's full form.

Gawain hacked at the tentacle grasping him—Excalibur's song echoed gloriously through the air—and called out, "Strike it from all sides! There are no eyes!"

Bertilak and the others in the dark trusted the location of Gawain's shout and rushed towards the beast, shields raised. The Green Knight swung low, hoping to catch its leg. A tentacle above him whipped and Gawain cried out; Bertilak blocked a heavy blow and continued his cut. His axe struck thick hide and flesh, but did not strike bone—though he knew the cut went deep.

The monster's form writhed and twitched. The dimming torchlight revealing just enough of it for the fighters on their feet to skirt about it and take blows when enough courage surged through them. Suddenly, the torch rose off the ground and Merlin's craggy, bearded face appeared in the glow. He puffed his cheeks and blew; the fire danced away from the torch, then swelled into a blast. The Dark Young's mouths shrieked as it ignited, sounding like metal shredding itself on metal. The fire worsened the smell, burning the throats of all who inhaled the fumes. It thrashed its tentacles, its grip loosening on the three captives. Gawain and the Pict landed on their sides; Bertilak assisted his fellow knight up while the Picts aided their tribesman. Dafyd's shout of surprise cut short as he plunged headfirst onto the ground. He moved no more from there.

The Dark Young spun and stomped, its lower body alight with fiery tongues. Above, its tentacles thrashed and reached out; the fighters gave their distance and hacked the slimy things in threatening reach. The shrieks proved to be a distraction; all who heard them grit their teeth and winced as their very minds were raked by the calls.

"Merlin, the tendrils!" shouted Bertilak. "We must get closer!"

The shaded form of the wizard stooped, but at the Green Knight's behest, he raised his arms. Like ants scaling a dying beast, the flames crawled up the Dark Young's body. More flashes of its hideous bulk were exposed; most of the party averted their gaze at the sickening surface of the thing. The wild head of butchered tentacles now bore a treacherous crown of flame. With a shout, Gawain flashed Excalibur and rushed forth, driving the point into the bloated flesh of the monster's middle. One of the mouths gnawed at him, but he withdrew and slashed. Arthur's legendary blade engaged in a sonorous duel with the rattles of the Dark Young. Bertilak and the other fighters joined him; the Green Knight finished his work severing the leg he cut.

The creature staggered off-balance, then fell prone. It suddenly thrashed and rolled across the ground; Bertilak, Gawain, Maxen Aled, and the torchbearer Pict leapt out of the way. In the dark, the other two Picts screamed as the mass of slimy, burning flesh crushed their bones.

A fury came over Bertilak as he chased the Dark Young down. He roared as he doffed his shield and bore his axe in both hands, chopping into his prone prey. He lopped away tentacles shooting towards him out of the dark. Soon, his allies joined in the *coup de grace*, moving with speed and fervency, giving the Dark Young as little a chance to retaliate as they could. With each stroke from the men, the cry of the creature escalated, until that, and faint notes of Excalibur's song, were the only sounds in the air. Even when the monster went still and its voice withered away, it resounded in the minds of the men.

The last of the firelight exposed the mutilation of the Dark Young: chunks of black flesh and bone white fangs lay in pools of sap-like slime. The body sank in on itself, for neither skeleton nor organs nor eldritch magic held it together.

Merlin shuffled over to the remaining men as they turned away from the monster. "There is no time to mourn or bury our allies."

Gawain looked about. "Where are the woodsmen accompanying you?"

Merlin sighed, gesturing to the Dark Young. "They were treacherous; their real faith hid in the shadows of their hearts and they tried to lure me to this scion of their god. I lost them in the flight away from their work. I am truly grievous, but we must reach the heart of their worship."

"Of course," said Bertilak. "We've only two days until the full moon."

Merlin's hand upon the Green Knight's shoulder elicited a sudden feeling of doubt within him. "Actually, there is less time," said the wizard. "Only a matter of hours lay between us and the knife that will cut your Lady."

"What?" Bertilak clenched his axe.

"This share of the woods, it belongs to something else, where even time is under its command to some extent," explained Merlin. "It can make men lose their way in the flow of time within this dim labyrinth. We must hurry and take care our minds and feet do not wander; have faith in yourselves and each other!"

Another torch came alight and the party continued forth, following Merlin. Gawain bowed his head and uttered prayers for the three fallen. However, his words felt quiet in this share of the woods, as if he spoke into a hollow dungeon with no windows. Bertilak and Maxen aided Merlin, who gulped in deep breaths; his limbs shook and his gait was a mere shamble.

"Follow the stones," he said. They passed the plinths, which leaned and leered like mute observers with plans unknown. The brunt of the Dark Young's stench faded with distance, but traces remained in the nostrils of the party members, joining the rest of the odors of the forest.

The path of the stones twisted through the trees. Every step warranted a quick survey of the area; things rustled and creaked in the distance; things that might have been words whispered on the wind. The massive, gnarled roots groaned and pulsed into the ground. Black sky melded with the branches of the stygian cathedral roof.

After many uncounted steps, the torch burned out; another took its place. Bertilak's heart pounded as the party progressed into halls of unending shadow. He sought at least a shaft of moonlight or definite sound to guide him. Merlin suddenly stumbled, threatening to fall out of his grasp. Bertilak caught the wizard and leaned his axe upon a nearby tree, then laid his hand upon it for balance. His palm made contact with a soft and wet thing growing on the bark; a puff of a dusty cloud brushed over his face accompanied by a new odor of sickly sweet fruit. He gagged, gently pulling off Merlin to clear his space of the smell. The more he fought it, the more it overpowered his nostrils, and entered his vision and thoughts.

The darkness before him rippled, the torchlight faded away. All stirring sounds dissolved. Bertilak knew he stood alone then, believed it truly. He rubbed the dust out of his eyes; his stomach churned from the lingering scent. Silver-blue beams descended through the branches, but the ground and bark on the trees remained black. Bertilak went to the nearest beam, and sighed as a cool breeze wove through the links in his mail. A lithe shade passed across another spot of light further ahead. He followed it; his feet made no sound on the soil. Again, the shade wove through another beam, then again, and again.

Bertilak's eyes whipped to-and-fro; his feet hastened along with his heartbeat. *Have I found her?* he wondered. For with each glimpse of the shade, something betraying it as his Lady appeared upon its form: a flowing train of a dress, a gold glimmer upon its finger, a flash of white teeth in a smile.

A single quick word cut through the silence, like the *snick* of a knife: "Bertilak."

The Green Knight froze in the middle of a beam. He moved his mouth to speak, but no sound emerged; and he could not force another step forward. His arms locked at his sides. The shade appeared in more places than one; his gaze moved with maddening speed.

With each appearance, his name sounded again, always in the same small, sharp tone: "Bertilak. Bertilak. Bertilak…"

They drew closer, but shadow always concealed their visages and attire. The smiles on them grew wider, but Bertilak's heart chilled and crept into his throat rather than warmed as it would have at the sight of his real Lady. The smell that guided him to this encounter bloomed inside his nose and into his mind. His stomach churned in response, and something hot and burning accompanied the feeling of his heart in his throat.

His eyes ached from remaining open and felt as though they would tear themselves out at the speed they sought the shades. The forms crowded him; one rose before him and locked his stare in a pitch black space above its smile. Two crescents formed like smaller smiles above the mouth—right where the eyes would be. Bertilak found himself torn between dread and hope if he would witness the eyes of his Lady. The crescents snapped open, and the Green Knight's jaw dropped in a soundless shriek of horror.

A pair of yellow goat's eyes stared back at him.

The chorus of his name morphed into an absolute babble. Drumming without rhythm supported it. His voice returned to his ears, but the sound he uttered was of a primal tone unlike anything he would dream of himself producing.

All went dark and quiet soon after.

Bertilak stared up at the single, baleful white eye of the night, lidded by clouds and veined with tree branches. Someone shook his shoulder.

"Bertilak." Gawain's voice brought some ease to his heart. But he took a draught of air to find it laced with the same odor as from the Green Chapel and the assault on Rou's village. He sat up, meeting the gazes of Gawain, the last Pict, and Maxen. All the men were filth-covered, bruised, and bore traces of blood on their graith.

"Where are Aled and Merlin?" asked Bertilak.

Gawain bowed his head. "Sir Aled fell in an ambush. We know not Merlin's fate, for we were taken in the same attack. After he nearly fell, you released him suddenly and wandered off the path. We followed you, calling your name, but you wouldn't heed us or wake at our touch. Far from the original course, you froze and screamed. Fanatics swarmed out of the trees, lashing us with nets and ropes. We fought, but there were many and Aled was overcome with rage. A noose caught around his neck and he lost breath, but he took a good number of our attackers with him…"

Though the remark of valor in death would have kept chins high, Gawain's next words were scant of any joy: "But they continued to come. Now we are here: their heart of worship."

The captives were in a cage of wood, shoved against the curved wall of bowled ground. A set of crooked moss-and-root-covered steps far to their left descended into the pit. Black trees lined the lip of the bowl, twisting over each other; their roots slithered along the walls, writhing like worms as they hung. Shadows moved between the trunks. In the base of the pit, fanatics danced and flailed about; groups of them engaged in orgies and choruses of fell chants. The one spot they avoided sat in the middle: a huge monolith laid upon its back. Bertilak's axe lay upon it, its butt touching the curved pommel of Excalibur.

Gawain looked to the sword with tears in his eyes. "I fear our King might not receive his blade ever again, and it is my fault."

"Not yours." Bertilak placed a hand on Gawain's shoulder. "Mine. In my own quest to save my wife, I brought you away from Arthur's side along with other men. Many have met their end in this and my heart aches for them…for Logres…for Britain…for the world."

A warped bellow split through the air out from the trees. At once, the fanatics halted their madness and gazed at the lip of the pit across from the table. There emerged a pale figure in a sheet of moonlight; Bertilak and Gawain gripped the bars of the cage.

"The Lady!" they both breathed.

She stood naked at the top of the pit, arms against her sides and her head bowed. The symbol of the perverted trinity adorned her supple belly in black paint. Behind her crept a darker form that kept just at the edge of the light. It looked like a crouched man, but tips of horns and points of claws weaved in and out of the beams. The Lady of Hautdesert beheld the cult and walked to her right along the lip; the furtive thing followed her. She came around to the steps and descended, now lifting her chin and wearing a solemn expression. A single tear winked silver along her eyelid.

184

Bertilak thrust himself against the cage. "My Lady! Release her! All of you be damned!"

Some of the fanatics cackled at Bertilak's raging. They stopped when the clopping of hooves sounded from the steps. The thing came into the pit. It held the familiar form of a man, but its legs were backwards and hooved like a goat's. Its elongated head bore a pair of spiraled horns sticking skyward. Long-fingered hands with filthy talons aided its weird gait across the ground. The entire skin coating it was black, akin to the black bark of the trees or the night sky.

"Damned?" it drawled out in a guttural alien voice, though it bore no mouth upon its face. *"This world is already 'damned.'"*

It looked to the captives and Bertilak screamed, for the hideous goat-thing possessed the same eyes that looked upon him in his vision.

"What sort of d-d-devil are you?" Gawain demanded, but his teeth clattered as he too beheld the eyes.

The monster slunk towards the cage; the captives shrunk back as it curled its fingers around the bars. *"No devil,"* it said. *"But a thing out of the first forests of the world. Your sages call me the Black Goat. I am the consort of Shub-Niggurath. Iä! Iä!"*

Every last fanatic echoed the chant of *Iä! Iä!*

"Her forests will return," the Black Goat vowed. *"Your spouse's blood will nourish the earth."*

Bertilak charged the front of the cage and gripped the Black Goat's throat with one large hand; its flesh was cold and clammy. The woody bars creaked against his force. He brought his other hand up to strike, but a troop of fanatics rushed to their master and harried Bertilak away.

"Yours will precede your mate's." The Black Goat pointed at Bertilak.

Gawain came to Bertilak's side as the cage door opened. "No!"

"It's alright. Have faith, good sir," Bertilak said quietly. Several fanatics dragged him out; he went kicking, shouting, and thrashing. "There is not one among you brave enough!"

he called out. "Not one who can take this head from my shoulders!"

The Black Goat came back beside the captive Lady. The cage door was closed shut; the men rushed to it and gripped the bars, watching in horror as the fanatics steered Bertilak towards the monolith. He continued to shout and jeer as they brought him around it, so he faced his wife and allies. They kicked the backs of his knees and shoved his head onto the stone. A fat, big-armed fanatic hefted the Green Knight's own axe off the table and walked around it. The fanatics went quiet.

Then, Bertilak laughed. It was a brief chortle. His executioner paid it no heed as he raised the weapon. Gawain's heart pounded, tears burned his cheeks. He looked to the Lady as she beheld the scene, but furrowed his brow at her reaction: a grin twitched at the corners of her mouth. Gawain looked back to Bertilak as the axe came down.

Thok!

The sound of the single stroke echoed through the woods.

The fanatics released Bertilak's body, letting it slump to the ground. His executioner leaned on the axe and grabbed his head by the long, curly green locks. Thick verdant blood drizzled from the stump and onto the ground. For a few moments, the tongue lolled out of the mouth and the eyes rolled upwards. Suddenly, the jaw on Bertilak's head dropped open, and he coughed. The executioner, startled, dropped his trophy to the ground.

Bertilak's blood and wisps of his ancient soul reached from his head into the earth. Ancient, beautiful, strong, dangerous power coursed into the ghost haunting his skull. All the roots of trees and plants whispered to him. They spoke with visions of who his soul was: The Green Knight. A warrior-thing reincarnated from pagan times. A being bidden to grow by the hand of God. Bertilak.

He felt as well the churning, terrible roots Shub-Niggurath planted in this share of the Caledonian Forest. And, further away, but drawing nearer, he felt resonations like drumbeats. Merlin, somewhere, performed a spell upon the last great

186

ancient pine who held out against the tainted part of the weald.

"Now," Bertilak's voice boomed throughout the pit, "it is my turn to cut off your heads!"

His body rose as fluidly as if it still bore a head and tore the axe from the executioner. He chopped through the man's neck, sending the house of his brains flying.

Gawain laughed. *Of course!* he remembered. *Only Bertilak is capable of such a miracle!*

The fanatics whooped and stumbled away as the decapitated knight retrieved his head. He placed it beneath one arm as he would a helm, a grin never wavering from his mouth. Bertilak rushed through the crowd, swinging his axe in wide sweeps. Many fled from him; those he caught were pushed away with gory gashes upon their flesh.

The Black Goat bellowed and grasped the Lady of Hautdesert by the arm. She laughed along with her husband, but her mirth was cut short as her captor dragged her, prone across the ground, towards the monolith. The beast pulled with one hand, clawing and pushing with the other at fanatics who stood in its way. Quicker cultists cleared the path and went after Bertilak.

The grin on his head warped into a snarl, and he turned to pursue the Black Goat, but fanatics formed a wall between Bertilak and their master. So he turned towards the cage. Bertilak barreled through several opponents in his way; the men backed away from the door as the Green Knight approached and cleaved the stiff bars.

Gawain leapt out—Maxen and the last Pict followed—and came next to Bertilak. "I'll hold your head; your axe cuts better with both hands."

"There is no man better than you to trust," Bertilak said as his body handed over his head to Gawain. Arthur's nephew took up a club in one hand as he ran with Bertilak into the crowd of fanatics between them and the end of their quest. Maxen and the Pict came up behind them, taking crude spears from bleeding victims of the Green Knight.

The troop of fighting men surged into the swarm, swinging

and stabbing with all the strength in them. Though their foes were many, they did not abandon their skill or faith, but married those qualities with their fury to press on. While they trudged through the masses, the Black Goat wove easily between its lackeys, sullying the Lady of Hautdesert with the filth on the ground.

Bertilak's head growled. "Gawain! To Excalibur! I'll make a path, but you must go with haste!"

The Black Goat and the sacrifice were steps from the monolith. The fighters stood a hundred yards away.

Gawain measured the distance as he fought, his head spinning in the flurry of battle. Suddenly, Bertilak's body jumped into the crowd before them and lashed about its whole self in several giant sweeps. A thin line of fanatics blocked the edge of the new gap.

"Go!" bellowed Bertilak.

So Gawain went forth with fury. He ran through the crowd, smiting two opponents in his way. His second strike landed so hard his club shattered in his hand; he let the remains fall. Once free, he sprinted, dodging the scattered fanatics outside the crowd. The Black Goat reached the monolith and flung the Lady onto it; Shub-Niggurath's consort raised its claws as moonbeams spilled into the pit.

"*Iä! Iä! Shub-Niggurath!*" it cried, then loosed forth a string of eldritch chants.

Gawain increased his speed, a little more than halfway to the monolith. The head of Bertilak clenched its teeth and jaw, grunting. The Lady mouthed a prayer. The Black Goat's claws shook, its voice grinding on mortal minds like the susurrus of the Dark Young. Excalibur's edge twinkled.

"*Iä! Iä!*" roared the Black Goat, its voice at its most guttural echoing through the forest. "*Shub-Niggurath!*"

"Lord God!" cried Gawain as he leaned into his run, striding with long steps. He came within spitting distance of the fell altar. He reached for Excalibur's leathern handle.

The Black Goat brought one claw down with its last utterance.

"No!" shouted Bertilak.

Gawain leapt. His knees exploded with pain as they broke his fall before the monolith. His hand fell upon Excalibur and he swung at the black shadow in the silver light. The sword sang a high, heartening note as it flew through the air towards the wicked claw. It ended with a tearing sound and sudden ring.

The Black Goat's shriek filled the air.

Its gnarled, twitching hand fell beside the Lady; dark blood spattered across her face and breasts. The Black Goat dismounted the monolith and slunk into a darker space. Gawain rose and flashed Excalibur towards encroaching fanatics; they growled like animals, arching their backs as if to pounce. He handed Bertilak's head over to his wife who accepted it gladly.

"Your presence is most loved, Lord," she said.

The head smiled. "My heart is a little more at ease. Gawain, remain at my Lady's side; to the stairs!"

Gawain helped the Lady off the monolith and brought her behind him. Fanatics leaping for him and the Lady met a swift end at the slashes of Excalibur, whose song rose high and sweet, even in this horrid battle.

Bertilak's body with Maxen and the Pict moved towards the stairs as well. All three men's bodies were cut and bruised as they hacked and stabbed through the crowd, fighting to meet their allies with fury. The trio convened with Gawain and the Lady with her spouse's head.

In the shadows, the Black Goat shrieked, repeating a new chant in strange words. The fanatics mimicked their master's cry.

Bertilak looked about the lip of the bowl; a pair of large shadows moved behind the trees towards the stairs. Appendages like thick branches flailed on the forms.

"Look out!" shouted Bertilak as the party reached the first step.

A Dark Young appeared at the top of the stairs. Another crept behind it. Their grave-stench choked the air, overpowering the musk of the Black Goat. The mouths of both monsters gibbered maddening nonsense.

The body of Bertilak took the lead, ascending with axe rested on its shoulder. The Dark Young rushed down the steps, its hooves tearing the moss and roots covering the stone. Gawain glanced over his shoulder, looking past the blood-covered face of the Lady; the fanatics approached the steps languidly, staring with grins up at the party as the Dark Young came to meet them.

Trapped on both sides, Gawain thought. *By God, we shan't shrink!*

Bertilak's body brought the axe over its empty shoulders and chopped at the great bulk of the Dark Young as it came down. The monster shrieked; its tentacles fell upon Bertilak's body, beating and slithering its limbs over his. Maxen and the Pict jabbed at the appendages constricting about their ally. Bertilak's head grunted as his body struggled out of the Dark Young's grasp. Behind the first one, the other descended to join it.

"Thank you for your faith in this doomed quest, Sir Gawain," whispered the Lady in Gawain's ear.

Gawain raised Excalibur. Bertilak's body hacked and kicked as the Dark Young's tentacles lifted it off the stairs; its mouths gnawed at his hard mail. *Once his body is gone, it comes for us*, Gawain theorized. *Oh Singing Sword, sing a hymn to glory this night.*

Up the steps, the violent rustling of branches sounded. The unengaged Dark Young roared as a tall, slender shadow came upon it. A flurry of heavy, needled limbs assaulted the hideous child of the forest; roots shot from the earth and tore at the soft, stinking flesh.

"The great pine!" Bertilak's head cried. "Merlin is here!"

Indeed, a robed form appeared behind the living tree, with arms raised and arcane chants in an old, noble tongue issuing from his mouth. With more heart, Maxen and the Pict shouted and rushed the Dark Young before them; their spears drove deep, spurting slime onto them. Bertilak's body seized a tentacle about his narrow waist in one hand and hacked it away with his axe. The Dark Young's grip faltered and his body escaped, landing on the steps and striking more blows

190

upon the hollow body.

"Go forth, Gawain!" the Lady shouted.

"For Arthur!" Gawain's oath of allegiance rang above the gibbering of the Dark Young. He charged with Excalibur's point unwavering; the keen tip went true into one of the hideous mouths. The teeth bit down on his mailed arm, but the blade drove deep; the Dark Young trembled as the wounds laid upon it tore away at its vitality.

"Around! Around!" ordered Bertilak. "There is no glory here! Let us away from these woods!"

Immediately, the headless body landed a heavy blow on the Dark Young before traversing around it. Maxen and the Pict skirted about it on either side. Gawain withdrew from the beast and kept himself between it and the Lady as he went up the steps. The pine wrestled with the other Dark Young, tearing and beating with its hard limbs while its foe slithered and constricted with formless ones. The tree pushed it away from the steps as the party ascended.

Merlin sighed as his allies came to him. "It is time we flee."

He waved his hands and the pine staggered upon its root-legs. The Dark Young brought its full weight and tentacles upon it in a grotesque embrace. The wood cracked and limbs fell.

"And so falls the last great pine in this share of the Caledonian Forest," said Merlin. "But its end is not in vain."

He waved his hands once more and the pine cracked asunder; splinters and needles tore through the grip of the Dark Young. The remains flew through the air in a cloud. It lowered before the party and coalesced into many smaller shapes—Elder Signs. The first Dark Young hauled its mangled body up the steps as the spell took form. Merlin held his palms up flat, then thrust them forth. A blast of wind followed his motion and the hail of Elder Signs flew at the Dark Young. The spawns of Shub-Niggurath screamed as the furtive warding runes ripped through them. The already wounded Dark Young tumbled back down the steps; the enemy of the pine staggered back, its tentacles drooping and hooves quivering.

"To the forest!" Merlin boomed in a hoarse voice. The party obeyed and rushed off, following Merlin's path of the stones away. Behind them the fanatics shrieked as they ascended the steps, crying to their god and cursing the interlopers. Above all of them, the Black Goat loosed its alien bellow, which, despite the growing distance between them, chilled the blood of each member of the party.

They traveled in darkness, with the occasional moonbeam trickling in through the branches; Merlin's shambling form guided them. Their own footfalls and heartbeats were so loud, they were unsure if anyone or anything followed them. Between the trees, branches rustled, roots groaned, and weird calls were issued. Nothing reached for them as they went deeper into the dark, their only true light being their faith in one another. Soon, clouds passed over the moon, and shadows wrapped over their forms.

"Hail, Sir Gawain!" called the lookout as Arthur's nephew and his escorts approached the camp. It sat upon a low, grassy hill, stirred heavily by the wind. A quickly-built wooden palisade surrounded the perimeter at the foot.

Merlin rode on his left; on his right rode Bertilak, with his head whole once again upon his neck, and his Lady sat before him on the same saddle. The Pict returned to Rou's land following the quest, but collapsed into a deep slumber once he arrived. Maxen said nothing the whole way back from the forest, and was returned to Camelot.

Gawain raised a hand in greeting as he arrived. Stable boys saw to the horses and squires guided the knights, the wizard, and the Lady to Arthur's tent. The King himself was situated at the heart of the camp. Within his grand shelter, a wooden copy of the Round Table—meant for transport—sat in the center. Arthur and the other knights were in discussion as Gawain entered with Bertilak and Merlin.

Arthur rose and threw up his arms. "My dear nephew! Good Sir Bertilak! You've returned!"

The Lady of Hautdesert entered and curtsied in a fine

travel dress, loaned to her by Guinevere. "Sire," she said. Each knight at the Round Table stood up at her entrance.

Arthur came around the Table. "You were successful? It humbles me greatly to meet you, Lady."

He kissed the Lady's hand and bowed as he came up to his guests and nephew. Gawain unsheathed Excalibur and knelt, presenting the brand with it laid out upon his palms. It glimmered and reflected, having been thoroughly cleansed of the black gore which coated it days prior. Arthur accepted his sword with a reverent nod.

"We have brought back the Lady of Hautdesert," said Gawain. "Put an end to the activity of those fanatics, but we lost many on the quest. And...what I witnessed, my King, I must admit...it shook my faith."

Arthur sheathed Excalibur in the empty scabbard on his belt. "Your faith might be shaken, nephew, but you are with good company now. Rise."

Gawain did so and gestured to Bertilak. "I was in excellent company with Sir Bertilak the whole way. I upheld my duties as Knight of Arthur and Protector of Women, but the *things* dwelling in the darkest regions of the Caledonian Forest...the sight of them and their rites made me feel so small, as if I were an ant plucked out of its hill."

"The outer things of primordial origin bestow such gloom," said Merlin. "They open gateways to perspectives no man would hope to understand or conceal from himself. They have always been in the cosmos, and always will be. I will not lie in saying rites such as what we witnessed will be tried again, and more things might occur regardless of our plans. I am one druid. Though I know much lore and spells, I cannot do it all alone."

"I would rather die than allow them to come after my Lady again," Bertilak laid a hand upon his spouse, "thus I will persist as a soldier in this dark war. Gawain's faith and company indeed kept my heart whole, though I too am shaken. It is his choice once more, but I would be glad to fight alongside him again."

The Lady of Hautdesert looked up to her husband and said,

"And woe would no doubt befall the hearts and souls of many if a similar fate befell others. I will stand by your side, my Lord, and give what strength I can to you."

Arthur gestured to the Round Table. "Come, let us talk more. All of a sudden, this campaign against the Saxons seems…petty. Greater shadows creep towards us."

So ends the tale of Bertilak the Green Knight's struggle against the Black Goat.

IN THE SHADOW OF GODS

Timothy Williams

The overcast sky seemed to reach down and touch the damp earth with a giant hand of gray fog. On a clear day he would have seen the earthen work and high wooden palisade that was the entrance of Camelot from leagues away. As it was, Palomides couldn't see more than an arm span in front of his horse's nose. After his voyage home and back and the long ride on horseback, Palomides was more than ready to deliver his message to the king and then find a warm fire and a soft bed. Despite the urgency he tried to impart to the beast, the shambling horse seemed to take a perverse pleasure in the weather-mandated slow pace as it would just randomly stop and lower its head to loudly snap up the wet grass.

Palomides felt he was somewhere between the liturgical hours, but on his honor, he couldn't remember which ones. It had only been a year since he converted under the Roman way in Frankia but now here in Britain, they had a slightly different way of worshipping that didn't focus as much on time. The hours had slipped away with disuse.

After what felt like an eternity a gruff voice called out of the fog, "Halt traveler! State your business!"

"I am Sir Palomides on the King's business! If you would be so kind as…"

"Palomides? I don't know any bearing that name."

Palomides was going to give the man a sharp-tongued answer till he heard the sound of a wooden bow being put under strain. His left hand quickly grasped the shield that hung from his horse's side as his right drew his sword and then he was off the beast and crouched low to the ground.

"Peace, Cadwyn! I know the name. Black as Adam's first sin he is. Light a torch and we'll have him come forward. I doubt even that damned Merlin could fake his visage."

Palomides cursed silently but moved forward when he saw the faint light in the gloom. The younger of the two guardsmen nearly fainted when Palomides came into view. While not the greeting he wanted, he was thankful for their help as guides to the gates of the stronghold. They travelled in silence, the one named Cadwyn constantly snatching glimpses of Palomides as he led the knight's horse. Thankfully the trek was brief and the gate stood open for them. Palomides ordered the two guards to see to the stabling of his horse. As he strode away toward the main hall he could hear the two men saying prayers to protect their souls from Saracens.

"Fire and damnation on you and all of heathenry! There is no spirit in the tree! God causes it to grow! Perhaps you weren't held under the baptismal waters long enough to cleanse your hellish soul!" Brother Aiden's voice boomed in the large, high ceilinged room that was both throne room and main hall of Arthur, king of the Britons. Aiden's voice was soon drowned out by the great booming laughter of the man who sat in the large oaken throne beneath the boar's head banner.

"The tree grows which means it possesses vitality of life. And even the Christ said the very stones would speak if they had mouths, therefore I say that by the Christ's own mouth the tree and grass and all else has spirit and it is you Aiden who follows heathenry!"

Palomides tried to suppress a smile at Brother Aiden's expense. Aiden was very learned for one so young, but his temper was as hot as the red flame of hair that crowned his forehead from the cut of his St. John's tonsure. Merlin seemed to delight in trying the man's patience.

The wizard was the first to notice Palomides' entrance and the knight couldn't stop the shudder that ran through his frame. Everything about Merlin seemed to be a contradiction.

196

His face and frame appeared young, yet his hair had turned to gray long before Palomides had come to Briton. He clung to his wooden and gnarled staff as if he needed its support for his frame but Palomides had seen the man use sword and spear as well as any knight. Most of all, he claimed to be baptized into the faith and yet he was the last of the great druids, darker stories circled the kingdom about the nature of his birth and Palomides did not know if this conjuror and necromancer had truly renounced his dark arts for the path of light. The gleam in the strange man's eye made Palomides wonder if Merlin could read his thoughts.

"Not quite." Merlin said, a smile tugging at the right corner of his bushy beard. Palomides stopped suddenly and gasped at the utterance. Even Aiden looked confused. "You see Aiden you take the words too harshly; it seems even Christ was a bit of a bard and as such would use a metaphorical phrase to reveal a deeper truth. Hold the words securely, yet gently, then you will see in fullness. But I go on too long. Arthur, it seems Palomides has returned."

In any other kingdom, Palomides would come to the dais and bow or kneel and pay homage. In Arthur's court the exuberant and burly king burst from his throne and closed the distance swiftly, catching Palomides up in a strong embrace while praising Jesu for his safe return. Palomides hugged the man back awkwardly, still not used to the informal ways of his new king.

He told Arthur of his voyage to Al-Andalus and the great fish of the sea he saw there and back, which delighted the young king more than the actual report of his bartering with architects and princes and merchants, until Palomides came to the conclusion, "Before Easter, ships laden with skilled workers and wise men will be here to erect you a fortress the likes of which even Rome would envy."

"Splendid!" Arthur said clapping his hands, "Palomides, you have done better than any knight before you. To have a memory of what we do here left in marble and stone, testament to the greatness of Camelot, future generations will speak of our grandeur in wonder."

A cool breeze came into the room as Arthur spoke and Kay strode in, his staff of office clacking harshly against the flagstones. From the pinched look on his face Palomides knew Kay had heard Arthur's words. "Your majesty, I have urgent matters that need your attention."

"Go on then." Arthur said absentmindedly drawing a small knife from his belt and began cleaning the dirt from under his fingernails with the tip of the blade.

"This news is not for all to hear." Kay said as he cast a significant glance at Palomides and Merlin. "Affairs of state need to be shielded from…outsiders."

Arthur looked up at Kay just as Palomides was going to speak but Merlin's voice was the first to be heard, "Your majesty, I do need to take your leave and ask that Palomides come with me. I have ancient scrolls I think may help with your project and need the use of another learned mind."

Arthur gave his leave with a wave of his hand, his eyes narrowing on Kay, and Merlin quickly hobbled to Palomides and walked with him out of the hall.

"They may be as different as the moon and the sun, but do not try to come between those two. They were raised as brothers and an attack on one will raise the ire of the other." Merlin spoke once they were out in the open air. The sky had darkened, portending rain, mirroring Palomides mood rather well at the moment.

"Leave me be, conjuror. I need neither your advice or your enchantments. You to your tower and I to my house and God will see us both safe this day." Palomides growled.

"No enchantments, I swear you would pay dearly for those, but my advice is freely given though only the wise would hear. To you, my sullen friend, I would say to remember to invoke Christ more in your speech, it strikes the ears of these Christians falsely to hear their king spoken of by his title rather than his name." With that, Merlin turned and made his way down the street.

Palomides tossed and turned in his cot. It seemed no matter how much he longed for it; sleep would remain elusive. He sat up and pulled on his boots, already fully dressed. Perhaps a walk about the grounds or some light training with the younger knights would finish tiring him enough that his dreams may find him.

Camelot at mid-day was vibrant. The weather had apparently changed its mind as the sun now shown brightly, having finally dispersed all the fog. Men and women who kept this fortress running were now moving about their tasks in earnest. Things here were very different from Al-Andalus or any of the lands that Palomides would recognize as home and belonging to Allah. There was little stone and no marble. Everything was timber and earth. In some ways this was the poorest kingdom that he had seen. And yet, as Palomides moved down the alleys to pass launderers and cooks and herdsmen and a score of other workers, every man and woman had a clean tunic. Arthur paid for everything. The lowliest servant was guaranteed clean clothes, a warm bed, and a full belly. That made Camelot unique among all the kingdoms Palomides had seen, a better standard of opulence. And Arthur's magnanimity extended to the countryside as well. All who claimed the Pendragon as their liege were given rights that other places would reserve for princes. Even in Europe, where the Empire of the Romans was breathing its last desperate gasps, they knew of Arthur and his generosity was spoken of as often as his martial prowess. Arthur wanted to draw the whole world under one banner. His easy way with people, even those drastically different from him, made Palomides believe he could do it.

That welcoming spirit didn't extend to his people. Palomides was reminded with every step that he wasn't the same as the others. The children watching him in wonder brought a smile to his face; it was the disgust in their parents' faces that darkened his mood.

His absentminded trek brought him to the small chapel that Brother Aiden maintained inside the walls of the compound. Palomides had to duck under the low mantel of the door and turn slightly so his shoulders wouldn't collide with the small frame of the door. Finding himself different than everyone else had other disadvantages besides foul treatment.

"Sweet Jesu!" Brother Aiden cried from the lectern where he stood before the small altar. "Announce yourself before coming in like that! I thought Merlin had asked his father for some demon to torment me!" the man laughed. Palomides suppressed an angry retort. Aiden was a good man; he didn't realize his joke just reminded Palomides that he was different.

"Sorry to intrude on your reading, brother. I think I came in to pray."

"You aren't sure?"

"It seems lately I am unsure of a great many things. Especially of my place here."

"It is difficult for one newly converted, so much to unlearn, so much to learn. How is your Latin coming along?"

Palomides let the conversation change to his studies. It was a pleasant enough distraction from his darker thoughts. Aiden allowed him to come up and practice from the gilded book on the lectern. Palomides pushed himself to read page after page, to understand the blocky forms on the page so different from the flowing script of home. The candles flickered as the flame touched the melted wax, finally alerting both men to how long they had been reading. Palomides still wasn't satisfied with his progress but Aiden assured him he was doing very well.

"Now that we have fed soul and mind, we will see to the body. Arthur has declared a feast for all tonight! The good news of your return put him in a good mood, then Yvain returned from his journeys in Pictland—and you know how he loves a good story. Lambs and capons and sweet pork, with enough mead and ale to drown the countryside." Aiden's face was beatific in the dying light as he imagined the feast.

Aiden gave him a friendly clap on the back and the two men walked out of the darkening chapel and into the shadows of a rapidly dwindling sun. Maybe it was the difference between the sunny land in the south and this colder isle, but the oncoming dark set Palomides' teeth on edge. He found his hand resting on the pommel of his sword, his fingers nervously playing with the red tassel that hung there. Aiden kept him moving, a constant stream of chatter rushing from his mouth that Palomides had ceased paying attention to long before.

A line of knights formed out the door of the main hall, talking boisterously of every topic under the sun. Good company and the promise of good food and drink—normally this was enough to make Palomides forget his cares. Yet his every step towards that hall felt like a step toward the gallows. As he scanned the crowd warily, his eyes met Merlin's. He saw his own alarm mirrored in those gray eyes. What could be affecting him and Merlin but no one else?

"Greetings, good knight and good brother. Would you do me the honor of your company at table?" Merlin's voice cracked as he spoke.

"Yes." Palomides rushed to answer before Aiden could make a sarcastic comment. *If this spawn of Iblis has done anything this night, I will cut his hands off and feed them to the crows*, Palomides thought darkly. The farther along they moved into the hall, the less suspicious he was of Merlin. His eye caught the way the wizened hands kept tightening their grip on the staff and when they were still, he could just make out the sound of Merlin's boot tapping quickly against the flagstones. Merlin's nervousness added to his own and each step into the hall increased that feeling of dread. He focused all his will on keeping his body from quaking under the tension.

The torches were bright in their sconces and the great hearth drove the chill from the air. Merlin led them to the table closest to the hearth. Aiden protested saying he wanted to eat roast not become it himself but was ignored. The light actually seemed to help Palomides' mood a bit, though he still felt as if a horde of enemies would attack him at any moment.

Kay entered the hall and called for quiet. It took a moment for everyone to settle down. The hawkish man seemed to make a mental note of everyone who spoke after his command. Gawain, several tables away, also took notice and made sure to keep talking long after everyone else was silent and punctuated his sentence with a rude gesture. Being the king's nephew had its perks.

"Everyone stand for his majesty, Arthur Pendragon," the seneschal intoned. Everyone stood to their feet and saluted with their swords as they cried loudly for God to save the king. Arthur strode to his table quickly, waving everyone down. The king hated the pomp but Kay was a stickler for proprieties.

Once the crowd had settled, Aiden gave the prayer for the meal, stumbling over his words with his desire for all the smells that wafted from the kitchen. Once done and all had taken their seats, Kay clapped and the servants burst forward with trenchers, goblets, and knives for the tables followed quickly by women carrying large pitchers of drink and then finally large men with tray after tray of meat.

The hall was filled with the good cheer of the knights, but Palomides swore he saw the torches lowering and the shadows stretching long. He picked at the capon before him but couldn't savor the taste and he didn't bother touching his cup. He glanced at Merlin and immediately wished he hadn't. The wizard looked more pale than normal, mouth mumbling words too low to hear; his eyes bulged and Palomides was left with the impression that Merlin was both unaware of the room and yet also very aware of more than he could see.

"Where is Yvain? We all want to hear his tale!" Arthur cried out around a mouthful of veal.

Palomides' eye quickly scanned the tables but did not see the youngest of knights. Then catching the hint of movement turned to see Yvain seemingly form out of a shadow in the opposite corner of the hall. The normally exuberant young man was dreadfully quiet and his once ruddy complexion was now gray, he had a sheen of sweat that drenched his hair and gave him the appearance of tears.

Underneath Palomides' tunic was a pendant of protection against the evil eye. A last gift from his mother before her passing, its cool stone touch against his chest had always been reassuring. Now though it felt like a hot coal on his sternum.

"Do you see?" Merlin hissed.

"He looks near death but none seem to notice," Palomides answered, his voice a bare whisper.

Yvain pulled his cloak away from his right hand once he stood in the center of the room. Palomides' eyes narrowed as he beheld what appeared to be a roughly carved lump of emerald, though one shot through with such impurities it was more black than green. Large eyes set over an even larger mouth with no neck to be seen. A potbelly with two squat arms ending in impressive talons. The potbelly seemed to rest on a coil of rope. It was a revolting figure, what little food he had eaten rebelled in his stomach. Despite all that, it triggered a distant memory that remained elusive.

Arthur and the others were all commenting on the fine craftsmanship and were obviously reacting to a tale that Palomides couldn't hear. Still he picked up on bits and pieces from the conversations around him. A knight fighting a creature is what they all saw. Bors and Gawain were having a loud discussion on whether the beast was properly called a wyrm or dragon.

"Both are but symbols of the Great Serpent himself, so what matter?" Aiden called out.

Palomides felt his breath catch in his chest. Not rope, snake coils! He hadn't been more than eight when he was travelling with his father and brother through ancient Carthage. Hunting small game and came upon that damned cave seeking the bird they wanted for dinner. The same carving but made of gold had stood on a marble dais stained brown by centuries of blood sacrifice. A robed man knelt before the figure, his arms raised in supplication till he turned in fright at the intruders in his sanctuary. His father had been swift, his scimitar cutting down the evil priest before he could utter a warning to whatever compatriots lay waiting beyond. Then he gathered the young boys up and fled.

Palomides reached into his tunic and pulled the amulet out. Slowly he stood, his body trembling. Every fiber of his being screamed for him to either sit or flee. He tried to remember the words to the prayers he had been taught by the priests and brothers as he made himself reach for his sword. Yvain turned to catch him in a wide-eyed glare, a strange glow came from behind those eyes. Palomides heard the voice of his mother when he was very young, "There is one God, and Muhammad is his prophet." It was the first thing he recalled her saying and it steadied him enough for steel to clear scabbard.

Yvain lifted the grotesque idol over his head and intoned, "Otkin aatarab utaalk!"

Palomides rushed forward with his father's own war cry on his lips, "Allah Akbar!"

Then all was darkness.

The whole world rocked violently and his head rattled against rough wood planking. Despite jarring to wakefulness, Palomides found it difficult to open his eyes. Something deep within him begged him to keep the world away from sight, to gently drift back into the insensate dark.

"If that didn't wake the bastard, then nothing will!" Merlin's voice pierced the quietude.

"Is there no peace even in death?" Palomides asked.

Whatever was carrying him stopped suddenly. He felt a hand on his shoulder and one pressed to his chest.

"Speak again! Right Now! Prove to me that Satan or other dark gods aren't toying with me! By your Allah I command you to speak!" The demands came in a flood of emotion that sounded close to hysteria.

Palomides forced his eyes to open, the lids parting slowly, to reveal the face of Merlin. His beard was bedraggled and the lines of his face were deep with worry where they weren't smoothed by swelling bruises. "I would think He would strike you dead for using His name"

Merlin's worried features changed to exuberance, "He just might yet, but let him wait till our quest is done."

Palomides found himself in the bed of a cart, lightly strewn with straw in a poor attempt at making a bed. Merlin burst into a psalm of praise as he reached into a pack and pulled out some dried meat and a skin of water. Palomides weakly accepted both.

"Eat and drink to regain your strength. I have your arms and armor in the front with me. We have many a mile till our destination. Christ willing, you will be hale by then."

As soon as Merlin was satisfied that Palomides wouldn't again fall to unconsciousness, he returned to the front of the cart and slowly got it into motion.

The meat was venison that must have been dried and salted before Noah boarded the ark, but the tough chewing brought him to full wakefulness. Looking about him, Palomides wondered if this was the same countryside he had ridden through a year before. The once verdant forest was now a withered heath of scrawny trees with bare branches clawing in empty fury at the sky. What animals they came by were sickly and pawed the ground in a vain attempt to find nourishment.

"How long was I asleep?"

"Two days, maybe three. The sun neither rises or sets. Once you destroyed the idol all was this constant twilight. I know not when tree, flower, and grass died. It seemed to be instant but when you look closely it appears nothing has lived for a long time."

From there Merlin let the story unfold. Palomides battle cry had pierced the illusion and everyone drew back in terror as he charged forward. Merlin's chanting had been an incantation of protection which moved through the room even as Yvain's words caused a purplish-black mist to fill the hall. The ferocity of magics warring against each other had scoured the room with violence. Yet the sorcery colliding in the room couldn't stop the cold steel of the sword already in motion. Yvain screamed as his idol exploded under the impact of the blow. Merlin was the only one still standing when all was done. The death that was meant for all of Camelot was halted but not defeated. All hung in limbo save Merlin and Palomides.

"Why were we spared?"

Merlin was quiet for so long that Palomides thought he missed the question. Just as he was going to ask again, Merlin said, "I don't know for certain. Maybe Christ protected us? We both come from other faiths and have travelled far, and there is great power in that knowledge. We both recognized the idol and the danger it posed. We are both also viewed as outsiders to Camelot and its faith. Finally, I had my spells and you that curious amulet."

Palomides recalled the amulet then and checked the leather thong around his neck. The blue and white eye of the agate stone had a significant crack in it, but was otherwise whole.

"I'll ask no questions, but whoever gave you that loved you dearly. You should know that." Merlin's voice was low and maybe a little wistful.

Palomides said nothing to that but instead, "So we two are the only ones on this quest. But where are we bound? More importantly, what do we do when we get there?"

"I was not idle the entire time you were asleep. I cast my vision far. The blighted land stretches down to York, east to Londinium, and north to Pictland. Only in the west does the land remain unmarred, in a tiny village that I'm not even sure has a name. It still has lush fields and forests."

"Sorcery! Must we use the enemy's own weapons to win?" Palomides asked with far more venom than he meant.

"Ah, ever the trouble between us. Two held apart from all else for being different must in turn hold each other apart for the same. Surely none in your old faith did ought to track the heavens, heal the sick, and find the hidden things of God to make life better. You will trust a miracle if it is a singular occurrence, but let it happen on command and it is from the devil. Your old faith and your new both tell of the prophets? They summoned extraordinary feats? I will gladly await their company in the fire to which you would condemn me."

Palomides was brought up short by all that, but whether Merlin truly was a prophet or not was beyond him. He moved to speak but Merlin beat him to it, "All forget that before shepherds were told of the savior, a cadre of mages went in search of the Christ to pay homage. Life is strange and the ways of God a mystery; so guard well the truth you find, but never think it will be *all* you find."

"You have given me much to think on sorc...Merlin."

The cart crunched along its way as the two men were quiet. "Do they not have telescopes or other devices for seeing great distances where you are from?" Merlin turned over his shoulder with a grin. Palomides swore violently, and then both men fell to laughing like happy children in a dying world.

Palomides knew not by what art the horses never tired and now that Merlin and he had found common ground he didn't care to bring it up. He and Merlin switched places driving when one grew tired. Only sleep and hunger served to tell them of the passage of time. Palomides slowly felt his full strength return and would take bouts walking beside the cart to make sure his body would answer all his commands.

He had told Merlin of his previous encounter with a similar idol. Merlin's eyebrows had lifted at being told how far the cult of this god had spread. The foul deity was known to Merlin as Crom Cruach but he knew it went by many different names and its cult was on this island before the first druid had touched mistletoe or tracked a star. Yet in all its ages none of the followers had tried something like this.

"The three faiths between us give portents for future events, conditions which must be met before events occur. Is it the same with this demon?"

"A fair guess and probably closer to the truth than we know. It will be something I will study when we return to Camelot in triumph."

"But will we triumph, Merlin?" Palomides asked with trepidation creeping into his voice. To that the wizard said nothing.

The scenery morphed gradually, gray and withered grasses slowly changing into the golden wheat of harvest as the perpetual twilight changed to true morning. Normally you would see men hard at work gathering all of this up for their stores, women and children walking the ever-shrinking perimeter to ensure not one good grain fell to be wasted. Instead the fields were empty, the air ominously still, and silence reigned over the entire countryside giving lie to the supposed tranquility. Merlin and Palomides slowly climbed off the cart, both preferring to walk. The horse pulled the cart slowly behind them. Palomides had crossed half the field before he realized that he could hear neither the cart behind them or the sound of crops being trampled under his own feet.

The gold of the field soon ended and lush green grass carpeted the ground to a wall of tall, dark trees. Each one was gnarled and twisted in on itself and the heavily verdant canopy made midnight under its boughs. Both men came up to the tree line, Palomides had walked forests and braved the dark many times, yet now it was difficult to take that final step. Even this perversion of bright day, somehow feeling as false as the previous twilight, was preferable to that all-encompassing dark.

"Can your eyes see anything mine have missed?" Palomides asked.

"No," was Merlin's only reply. He stepped over to the cart and reached onto the seat for the leather wrapped bundle. Palomides walked up to him slowly so that Merlin could squire for him in the putting on of his armor.

"The cart should stay here; I don't think it or the horses will help in this." Merlin said.

"We will move quieter on foot anyway."

"We won't surprise anyone. Know, Palomides, we are already marked. I can feel a pressure in the air that impresses me with cunning. We are on ground consecrated to a foreign god and our approach is unwelcome."

Palomides looked at Merlin flatly, trying his best to come to terms with the situation. Finally, he drew his sword, "No reason to pretend hospitality then." Merlin answered with a slight smirk and the two men moved slowly into the line of trees.

The dark hugged so closely about them that they couldn't see each other, though they weren't more than an arm span apart. No light made it to the earth below, but at least no animal seemed to stir either. Merlin had taken the lead, feeling along the ground with his staff, sniffing the air like a hound, using all the knowledge of the old wood that was the birthright of the druid.

They walked till their legs ached but neither could really tell how much ground they had covered in their slow trudge.

Just as Palomides had thought to ask for a stop, a sound broke the stillness.

A horn blew a single note which reverberated on the air and stayed hanging all about them. Then drums, low and struck in a slow deliberate rhythm, which was felt in the chest more than it was heard. Clanging metal as if blades were striking other blades raising an aprosadic counterpoint to the low bass of the drumming. Then came the voices. Palomides couldn't make out the words but he doubted it was Briton or Latin. A chant filled the air in distinction to the other sounds filling the dark around them. As if multiple songs were being played at the same time.

Even as the voices grew louder, the language was still strange, but Palomides felt the intent of those alien words. The infernal cacophony that assaulted his mind conjured images of the most dreadful monsters being worshipped in unholy rites, whose name was called upon battlefields making the slaughter of both sides a profane offering, of people so debased they were more animal than man. This is what they were up against, a group that had sacrificed their very humanity to gain this dread god's power.

Proof, if it had been needed at all, came as they neared the glade in which the village had been built. A rude palisade had been erected in a haphazard fashion, though many of the rough logs had dislodged from the earth and bent forward only held by the press of logs on either side. What parts were standing appeared hazy in the gloom of the dusk falling over the glade. The music was overpowering, through the gaps in the palisade they saw the orange flicker of a great flame, this occasionally eclipsed by dark figures, all of it putting Palomides in such a state of dread it was all he could do not to retreat.

"May heaven empty of angels to come to our aid," Merlin whispered. Palomides followed his line of sight back to the front of the palisade, immediately he wished for the haze of distance to return. All the beasts of the forest which had been marked for their silence were nailed to the rough timber. Everything from the smallest creeping salamander to a whole buck, every type of bird Palomides could name was crucified, and then to his final horror, people. What bare wood could be seen was brownish red in all the blood. Some of the creatures were still struggling to move despite being beyond all hope.

"Come in! All are welcome in our village!" a high clear voice called from inside the village. A panel of four timbers swung out to allow entry.

Palomides and Merlin shared a look, Palomides wondered if the fear and disgust he felt was as visible in his face as it was in Merlin's.

"They will slay us," Palomides stated flatly.

"If we are lucky that is all they'll do," Merlin retorted. "A sword and a staff and two willing hands, is it enough?"

"It must be, for it is all we have. If this is to be our end, let us make it worthy of a song." Palomides felt a grim smile cross his lips as he felt the familiar tension that precedes combat.

"If we die here, Palomides, they better write a whole chronicle."

Merlin and Palomides both steeled themselves for what was to come. Long years of practice forced the worry and dread from Palomides: all was the mind of battle now. The two men charged toward the entrance, war cries tearing from their throats, only to be drowned out by the sound of the crowd rushing at them. Men, women, and children, all carrying knives or hatchets or whatever other tools they would have at hand. The burning red of the setting sun lit their eyes with a strange fire.

Not breaking stride, Palomides reversed his grip on his sword. The long thin blade now held tightly in his gauntleted hand; he brought the pommel down on the head of the first man close to him. It wasn't ideal—many may yet die—but he saw no honor in using a naked blade amongst this rabble.

Merlin was at his side, his staff a blur as it lashed out, sending someone to the ground with each crack of wood on bone. The ferocious press of these people driven mad by this demon tried to pin the two men in place but cool precision met brute savagery as knight and wizard scythed their way through the crowd. Gaining the entrance of the gate, a word from Merlin conjured a wall of flame to rise up in the space, locking away all those still standing on the other side of the palisade.

Palomides faced the great bonfire that sat in the open square between the ramshackle houses and stable of the village. Twelve men and women danced frantically around the flame, their voices raised in a deranged hymn. Just before the fire was a stone plinth on which stood a larger version of that horrid idol that Yvain had brought into Camelot.

"Very good! The warriors of Arthur are every inch the legends I have heard. Perhaps you need not die here today." The speaker stepped out from behind the nearest house. In the baleful glare of the great fire, his every feature was thrown into stark reality. His corpse gray skin was pulled too tightly around his head, smoothing the nose to not more than two slits. Where his face was impossibly thin, the middle of him was grossly large, should have been too large to stand let alone move. His excess bulk was as tight as a pregnant woman's belly, except when whatever was inside the man stretched or moved, pressing out of the man in a display that had Palomides desperately swallowing his gorge.

"We come not to treat with a simple village, headman. Where is the false god who dared strike at his betters?" Merlin challenged, seemingly unfazed by the grotesquery in front of them.

The creature's laugh sounded more like a sobbing wheeze and its mouth opened unnaturally wide, showing every rotted and yellow tooth in its head.

"Grand words but neither your king nor your god have any power here to command such as I. I am Slajormmangede, he who engulfs the world! Ancient before the land of Nazareth knew a divine whelp. It will please me much to kill you haughty upstarts."

"Foolish bug!" Merlin snapped and slammed the butt of his staff against the ground. A circle of eldritch light appeared on the ground around him with runes and sigils from more languages than Palomides recognized, though the ones he did gave him cause to shudder. "I come not for any king or his deity. You dare to bandy words with Merlinus Infernalis, son of the Fallen? Leave this place now or I shall cast you to the outer dark!" and from his staff a reddish light flew as a javelin and struck the idol, shattering the abomination.

When Palomides' vision cleared he looked up and saw that all the light had died and the blackness between the stars had been brought down to earth. All he could hear was the screaming of that horrid being and a sound of something wet tearing open.

Feeling a burning at his chest, Palomides pulled the amulet out to rest over his mail coat. It glowed, and was hot to the touch. He immediately regretted the light it cast as he saw the dreaded monstrosity in all its unholy glory. It was even less human than the idol had indicated, a gross caricature of human form painted by a demon possessed madman. Nor was the headman not all that changed, for the men and women that had danced before the fire were now far different from what they had been. Palomides could make out gigantic maws with row after row of spear like teeth and tentacles that lashed about all on an amorphous mass that shambled toward him.

"Those creatures' belief in him are all that holds him here now. Slay them, for their souls have long since departed, and we may yet win this night. I will distract him." Merlin said and then strode toward the beast. As he did his cloak billowed around him before blurring till the man was gone and a great red dragon was in his place. Magnificent rose-gold wings unfurled and in one great movement the beast was airborne.

"You are beyond your depth," Palomides chided himself.

The creatures moved faster than it appeared at first. The two closest were already so near he could feel the foul heat of their breath. He ducked one lightning fast tentacle and swiped at the second with his sword. The blade sliced cleanly through the oily appendage making the monster howl. He said a prayer of thanks that these could be pained by cold steel and then went to work.

It was the way of many westerners to square up against opponents and trade blows, but Palomides had learned his killing art far from western lands. He was fluidity itself as he danced among his prey, his feet moving quickly, his body spinning and contorting away from an attack only for his blade to leap out unexpectedly with precision. The ground was soon slick with ghastly ichor, occasionally set aglow with the sorcerous battle taking place above him.

Rain began to fall from above, Palomides wasn't concerned. Despite Merlin's dire warning this night had gone well. Every limb had been struck from the creatures and he could now slay them at his leisure. He wiped at the rain on his face—the drops felt thick and viscous—and he held his hand before him and let out a gasp of shock. He looked up and saw the snakelike monster coiled about the dragon, it's taloned hands tearing through scales, showering the ground below in blood. He cursed his overconfidence but before the oath had fully left his throat, he felt something cold wrap his ankles before he slammed to the ground.

He was dragged across the sharp stones, his armor protecting from cuts until other tentacles lashed out at the iron links, tearing through them with ease. He fended off the next several strikes, howls of pain split the dark again as tentacles piled the ground but just as soon they grew back before his eyes. Quickly cutting his feet free, Palomides stood up just in time for one tentacle to strike his back. He shrieked as he felt skin and muscle separate down to bone.

One creature lunged then, trying to deliver a fatal bite and Palomides thrust his sword forward in desperation. He felt his weapon sink into what passed for flesh. It spasmed and then collapsed in a flood of ooze.

A shout of praise erupted from Palomides' lips and he began his dance again, slower than before, slower still with each kill, as he couldn't trust the ground beneath him. His careful step allowed strike after strike to fall and when the last monster died, he collapsed to his knees, blood pouring freely from deep wounds.

He thought the sky should be clearing—he had done it, they had won. Yet the dark remained. A burst of sickly yellow light and then he saw the giant dragon crash onto its back not three paces from him. The form shimmered in the soft glow of the amulet and then Merlin laid before him, naked and as deeply gouged as himself. Palomides used his sword in a dragging crawl to reach Merlin's side. Above but out of sight, they could hear a bestial cry of triumph.

"You...lied," Palomides barely whispered.

"No...merely...hoped," came the faint reply.

Palomides felt tears well up in his eyes. What was hope in the face of such odds when prayers to any god echoed hollow in the sky above? How could weak men contend with beings that could blot out the sun and blight the land? Where the God of Islam, where the Jesu of the Christian? Stories told to insulate children against that which lurked in the dark.

His despair changed to rage and he grabbed the amulet at his chest and tore it from about his neck. If there was any truth at all in the stories he had dedicated his life to, let something at least witness his final rebellion against the eternal dark. With the last of his strength he hurled the small stone up and into the vastness of night. The amulet flew quickly, a shooting star in the void, and to Palomides amazement it disappeared into a great wound that Merlin had given the fell creature.

The cruel joy of Slajormmangede instantly changed to terror as it clawed at the wound, desperately searching for the small bit of stone. Its skin began to glow with the blueish white light of the amulet and it howled in agony. The light grew brighter and brighter till Palomides was forced to cover his eyes from the intense glare, then Palomides knew no more.

Pain brought Palomides back to the waking world. He opened his eyes to find himself in a soft bed with a young woman changing his bandages. A sharp cry to his right surprised him and he turned to see Merlin receiving the same treatment. The women were as gentle as possible in the applying of salves and new dressings but it was still a living hell for both men.

"I have questions," Palomides said once the angels of misery had left. Merlin told him briefly of how once out from

214

under the influence of the beast, the people they had spared outside of the village had saved them in return and brought them back to Camelot. That was all well and good but not what Palomides wanted to know.

"What can be said that would satisfy? Am I truly a son of hell or did I just lie to try and disconcert an enemy? Did some small magic destroy a great evil or were our prayers finally answered and we granted a miracle? Is all we know truly that easily upended and torn away by forces beyond our kin? Truly Palomides, which question would you have me answer first?"

Palomides thought for a long time and Merlin gave him the space to do so. The evening meal was brought to them and though neither man could eat much, the broth was good and restorative. True night had fallen outside and in their room the candles flickered as they burned low.

"Are we safe now? That is the question I'd have answered. Are we safe now?"

Merlin fixed him with a sad but kindly look, "Palomides, gather your strength and reclaim your arms and armor. You have seen more than mortals were meant to, and so now I answer you with a question that has more truth than either of us would care to guess. You ask if we are safe now, but were we ever truly safe at all?"

AN ENCOUNTER IN GEIFRVALE

Tim Mendees

It looked as though Gawain would never get to keep his date with destiny, and the Green Knight, after all. He knew he was going to his death, but what choice did he have? He was a man of honour and duty; his word was his bond. Unfortunately, it was that same sense of honour and duty that had landed him in the steaming mess that he was currently neck-deep in. Now, he was lost, alone, and separated from his faithful steed, Gringolet. He should have never gone charging off into the woods during a storm. He should have stayed in the strange little village... or, at least, retrieved Gringolet from the barn. Sadly, once again, his sense of duty had bested his survival instincts. When he heard the cries of a damsel in distress he was off like an arrow before you could say 'Camelot.'

What he had heard was no damsel... and the only person in distress was him.

Crack!

Gawain's hand shot instinctively to the hilt of his sword as the sound of a snapping twig echoed through the trees. "Show yourself!" he demanded as his chest heaved against his breastplate. Each ragged breath of the frigid night air burned as he fought to steady himself. When no answer came, he drew his sword and stepped gingerly between the trees. Skeletal branches whipped and thrashed as a roaring gale swept through the forest. Boughs creaked and trunks groaned joining the rain and thunder in a dizzying cacophony.

Rain lashed down upon the dense woodland turning the ground into a treacherous quagmire. Gawain had erroneously taken the sudden thaw as a change in his fortunes, but it seemed as though the opposite was true. The journey past the Anglesey Isles and the Holy Head had been arduous enough, but since he entered the great Forest of Wirral, it had turned into a nightmare. Every step had been fraught with danger, and what he had taken as a welcome respite had, in fact, been a diabolical trap.

With his feet churning the sticky mud, Gawain lunged forwards and caught hold of a tree-trunk to steady himself. The courage he had flaunted so dramatically just under a year ago in Arthur's court was deserting him rapidly. Cold and alone, he stared through the trees in an attempt to discover just *what* was stalking him. Shadows cast by the flailing trees shrouded more furtive shapes that lurked just beyond his vision. The dancing shapes played tricks on his vision and he could no longer trust his own eyes.

"In the name of King Arthur, I demand that you show yourself, coward!" His words sounded weedy and tremulous as he shivered from the winter chill that gnawed at his bones. Suddenly aware of his fear, Gawain tightened his grip on his weapon and swallowed before taking another hesitant step into the gloom. The sound of the rain was deafening as it thundered against his helm, relieving him of yet another of his senses. He wasn't sure that if anyone replied to one of his cries he would be able to hear a damn thing over the relentless thrum...

Then, he heard *that* sound again.

"Hello?" It sounded like the garbled and distorted bleat of a hundred rampant goats. Gawain felt the icy claws of fear rake down his spine, scratching every ridge and valley. It had sounded like a woman screaming the first time he had heard it, then had steadily degenerated into something ghastly and unearthly. Straining his ears, he tried to pinpoint the source of the sound, but it was impossible, it seemed to come from everywhere at once. "Show yourself, so I can split you open from neck to navel, foul beast!"

A mighty flash of lightning and rumble of thunder was followed closely by another sharp *crack* from amongst the trees. Spinning around, Gawain pointed his sword in the direction the noise came from. "Step closer, let this be your end!"

Crack!

The noises rose in frequency and seemed to be getting closer. Gawain adjusted his feet as best as he could on the shifting ground into a fighting stance. With his blade ready, he took a deep breath as what sounded like footsteps neared his position. They were heavy and ponderous, seemingly running towards him.

"Reveal yourself... damn you!" Gawain's blood was up. His youthful vigour and pugnaciousness were about to boil over into violent bloodshed. There was another loud *crack* and a shambling shape appeared between two gnarled yew trees. Gawain prepared to strike...

"Ye!" The dishevelled and bleeding form of a local man burst from the trees and slumped onto his knees. His face was a mess of scratches and scrapes, blood had flown down his weathered features and soaked into his filthy smock. "This is yer doing, knight." The man spat a gob of blood and saliva onto Gawain's shield. It landed in the centre of the gold pentangle design with a disgusting *splat*.

"What are you saying, man?" Gawain levelled the point of his blade at the man's face. He recognised him instantly, he was the brute with the woodcutter's axe that had nearly done for him that morning before fleeing into the forest. "Speak!"

"It was ye that brought this down upon us... bloody fool!" The man coughed and spluttered, then slowly got to his feet and steadied himself on a branch. "If ye hadn't come 'ere stickin' yer nose into business that don't concern ye, none of this would be happening... now we are all damned!"

"Explain yourself, damn you!" The tip of Gawain's sword had started to waver as horrible realisation started to dance around his brain like a horde of devilish imps.

"Hah! ... Ain't ye figured it out yet, *knight*." The man's words oozed with contempt. "Ye should have buggered off back to Camelot when ye had the chance!" Tipping his head back, the man roared with manic laughter, his body shook and trembled as his eyes danced like flames.

"Stop!" Gawain demanded. "Stop, or I'll cut you down where you stand!"

Splat!

The man's stomach erupted in twin gouts of blood and intestines as two branch-like horns burst through his body from behind. Gawain yelped in horror and revulsion as his armour was showered in the man's viscera. As he gazed in shocked awe, a shadowy form suddenly loomed up behind the screaming woodsman. Its enormous bulk rippled and undulated as it rose up almost as tall as the trees.

Swinging his sword wildly, Gawain backed away from the looming horror. The twin horns lost their rigidity and folded back upon themselves like glistening tentacles that snapped around the man's midriff as his arms flailed in panic. A scream of abject terror escaped from Gawain's throat as the appendages tore aside and bisected the unfortunate local.

Gawain lowered his head in silent prayer before gripping his sword with both hands and raising it above his head. If only he hadn't strayed from the forest trail... if only...

"Chin up, Gringolet... we will find shelter soon." Gawain patted his horse gently on its flanks as the wind tore through the trees like an attacking army. The steep gradient of the climbing terrain was proving to be hard to navigate. They had been on the road since daybreak. A meagre repast of roasted squirrel and a wedge of mouldy cheese had been hardly sufficient and hunger growled in his guts like an angry beast.

Gringolet's hooves slid in the mud as he tried to gain traction and climb the steep incline. Snorting and whinnying, he struggled until Gawain called him to a halt. They had been following an old hunter's trail that, as the villagers in the last settlement informed him, would lead them onto the high peaks to the north. From there, it should be an easy journey on to the Green Chapel and his almost certain death.

"Looks like we will have to go around." Gawain peered off

to the left, there the land levelled off into a kind of rough plateau. Clicking his tongue against the roof of his mouth and giving a stiff yank on the reins, Gawain steered Gringolet off the slope and onto a much flatter surface. Gringolet swished his tail in appreciation and twitched his unusual red ears. "That's better, isn't it? I'm sure there will be another way around."

Following the contours of the hill, Gawain and Gringolet found themselves snaking further and further into the trees away from their intended point of elevation. It couldn't have been much past midday but the sky was low and glowering making it appear like dusk. It didn't help that the trees were so dense in this part of the forest that it was as though they huddled their wizened bodies together for protection against the savage elements. He had expected his journey to be miserable, but this was taking misery to a whole new level of human endurance.

They kept true on their diversion until something tickled Gawain's nostrils and he pulled sharply on the reins. "Hold... Do you smell that, Gringolet?" He inhaled deeply then smiled. "Woodsmoke! There must be a hamlet nearby... Onward, Gringolet!"

Trotting with renewed vigour, Gringolet carried Gawain towards the source of the smoke. It didn't matter that they were heading further away from the track, they were weary and in dire need of rest and sustenance. With any luck, they would be able to trade for some food and shelter. They could easily retrace their steps on the morrow after a good night's sleep. The rhythmic *thump* of the white charger's hooves in the sticky mud was soon joined by the lively twitter of water as they neared a tributary for the large river to the south of their position, fording that had been a struggle, to say the least.

As they tramped through the mounds of rotting vegetation and tangled branches to the source of the water, the smoke thickened. Gawain's moustache twitched as several familiar scents reached his nostrils. The smoke smelt of apple-wood, birch and yew, but there was something else that made his neck prickle... sage. He hadn't smelt burning sage since the last time he had encountered Morgan Le Fey; that wicked woman always reeked of the stuff. For that reason alone, Gawain always associated the distinctive smell of burning herbs with witchcraft.

"Have a good drink, Gringolet... We will follow the river, there must be some kind of settlement ahead." Gawain refilled his waterskin from the crystal waters and slaked his thirst before remounting and following the smoke once again. Back from the bank, the ground rose sharply into a dense cluster of trees. Gringolet jumped dexterously and clattered through the branches then came to a skidding halt...

On the trail ahead, staring at them with unblinking eyes, was a goat. Gringolet snorted and shifted his back legs around. "Hush, Gringolet... It's just a goat." It wasn't *just* a goat, it was a large and sinister goat; black as the night sky with twisted horns, emerald eyes, and a long trailing beard.

Gringolet stamped and snorted as the goat stood its ground. It never flinched nor blinked, it just stood there... staring. "Off with you!" Gawain yelled at the beast and shook his fist. His gauntlets clattered and rattled, but still, the goat stared a hole through him. His horse was starting to become skittish, its stamps and whinnies becoming increasingly frantic. Something about the goat was scaring the steadfast horse out of his wits.

"Shh, shh. Easy, Gringolet." Gawain leaned forward and stroked his nose and whispered in his ear. "It's just a goat... nothing to worry about."

When Gawain looked up... the goat was gone.

Looking around, Gawain's scalp prickled as he tried to see where the animal had trotted off to. It was nowhere in sight. It had seemingly vanished, carried away on the drifting smoke. Gawain smiled but couldn't help feeling unnerved by the encounter. He wasn't a superstitious man in nature but he couldn't help feeling that the black goat was some kind of ill omen.

Gringolet had got over his attack of nerves and had started to trot along the rough trail towards the smoke when a piercing scream shattered the quiet and sent winter birds into the air in alarm. "That sounded like a lady in distress!" Gawain exclaimed. "Onward, Gringolet!" He tugged sharply on the reins and kicked the horse's flanks. Gringolet took off through the woods, his hooves sending plumes of mud and debris into the air behind him.

Another scream accompanied by the angry growls of several men became audible over the thunder of Gringolet's hooves as they burst into a small clearing. A young woman in a filthy white gown was on the ground struggling with two men in the garments of hunters or trappers. Another two men with axes stoked a roughly-built pyre in the centre of the circular space. Gawain roared with anger and jumped down from Gringolet's back.

"Let her go!" Gawain demanded as he drew his sword and rushed towards the two struggling with the woman.

"This is no business of yours, knight!" One of the men by the fire growled and gripped his axe with both hands, ready for action.

"Leave the girl be!" Gawain raised his sword to strike at the man currently wrestling with the girl.

"You don't understand!" The man with the axe replied as he advanced.

"Oh, I understand only too well, you filthy dogs!" Gawain kicked out at the man on the floor. He let the girl go and sprung to his feet clutching a dagger. He shifted position and stood shoulder to shoulder with the other ruffian. Gawain stared them down. The odds were against him but there was no way that 'The Maiden's Knight' was going to let four brutes have their way with a helpless damsel

For a few tense moments, everything was still... then, one of the two swung for Gawain's head with a rough cudgel. Gawain blocked the blow with his shield then punched him in the face with the hilt of his sword. Blood and teeth splattered the floor as the man roared in agony. The second man lunged with his dagger. With a deft sidestep and a quick boot to his attacker's groin, he soon had two of them reeling.

"Bastard!" The man with the axe bellowed as the head of

the weapon whooshed past Gawain's ears. He spun and parried with a swing of his sword. He overpowered the woodcutter and wrenched the axe from his grip, it fell to the ground with a dull *thud*. The second man who was over by the fire swung his axe in Gawain's direction. Dodging the attack, Gawain countered with a thrust directly to the man's abdomen. It punctured his skin like it was parchment.

Dropping to his knees, the man's eyes rolled back in his head as blood gushed from the savage wound in his belly. The first man, the one with the club, grabbed Gawain from behind. "Kill 'im! Kill the son of a whore!" He instructed the first man with an axe. Gawain swung his head backwards and smashed the man's nose with the back of his helm. Before his assailant could recover, Gawain pivoted and swung his sword in a smooth arc that neatly cleaved the man's head from his shoulders. It tumbled across the floor and rolled into the fire with a wet *sizzle.*

Gawain regained his balance and waited for the next attack... The two remaining men looked at each other, looked at Gawain, then ran off into the trees like scolded dogs.

"Don't come back, you cowardly beasts!" Gawain snarled at the disturbed branches they left swinging in their wake. "Are you okay, madam?" Gawain sheathed his sword after wiping the blood off on one of the dead men's garments and offered the distressed lady his hand. "I don't think you will be having any more trouble with them."

Blinking her startled emerald eyes, the raven-haired woman edged from under the branches she had been cowering under. She didn't speak as she rose to her feet. The poor girl looked petrified.

"You have nothing to fear." Gawain smiled as he laid his shield and helm on the ground. "I am Sir Gawain, a knight of Camelot... at your service, my lady."

Gringolet stamped his hoof and snorted. He had seen his master turn on the charm many times before and knew where it, more often than not, led. He wasn't called *'The Maiden's Knight'* just because it sounded good; he had left many a distressed female behind when he had left on his potentially fatal quest. If a horse could roll its eyes, Gringolet would have done so at that precise moment.

"Brangwen... my name is, Brangwen" The girl whispered. "They were going to..."

"Hush, it's over now. Do you live nearby... a settlement perhaps?"

With a tremulous finger, Brangwen pointed to a trail that led away to the south. "A small village... it's not far."

Thunder rolled overhead, Gawain looked up at the angry black clouds then gestured towards Gringolet. "Are you well enough to ride?"

Brangwen nodded.

Gawain picked up his shield and put on his helm as he led her over to his horse. As Brangwen placed her hand on Gringolet's hide, the stout equine flinched and started to shift his front legs uneasily. "Shh, Gringolet." Gawain tickled his ears and rubbed his snout. "Pay no heed to Gringolet, he's had a trying morning. I'm afraid the poor fellow's nerves are frayed... He'll be fine after a good rest."

"It's most likely the storm." Brangwen smiled. "The weather around 'ere tends to send the animals a little mad."

Once Gringolet had got over whatever had shaken him, Gawain helped Brangwen onto his back and saddled up. As the rain started to pour through the sparse canopy, they joined the trail and trotted towards the isolated village.

"Welcome to Geifrvale, Sir Gawain... I'm afraid it's not much to look at." Brangwen spoke for the first time since the clearing as they passed through a natural gateway of interlinked branches and into a ramshackle collection of huts and animal shelters.

Gawain sniffed as the fruity aroma of pig-muck assailed his sinuses then flashed one of his winning smiles. "Nonsense, my lady. It appears quite charming." Despite his obvious charms, Gawain was a terrible liar. It wasn't charming, not in the slightest. The wooden dwellings were thick with grime and black mould. What classed as a village square was a pile of rotting fruit, chicken feathers and a well-used chopping block stained brown with old blood. A large black raven perched above the eaves of passed for a chapel cried in irritation as Gringolet came to a stamping halt.

With his armour clattering and sending a group of scrawny chickens running for cover, Gawain leapt down from his horse and landed with both feet in the mud. After helping Brangwen down, he took a step towards the centre of the village as the rain hammered his helm. There was no sign of life, but he got the distinct impression that behind every dark and gloomy doorway lurked several pairs of furtive eyes. There was something sinister and oppressive about his surroundings. It was a place untouched by the outside world, even the chapel seemed to hark back to dark and ancient times.

"There you are, my daughter... what has kept you so long?" The crow-like tones of a bent old woman made Gawain turn sharply in the direction of a large dwelling. She was standing in the doorway, backlit by cavorting candlelight.

"Sorry, Mother," Brangwen said brightly. "I was waylaid by four ruffians, but this brave knight saved me."

Brangwen's mother stepped out into the dismal daylight and peered at Gawain with her rheumy eyes. "Oh... and who have you brought to us, then?" She grinned a wonky rictus, baring her gnarled yellow and brown teeth. "He is a dashing young fellow, indeed."

"Mother, this is Sir Gawain, from Camelot."

Gawain bowed. "A pleasure to meet you, madam... I wonder if I may be so bold as to trouble you for shelter and perhaps something to eat?"

The old woman chuckled. "Of course, of course... It's the least I can do for saving my sweet Brangwen."

"Many thanks, madam. Is there somewhere that Gringolet here can get some food and shelter?" He patted his horse tenderly on the rump.

"Of course," Brangwen answered. "I'll call Gregory... our stable hand... Gregory!" Her voice became shrill and offensive as she summoned a bent and gaunt chap from a small hovel that looked to be one gust of wind from collapse.

"Uhh... yes... madam Brangwen?" Gregory stammered. Gawain was taken aback by the man's appearance. Though he was in reality only aged around twenty-five, he looked far older. In fact, he looked to be in worse shape than his dwelling. His hollow cheeks, studded with vile pus-filled spots and sores, hung loose like a turkey's wattle. The man's attire, fashioned from sack-cloth or similar dun-coloured fabric was stiff with mud and animal droppings. Gawain wrinkled his nose, Gregory stunk to high heaven. Gregory reached out a red and blistered hand for Gringolet's bridle.

"Hold!" Gawain barked. "I'll take Gringolet, you just show me the way."

Gregory's eyes, wide and bloodshot, darted over to the bent matriarch for approval. Gawain got the distinct impression that he was terrified of the woman. Clearly, she held some kind of sway over the village, head-woman perhaps. He had come across many of these tightly-knit communities in the past and while they often had a head-man or laird it was just as often the man's wife who was the power behind the throne, so to speak.

"That's quite alright, Gregory..." She waved him away with her withered paw. "You will find the stables behind the chapel. Now, if you will excuse me, I must get back to the fire, I'm afraid the winter air makes my joints ache something terrible."

Gawain looked at the woman and Brangwen. The pretty young woman had addressed her as 'mother' though there was little in the way of family resemblance. She was short, mousy and with hazel eyes where Brangwen was tall, dark and with green eyes. Their faces were also a completely different shape, the old woman had a rat-like visage where Brangwen was beautiful. As they went inside, Gawain turned to Gringolet and whispered. "Come along, then... Let's get you indoors."

Gringolet snorted nervously.

"Don't worry, they are just a little isolated out here, there is nothing to worry about. As soon as the storm passes and we have had some rest, we will be on our way."

Rain hammered the ground turning it into little more than a glorified bog. Gawain struggled to keep his footing as he led his horse across the square. The crooked chapel loomed overhead, casting the square in shadow. Gawain felt a shiver race down his spine as he gazed at the odd carvings above the stout oak doors. They depicted oddly formless creatures consuming what looked to be cattle. He had no idea what faith these people subscribed to and he had little desire to learn.

A cluster of sodden chickens clucked and scrabbled frantically as Gringolet clomped his way past their hiding place under the chapel. Gawain looked at the poor creatures, there was scarcely an ounce of meat on them. Still, he wondered if he could maybe purchase a couple of the healthier specimens for his journey. As he salivated over visions of fire-roasted fowl, Gringolet suddenly let out an ear-splitting cry and reared up, nearly sending Gawain onto his rump in the mud.

"Woah, Gringolet. What in the name of Camelot is the matter?" As he tried to regain control over his skittish steed, Gawain glanced behind him and nearly leapt into the air in surprise. He was being glared at by *two* sinister black goats with emerald eyes...

"Go! ... Away with you!" Gawain kicked at the mud, showering the unblinking creatures. Neither goat moved. Gringolet started to stamp his hooves and snort in anger. Gawain swiftly cradled his horse's head and whispered soothing words into his twitching crimson ears. He had to get him under control; there would be no chance of shelter and sustenance if the brawny charger started flattening the village on one of his violent rampages. Gringolet was a force to be reckoned with on the battlefield.

"Stop, Gringolet... They are just goats, they pose no threat. Watch..." Gawain turned to approach the goats and was bewildered to find that once again, they had vanished into thin air. "What?" Gawain ran forwards and peered around the side of the barn. There was no sign of them. Returning to Gringolet, Gawain seized the reins and led him into the barn.

Gawain was pleasantly surprised to find the barn kitted out

with feed and water. "Here you go, Gringolet." He said, tying his horse to a splintering beam. "And it looks like you have company..." There was an old nag in the end paddock. She looked a tad weather-beaten but healthy enough. "Now, don't you go getting frisky, you hear... I want you in good walking condition on the morrow." As he chuckled heartily, Gawain turned and almost leapt into the air bellowing like a wild boar as he came face to face with Gregory.

"Ye shouldn' o' come 'ere." The man's eyes were wild with fright. He grabbed Gawain by the shoulders and shoved his manky features close to Gawain's ear. "There are bad things 'ere, Sir Knight... *Very* bad things."

"Let me go, you damned fool!" Gawain shoved Gregory back and almost struck the man across the side of the head but managed to get his temper in check just in time. "What are you rambling about?"

"Out there..." He pointed a trembling finger at the village and the impenetrable woods beyond. "Things that shouldn't be... Get away before..."

"Gregory!" A sharp cry from the far corner of the barn stopped Gregory mid-sentence. The man yelped in surprise. Gawain peered into the gloom as a woman in a white gown appeared from one of the stalls. "Leave our guest be... We have had quite enough of your diseased ravings for one day!"

Gregory babbled and ran from the barn like his pants were ablaze.

"Brangwen?"

The woman tittered musically and ran a hand through her tumbling black locks. "No, Sir Knight... I'm Elain, Brangwen is my dear sister... I understand that I have you to thank for her safe return?" She moved gracefully through the mounds of straw and manure and placed a hand on Gawain's chest plate. "My, you are a handsome one... I hear you will be staying the night... Perhaps we will become better acquainted." Turning, Elain walked from the barn still toying with a lock of hair.

Gawain swallowed. Something in the way the woman looked at him had rendered him speechless. Watching the way she moved brought a smile to his lips. "Well, Gringolet... it looks like we both might have a bit of companionship for the evening."

Gringolet snorted and stamped a hoof.

"Oh, don't be such a prude." Gawain left the barn with his spirits a little lighter than when they entered. He crossed the village with his belly rumbling and his loins tingling, maybe this detour wasn't such a bad idea after all...

Gawain's heavy eyelids snapped open as a strangled scream rang out from somewhere behind the old woman's shack. His head was spinning and his guts were on fire. "What? ... what's going on... I don't remember going to sleep." He rubbed his eyes with his palms and sat upright on the straw cot he found himself lying upon. Rain pounded the wooden roof and dripped from holes into various buckets and bowls creating a hypnotic cacophony.

Peering through the gaps in the boards, Gawain realised that night had fallen. The last thing he remembered was tucking into a hearty stew and a flagon of the local mead. He had knocked on the door and had been welcomed inside by the old woman, who was apparently named Rhonwen. He had joined her and her twin daughters at a small rickety table by the kitchen. The stew had been a mixture of root vegetables and goat meat and had been heavily flavoured with various herbs and bulbs. He had enjoyed it immensely but everything became a blur after that...

"Drugged..." Getting slowly to his feet, Gawain was shocked to find that his garments had been loosened... what else couldn't he remember?

Before he could puzzle any further over his predicament, the scream sang out again. Buckling his clothing and putting on his armour, Gawain prepared to leap to a lady's aid once again. His mind was befuddled by whatever was in the stew, so much so that he didn't register the strange unearthly cadence to the cries. With his sword around his waist and his shield in hand, Gawain raced from the dwelling and into the night...

Gawain stood with his sword ready as the monstrous bulk loomed above him. Its body shimmered and rippled as hundreds of anemone-like fronds sprouted from what counted as its back. Several larger appendages thrashed from side to side, splintering and shattering wizened tree-trunks and branches. The bisected remains of the axe-man from the clearing steamed at Gawain's feet, its blood and fluids mingling with the foul mud and decaying leaves. All around, the forest cracked and creaked as the preternatural gales rushed towards the village of Geifrvale.

As the creature reared back and prepared to strike, another man suddenly appeared at its rear and threw a dagger into its hide. "Run, ye stupid bugger!" the man shouted as the horror turned in his direction. Gawain seized the moment, turned and fled. From behind, the creature howled in fury as the other man dodged and weaved through the trees.

Choosing to run with the wind, rather than against it, proved to be a good move. Gawain soon found himself on the outskirts of Geifrvale. When he left, there had been fires and candles illuminating the dwellings, now, there was not a single point of light to be found. In the all-pervading darkness, the twisted structures looked like the silhouettes of a line of skewed gravestones.

Stepping between two leaning hovels, Gawain's foot connected with a collection of farming implements that clattered noisily as they hit the ground. Gawain could smell death on the air, the atmosphere was charged with encroaching horror. Holding his breath, Gawain peered around the building then stepped out into the square. It seemed deserted, the barn was on the opposing side, all he had to do was get to Gringolet and make his escape.

As he started to walk forwards, a sudden *snap* from behind made him turn, waving his sword at the empty air. There was nothing there, his nerves were playing tricks on him. Returning to his forward trajectory, Gawain suddenly stopped and screamed in surprise. The once deserted square was now home to hundreds upon hundreds of black goats. Each one stared at him maliciously with their piercing green eyes.

"Back..." He demanded. "Keep back... I'll slay you all if I have to!"

Taking a tentative step, Gawain suddenly felt a soft hand upon his shoulder. He screamed again and snapped his head around. Standing there with an amused smile playing on her lips, was Brangwen... or was it Elain? In the darkness, he couldn't tell.

"Don't excite yourself, Sir Knight... you have had a strenuous day." He could tell by the husky voice that it was Elain that stood before him, her drenched white gown clinging to her curves.

"What? ... Where did you?" Gawain gabbled. His tongue was still twisted by terror and the effects of the stew. "We have to get out of here, where is your sister?"

Elain tipped her head back and laughed throatily. "Oh, she's around here somewhere... I thought we had worn you out?"

"What?"

Again, Elain laughed. "You performed well, and your seed is greatly appreciated, Sir Knight, and now you must go to meet mother..."

"What? ... Rhonwen? Why?" Gawain's head was spinning. He had started to back away from Elain but found his way blocked by several large goats.

"She is not my mother." Elain grinned, her face taking on the aspect of a satyr. "She is a wet nurse... nothing more." She swept her arms wide and gestured to the mass of glaring goats. "*We* are the thousand young of the goat mother and you will make a great offering." With a sharp jerking motion, Elain took a large wavy dagger from her belt and lunged at Gawain, screaming like a banshee. "Iä! Shub-Niggurath!"

Before she could strike, a dagger flew over Gawain's shoulder and struck Elain in the throat. Black blood bubbled from the wound in thick sticky gouts. Gawain turned and saw his saviour, it was the man he had met twice before; once when he saved his life in the woods and, Twice, when he kicked him in the plums when he rescued Brangwen.

"Don't just bloody stand there, follow me if ye value yer

life!" The man beckoned Gawain to follow him as he took off towards a cluster of buildings to the east. Gawain did as he was told and charged after his unlikely ally.

Elain dropped to her hands and knees, the viscous substance still pouring forth and coating her body. Soon, she was a strange iridescent mound of pulsing matter. Gawain risked a glance and instantly wished that he hadn't. Elain rose up on four goat-like legs with appendages sprouting from her body. She was the twin of the beast in the forest... Brangwen.

To his horror, each goat split down its back and its true form bubbled to the surface. They stayed relatively small but there were hundreds of them. Each one piping and screeching furiously as their tendrils searched for meat.

Crashing through a doorway, Gawain was suddenly pinned to the wall by his saviour who now held a knife to his throat. "Ye stupid bastard!" The man hissed. "I ought to slit yer throat and feed you to them things. If ye'd let us deal with *that* witch, we would have saved the forest. We have been in terror of the thousand young for too long, and when we finally have a chance to end this, ye come in and ruin it!"

"I... I'm sorry..." Gawain's lip trembled.

"Tell that to the brave lads, that ye cut down like dogs!" The man spat on the floor at Gawain's feet. "For generations, the children of the goat mother have been luring men here to mate with and add to their unspeakable brood. If they are not stopped, their malignance will spread across the land like a plague. Ye have to help me finish this!" It wasn't a request, it was an instruction.

"Yes... but, what can we do against those... *demons*?"

Letting Gawain go, the man pointed over towards the chapel. "In there... The old woman, she's the one who summons Shub-Niggurath. She has a scroll. If we deal with her and burn the scroll, maybe..."

Gawain suddenly felt the surge of power that came with a righteous quest. Gripping his sword tightly, he stepped out into the square. "Right, follow me... Charge!"

"Ye can't be serious?" The man questioned as Gawain raced off towards the chapel whacking and slashing at any glistening pseudopod that happened to come within reach. With a dagger in each hand, the man charged after the headstrong knight, roaring like a bear.

Filth and ichor filled the air as Gawain cut his way to the chapel. "Open the door, I'll hold them off!"

Slamming his shoulder against the fragile timber, again and again, the woodsman soon had the chapel door open. A rush of foul-smelling air hit him in the face as he crashed through into a candle-lit space. Gawain ducked and parried snake-like tentacles, cutting and hacking to keep the thousand young at bay. "Quickly, inside!" The woodsman bellowed. Gawain flung himself back up the two small steps, landing flat on his posterior on the inside of the chapel.

"Close the door!" Gawain yelled as the other man tried to help him to his feet. "I can manage!"

With a growl of exertion, the woodsman gripped the door with both hands and... stopped.

"What are you waiting for?" Gawain cried as he got to his feet. He rushed over to the woodsman and peered out into the night. The creatures had stopped advancing. They had formed a perfect circle around the chapel. The twin abominations that had been Brangwen and Elain towered over the rest, they linked appendages and shook with what could have been laughter.

"Why have they stopped?" The man asked in hushed and terrified tones.

"I think we are right where they want us to be..." Gawain swallowed and turned around. They were standing in a blasphemous parody of a chapel. The floor ended a couple of feet from their position in a circular pit that belched a foul miasma into the structure. There was only a narrow walkway around the abyss and on the other side, standing over the bloodied remains of Gregory the stable-hand was Rhonwen.

"I have been waiting for you." She cackled. "The goat mother hungers for your flesh."

Something in the pit shifted... it sounded huge and hungry.

Gawain said nothing but motioned for the woodsman to edge around the opposing side to him. Shuffling like a crab,

Gawain hastened towards the evil priestess of Shub-Niggurath.

Crack!

Without a warning, a thick wiry tentacle cracked like a whip from the pit and coiled itself around the woodsman's left leg. He screamed in terror as it yanked him into the air with a sharp tug. Gawain could do naught to aid his compatriot and instead grasped the moment that the distraction had offered. Nimbly, he leapt the rest of the way and landed by the blasphemous altar that was decorated in the hapless villager's innards. He snatched the scroll from the witche's hand and reached for a candle...

The witch laughed. "That won't work, you fool... she is already here!"

Gawain picked up the candle and went to throw it at the witch's head, but in doing so, brought it in front of his pentangle shield.

Her eyes wide with fear, the witch screamed as the pentangle flared with a brilliant white light. "No! Not the Elder Sign!"

Gawain looked at his shield, the pentangle had become stretched and distorted by all the damage and the pouring rain. It flared and sizzled when he held the candle in the centre of the twisted design. Seeing the witches fear, he brandished the shield and candle at her. Screaming with agony, the witch burst into a strange green fireball that spread across the walls of the chapel like a liquid.

The thing in the pit roared as he directed the Elder Sign down the abyss. With a mighty roar, the pit erupted like a volcano. Gawain ran into the night, with the sign in front of his face. The screams of the creatures became deafening as one by one, they were immolated by the purifying flame of the Elder Sign.

Gawain was blown backwards as the creatures burst and popped, striking his head on the timbers of one of the buildings... everything went black.

It was morning when Gawain next opened his eyes. The rain

had stopped and the air was fresh. His body ached and his mind was in turmoil. For one glorious minute, he almost believed that what had happened was nothing more than a fever dream brought on by the cold weather and malnutrition...

He sat up sharply and held out his shield in defence, but nothing happened. Looking around, he could see no sign of the thousand young. In fact, the only evidence that anything had happened was the smouldering wreckage that had once been a chapel.

Panic suddenly took hold. "Gringolet!" He leapt to his feet and ran to the barn. Using all of his remaining strength, he yanked the doors open. "There you are!"

Gringolet snorted happily and swished his tail as Gawain untied him.

"Thank goodness, you are safe!" Gawain caressed Gringolet's nose. "Let's get out of this nightmare."

Saddling up, Gawain led Gringolet from the barn and onto the track that led back the way they came. "You know, Gringolet, I don't think Arthur will believe what happened here..."

Gringolet snorted.

"Quite right." Gawain tickled his ears. "I will tell him it was a dragon or trolls... Arthur will believe that."

A SUNDERED PEACE

Tim Hanlon

*So then they departed, and came to Sir Mordred, where he
had a grim host of an hundred thousand men.*
—Le Morte d'Arthur by Thomas Malory

The warriors waited on a hill far to the north of Hadrian's
Wall and Mordred reined in to examine them. The afternoon
sun shone weakly now and he could feel the sweat drying on
his skin under his gambeson. Mordred would have loved
nothing better than to shed his armour and rub himself dry but
Arthur, the Emperor of the Britons, insisted that all members
of his Comitatus go fully armed when beyond the walls of
Camelot. His men must be prepared to join combat at any
time but, more importantly, they were a symbol of the peace
by might that Arthur had brought upon the land.

"Picts," said Dunstan, his scutarius, beside him. The
younger man patted the neck of his horse as it caught the
scent of the others and snorted derisively.

Mordred nodded his head. His blonde hair, a little beyond
regulation length, brushed his handsome face and the knight
flicked it back with practiced nonchalance. "Let us see what
they want, Dunstan."

They urged their horses forward and the four riders came
to meet them. On a patch of flat ground at the base of the hill,
one of the Picts pushed ahead with a battle cry in his throat.
His tattooed arms wore dark swirls and in the gloom they
seemed insubstantial. However, the war spear the warrior

237

raised overhead was hard and deadly and present.

"Your spear, my lord?"

Mordred shook his head and donned his helmet. He kicked his own mount forward and slipped his shield from his back and onto this left arm. The knight made no move to draw his sword. The Pict bearing down on him was young and strong and his cry held a martial delight. Mordred, perhaps not that much older, was silent.

The drum beat of hoofs joined in rhythm as the two horses bore down on each other. Mordred watched the young tribesman draw his arm back and his form was perfect as the spear hurtled the distance between them. Mordred appreciated the hours of practice that went into such a throw on horseback but it did not stop him from raising his shield and flicking casually at the lance, so that it tumbled harmlessly away. He turned his stallion into the Pictish horse and Mordred's charger, bred for size and strength, sent the other beast stumbling. The warrior tried to draw his sword but Mordred kept the pressure on the other man and reached across casually and grabbed him by the neck. Mordred danced his horse aside and, with a heave, threw the Pict to the earth. The young man grunted with the hard blow of solid ground and lay still.

Mordred reined in and sat quietly upon his beast as the other Picts trotted over and halted. The only noise was the puffing of the horses in the murk of the cooling afternoon as the sky darkened like steel blued by a flame. Two were warriors, older men with tribal tattoos marred by age and battle scars. One was young and slumped as if ill, his wrists bound to the saddle bow by a length of hide rope. The leader, with a beard almost fully grey but shoulders still broad and hard, raised his hand and spoke with an inflection foreign to Mordred's ears.

"You are Arthur's man?"

"He is Lord Mordred," called Dunstan from behind. "A knight of the inner circle of the war-band of King Arthur."

"We did not know, Lord."

Mordred flicked his own hand towards the young warrior

wheezing on the turf. "That is why he still lives," the knight said. "I normally deal more harshly to those who offer me such offence."

"You are earlier than expected, Lord Mordred," said the oldest Pict. "We were told it would be long past this new moon before one of Arthur's band arrived."

"We had a swift journey," said Mordred. "The men of Arthur's company are used to hard riding."

The grey beard nodded. "Just so," he declared. "It was but luck that we saw you crossing the valley."

The old warrior looked at the third man who swung himself from his horse and bent to the fallen tribesman. This one propped the young man against his knee until the panting eased, then cuffed the youth across the back of the head. Dunstan rode up with the reins of the loose horse in his hand and the warrior swung himself upon its back. His face was as dark as the sky behind him but then the young Pict laughed suddenly and his face opened to the sun.

"You will have to teach me that!"

The handsome knight returned his shield to his back and laughed too. "Gladly," Mordred replied.

"I am called Ougen," said the grey beard. "That is Drosten. And the young fool is Uuen."

"I have never met one of Arthur's men before," called Uuen. "I see the rumours are true."

"Dolt," barked Drosten.

The grey bearded warrior sat comfortably on his mount. His sword, lighter than the models used in the south, lay across his thighs in a beautifully wrought scabbard and his fingers traced the design as he studied Mordred.

"We are of the Fortriu tribe. It is our honour to be your guides to the monastery. The land surrounding it can be treacherous and what looks like solid earth can swallow an unwary man and horse in the time it takes a bird to cross his sight."

Mordred indicated the youth bound to the pony. His head hung upon his chest and the captive had not deemed to raise it throughout the discussion. The grey-bearded warrior said, "He is a serving lad, entrusted to the monastery by his parents. He had a different notion but we are returning him to his home now."

"Against his will?" asked Mordred.

"A wayward youth, Lord. It was his parent's wish that he learn of the Christ god."

Mordred studied the group for the time it takes a leaf to fall to the ground. "I will enquire of the abbot at the monastery," he said eventually.

"Just so, Lord Mordred," agreed Ougen.

Ougen turned his mount around and began to trot around the hill. "We can make it before night falls," the Pictish leader called. "If we do not tarry. We who follow the old ways do not care to be out on nights when the stars fall from the sky."

"The comet?" asked Mordred. "It holds no prophecy. It does not affect the lives of men who follow the Christian path."

Ougen merely shrugged his shoulders. "We Fortriu believe differently."

The group sorted itself into a line and there was little further talk as they set their horses' heads away from the setting sun. Eventually, Uuen dropped back so that his horse was beside Mordred's and they trotted in time.

"That is a fine beast," declared Uuen when Mordred's stallion, tired of the intrusion, nipped the other mount's shoulder.

"They are bred for battle," replied Mordred. "Arthur insists on only the finest of stock. The King is a man of few compromises and, with horses, none."

Uuen watched the fine Briton horse for some time then said, "Some say he is your father." His voice rose at the end for he had not yet mastered his emotions, the young Pictish warrior.

"Some do," said Mordred.

"So it could all be yours? When Arthur dies. The kingdom."

"I wish only to serve," said Mordred and this time his voice was flat like a blacksmith's anvil and with as much give. No-one could read his thoughts when his face shut and that was how Mordred wished it to be. He nudged his charger with his knee and the well-trained horse turned its shoulders into the smaller beast. Uuen's horse stumbled on the edge of the path and the Pict let go a small shout of surprise.

"Uuen!" called Ougen from the front. "Go ahead and inspect the causeway. Now, boy!"

He watched the young warrior prod his mount forward and gallop off in a spray of soft grass. The grey-bearded veteran did not turn his head immediately but continued to examine Mordred for a dozen beats of a resting heart. The knight returned the stare but the other man's eyes were shaded in his sockets like a bright stone pressed into mud and Mordred could not find a message within. Finally, Ougen turned away without speaking.

"These are our allies, Lord Mordred?" asked Dunstan behind him.

"Yes," replied Mordred as he watched the men trotting ahead.

"Good," said Dunstan quietly. "I was not quite certain."

The monastery sat on a tidal island connected to the mainland by a narrow land bridge, wide enough only for one rider to travel safely. A huddle of round-houses welcomed the visitor at the end of the causeway. A path grew from these and snaked up the side of a large hill and the building rested upon it like a frog on a too small rock. Its buildings dominated the surroundings, stretching to all points of the hilltop and mainly of stone, a remarkable feat for a place so isolated on this inhospitable stretch of coast. It had the look of a repurposed fortification, no longer needed with the peace but unwilling to let go of its original meaning for existence, so far from the safety and solidity of Arthur's Logres.

The riders picked their way down the slope and onto the beach. Beyond the island the sea sent foaming horses racing towards the shore and the crash of hard-driven waves against the rocks was a stampede of hoofs. In this late afternoon there was little difference between the ocean and the sky above it, so that the island was framed by a solid sheet of slate.

They walked in single file along the causeway and Mordred could see that the monastery would be cut off from all but the most determined when the tide was up. From this close it did indeed look more fortress than place of worship.

At the round huts the three Picts pulled aside with their charge and sat upon their horses. Smoke rose from the roof holes of the buildings and it was redolent with a fragrant wood that Mordred could not place.

Ougen gestured to the path that continued up the hill. "Lord," he said, "we go no further. We do not follow the way of the hanged god and do not care to enter his sacred places. This one is to stay with us until he learns some gratitude."

Mordred inclined his head in thanks and the knight and his shield-bearer left the painted-men there. The path was unkempt and seemed almost unused and the horses picked their way carefully through the stones and other debris. Mordred examined the monastery as it loomed overhead but the knight could read nothing in the dark stone walls.

The monastery gate was closed. Dunstan slipped from his mount and thumped his fist against the wood. "Open in the name of Lord Mordredof the Comitatus of the Emperor of the Britons, Arthur Pendragon."

They waited and it was longer than either of them deemed appropriate. Dunstan drew his dagger and used the pommel to hammer once more on the solid wood. The sound was remote and it spoke of a thick piece of well-aged timber. The scutarius pounded a third time and when there was no response, the younger man swung back onto his horse and looked towards his master.

Mordred's face was set like an artist's rendering of a handsome warrior but Dunstan knew that underneath the knight would be boiling. Mordred could stand many things but to be ignored pricked his still youthful pride. Dunstan had seen more than one man regret such an action. The scutarius watched his lord but remained silent.

The shadows had moved a pace when finally there was a faint grinding behind the door. It cracked slightly and a face appeared, round and tonsured. The monk looked at the two warriors and his puffed cheeks crinkled with questions.

"Who goes…" the monk began but then squeaked like a rodent as Mordred pushed his charger through the gap. The beast's big shoulders swung the door away and the round monk tumbled to the earth. The skirt of his habit flew up and exposed legs as white as a fish's belly. Mordred ignored the floundering man and trotted into the monastery's courtyard, Dunstan at his heels.

The hoofs of their mounts and the jangle of their equipment reverberated in the enclosed space and it could not be ignored. Mordred reined in before the largest door of the monastery as more monks stepped through. Their robes were simple and of brown dyed wool and their faces displayed a lack of shock that made Mordred check his sword's position. At the head of the pack was an old man and another fellow, tall and solid, with a warrior's carriage.

Dustan cried out again, "Make way for Lord Mordred of the company of King Arthur. Make way!"

The old man raised his hand. "My Lord Mordred," he said loudly, "please accept my most humble apologies. We begin Vespers early this far north and were not aware of your arrival. We did not expect you so soon."

Mordred examined the old man with his face still set and unyielding. The man seemed genuinely contrite, almost embarrassed, but Mordred saw, too, the big monk beside him and how that one gripped a solid staff with scarred hands.

"Do you not have a gatekeeper, Abbot…?"

"Bernard," said the old man. "And we have no need, Lord Mordred, we so rarely see visitors. Particularly none as important as yourself."

The knight nodded his head, mollified somewhat. He swung his long legs over the saddlebow and slid down gracefully. Mordred did everything that way; with a smoothness that made people stop and watch. Behind him Dunstan tried to emulate his master with a little less success.

Abbot Bernard indicated the doorway. "Brother Bartholomew can show you to your rooms, Lord. Perhaps you can wash away your journey while we finish our service and then you can explain why we have a visit by such an august individual."

Mordred followed the big monk into the monastery. From somewhere a hymn began that the knight did not recognize. Voices rose joyously skyward but on Mordred's shoulders settled an unease he could not justify.

Once in his rooms Mordred paused. He looked out the slitted window at the ocean and its unruly spirit mirrored what was within and would never be seen without. Mordred seethed at the menial task he had been given; it was beneath one who was, although never acknowledged, the true and only heir to this new kingdom. The knight had fought and bled for his father but he had been bestowed nothing but scraps in return. The sea thundered and Mordred's spirit joined in accord.

Dunstan entered with warm water for washing and Mordred turned from the window and his face was again a handsome mask for all to see.

The Abbot's chambers were larger than Mordred expected and more opulent. Glossy tapestries hung on the walls and trapped the heat from the generous fireplace within the room. The men drank from glass, imported from the Middle East the Abbot informed him. The room was high on the north side but Mordred could still hear the voices of the monastery choir, raising praise to the night sky. They had continued as the knight and his scutarius had washed the sweat and dirt from their libs and donned fresh tunics. Even in the high room, Mordred could feel the power of the worship like heat from a bonfire.

"Impressive worship tonight, Abbot Bernard," remarked Mordred. "Is this usual practice?"

The abbot turned his head to the window high in the wall and shuttered against the night. The old man cocked an ear like a dog hearing its master's call. "No," he said quietly. "It is not the usual. Lord Mordred. Not the usual at all."

"A saint's day?"

"No."

Mordred looked at the old man's closed face and asked no more. He had found that many churchmen like to keep mysteries that were anything but significant, in the hope of fooling the masses who came to worship. This bent old crow was probably such a one and Mordred would waste no further time.

"I have been sent here by the Emperor…"

"Your father?"

"By the Emperor of the Britons, to investigate rumours of strange practices within the bounds of this monastery."

"Strange practices?" asked the abbot. "How so, Lord?"

"That is what I am to determine," stated Mordred shortly. "As I just said."

The abbot's head flinched then, much like a crow in fact, and he stared at the young man. The singing rose around them until Mordred was sure he could feel it pressing onto his skin like a storm saturated cloak. Mordred rose from his chair and crossed and opened the door to the chamber. Dunstan waited outside the door, as instructed.

"My lord?"

"You do hear it, Dunstan?" asked Mordred. "The singing?"

His scutarius nodded his head. "The monks, Sir? Yes, faintly."

Mordred placed his hand on the younger man's shoulder. "Stay awake, Dunstan," he said with warmth. "It is a strange night."

The handsome knight closed the door. Abbot Bernard sat with his back to him now and Mordred could see the pulse in his thin, pale neck. It ticked against the old man's skin, too rapidly for a man in the comfort of his own chamber. The voices rose higher again and Mordred could feel his own blood quicken.

"You may, of course, examine any aspect of the life of this place of worship," declared Bernard. "We have nothing to hide. In the morning I will personally escort you anywhere you wish, my lord, and answer any questions you may have."

"Why not start now? Arthur says that the best time to start

something is when it is needed."

"Ah, yes," said Bernard, "the Emperor. The saviour of the land. He has brought peace to the people after so many years."

"He has," agreed Mordred, "with the help of many true followers."

The old man inclined his head. "Very true, very true. But my fear is, here so far from civilization, who will take over when the king is no longer?"

"We do not speak of his death, Abbot Bernard."

"Yes, yes, of course. But is there none of his line to take on his role and set the land on its true path."

"Set, Abbot?"

"Maintain, my son. I, of course, meant maintain. It would take a man who truly has the blood of the dragon in his veins to maintain the peace so bloodily wrought. I know of only one man, Lord, if I may be so presumptuous."

"You may not." Mordred touched his brow. Sweat lounged at his hairline. The room was not hot, merely pleasant, and he was not prone to perspiration. The edges of his vision were suddenly unclear, like looking through the abbot's thick glass cups, and Mordred thought that he should drink some water but had no wish to rise from his seat. The singing lulled him now and his head lolled back.

"The runaway youth…" began Mordred but he could not finish the question for his eyes blinked and they closed and, for a moment, Mordred was not of the world.

It was the cry that brought him back. Mordred heard it even above his stupor and through the closed door. He recognized the voice though it was twisted with pain. He turned his head and his vision swam but he stayed afloat. Mordred saw the abbot open the door and the big monk was there and the scarred brother dragged Dunstan into the room. The blade of the dagger pulled from his scutarius' throat was long and dark now with the younger man's blood.

"We needed but one more day," Mordred heard the abbot say to Bartholomew.

"After tonight nothing will matter," said the big monk.

246

"You could not turn him towards us?"

"I circled it. But on the surface he remains loyal."

Bartholomew dragged the corpse of Dunstan further into the room for its foot still blocked the door. "It is of no matter now the true lord comes. Him?"

"Yes, as you say, it does not matter now. Kill him and join us." The abbot swung through the door without a backwards glance.

Mordred closed his eyes as the big monk approached. His head roiled with whatever he had been given and his limbs seemed distant. However, he had seen the body of the lad entrusted to his care and the wound that tore through Dunstan's throat and he did not give up easily. He was a knight of Arthur's inner circle, so he prepared to give his life at some cost.

The scarred monk held Mordred's head by his thick hair and brought the dagger to his throat. Mordred grabbed for the knife hand but he missed and found only the other's sleeve. Mordred held on as the big man, startled by the sudden show of life, drew his arm back. Mordred went with the force and in his own right hand and he grasped the Abbot's glass goblet. Mordred smashed it against Bartholomew's head and the big man went down. Mordred went with him and the broken glass now found the monk's throat and Mordred slashed furiously until the blood made him lose his grip and the big man was dead.

Mordred came up to his hands and knees but his head was not in the room and he fell again. He blacked out once more and when he regained his senses the dead monk's blood was sticky with the passage of time.

The knight got to his knees again and, with a hand on the abbot's desk, pulled himself to his feet. Mordred bent over and jammed a finger down his throat and the contents of his stomach joined the blood on the floor. Mordred felt a little better and when he saw Dunstan's body cold on the chamber's floor he knew he was well enough to kill.

The hymn was back in his ears now and Mordred would let it be his guide. He first went quickly to his room and buckled his sword belt to his waist and gathered his shield. A jug of water tipped over his head revived him even more.

He let the beautiful voices lead him down through the monastery. Lower and lower the knight went as the chorus rose in volume. The stone walls on the monastery were damp now and Mordred could taste the tang of salt sea on his tongue. His brain was feverish with revenge for the killing of his companion and the insult to himself.

A door appeared and Mordred knew that what he sought was just beyond. He pushed slowly and it swung open on well-oiled hinges. Mordred stepped through into shadows and what he saw stopped him.

The space was vast and open to the ocean. Waves pounded at its entrance and the spray washed over those gathered within. It was carved from the earth but nothing so large could have been accomplished by human hands. The walls were smooth and designs alien to the knight decorated all points. Torches burned around the perimeter to throw dancing shadows to all corners.

Mordred was unnoticed, for all looked towards the mouth of the immense cave. Every man sang out as they swayed with the rhythm and it was beautiful and terrible all at once. On a platform stood the abbot. At his feet lay the young man Mordred had first seen slumped on the pony. The grey-bearded Pict, Ougen, held the youth to the rock floor and the other two warriors stood at the base of the raised area as if on guard.

As Mordred watched the old abbot drew a knife from the folds of his habit and held it aloft. The man did not seem so frail now but a fervour strengthened his limbs and straightened his back. The youth below the old man did not struggle and Mordred knew what they had given him to obtain such acquiescence.

"Father Dagon," the abbot called, "take this offering. Come to us here, for we are your servants and we have prepared the way. Bring your might to this land, for it is a shadow of what it once was and it has lost its way. Strangers have brought the god of the desert to this land, but we do not forget who we are. We beseech you, mighty Dagon, to make this land your own and us your humble servants."

Mordred found his breath was trapped in his lungs and his blood was too hot for his veins. He could not look away, for beyond the mouth of the cave the sea began to boil and swell as if something was forcing its way to the surface. In fascination and dread, Mordred stepped towards the platform at the mouth of the vast alien cave.

A monk saw him then raised his hand and yelled. The brother beside Mordred grabbed the knight by the shoulder and the spell was broken. Mordred drew his sword and backhanded the monk across the face; the man fell and his scream tore at the song around them. Mordred waded into the press of men, monks fell and the song was lost in the spray of sea and blood and the old stones were slick underfoot.

The abbot pointed towards Mordred with the knife and Ougen shouted at the two warriors below the platform. Uuen sprang forward in an echo of their first meeting and he threw his spear. Mordred knocked it aside and was upon the young warrior and the knight's sword cleaved his chest. He had fared no better, Uuen, but he did not rise this time with a smile.

The monks were running heedlessly around the cave and one of them grabbed Mordred's shield. The knight slammed the cross-guard of his sword into the man's face and he fell away but into this distraction stepped Drosten. His sword was quick and he was brave but he was not one of King Arthur's Comitatus.

Mordred met his sword-stroke with his Linden-wood shield and he let the war-board twist in his grip and clear the man's sword as he swung his own blade in a reverse arc over his own head. The keen edge of his sword bit into the Pict's skull beside the right eye socket and the brittle bone there snapped and the steel carved its way through the warrior's brain. Drosten was dead before his sword rang off the rock floor of the cave.

"Surrender!" called Mordred to the abbot. "Surrender and you will have a quick death."

"Join us and help us rule this land!" returned Abbot

Bernard. His eyes were wide with zeal as he loomed over the fallen youth.

"You fool! You are too weak!"

Mordred saw the ocean bubbling behind the old man and he could feel a presence foreign to his experience. It twisted in his mind and the knight did not know who he was for a moment. He forgot that he was the loyal retainer of a king who had brought peace to the land but remembered that he was the only heir to a kingdom that could give him power he had only imagined in the dark hours of the mornings when men were their most honest. The authority that emanated from the crash and surge of water held him to the cave floor.

The abbot's zeal overplayed his hand and the old man did not wait. The abbot yelled "Kill him!" as he plunged the knife at the youth's chest. The abbot rushed, missing, his blade only scouring the ribs of the young man; the sacrifice jolted at the pain and grabbed the abbot's arms. They rolled across the platform and then Mordred could see no more for Ougen filled his vision as the leader of the Picts sought his life.

Ougen came on with a calculated step. He had a beard of grey because he had survived countless battles and skirmishes. He had no doubt in his ability and feared no man.

"There is power here," the tribesman said as he approached. "You must feel it?"

Mordred shook his head. "You shame your position as a warrior. To fight for such evil."

"It is no evil! It is our way and has been since this land was forged. It is the way of strength and of conflict. We will not let it be destroyed by your foreign god, nor the weak gods of other Picts. Only we will stand."

Mordred had nothing more to say and he leapt forward because he would not let the other man set the distance. Their swords struck and their shields boomed in the enclosed space and, as happened when two expert swordsmen fought in earnest, it was over quickly.

Ougen cut down at Mordred's neck but the knight counter cut at the same angle. Mordred caught the blade on his own and Mordred twisted his sword hand from thumb up to thumb down, lancing the point of his sword forward. The steel went unerringly to Ougen's throat and the grey beard was dyed red by the Pict's life blood. The older warrior stepped back and sunk to the floor of the cave and turned on his side and said nothing more as he slipped into death.

Mordred jumped onto the platform where the two still wrestled and in a quick stride he kicked the old abbot in the side of the head. The man rolled away and curled into a ball. The youth sat and held his ribs where the knife had sliced the skin and cried.

The sea erupted, water washing into the cave. The three were alone. Mordred shielded his eyes from the spray and when he dropped his arm he could not move. Mordred could not raise his arms again nor put one foot in front of the other, for in the dark water before him rose a being of such enormity that his mind could not encompass its presence. It reared as high as the cliff before it and was vaguely human in shape but its skin was dark like oil and webbing stretched between fingers of hands that could crush a bull with little effort. Of its face, Mordred could not see clearly and within the small recess of his mind that still held conscious thought he was glad for that mercy.

The waves crashed but it was within his mind that the sound appeared and gradually Mordred, a knight of Arthur's band, began to hear the words. They formed slowly, as if the being was unused to such things, but they held command and they held promise.

"Do you deny me now, Mordred, as you deny your rightful place in this land? Lord Dagon, my servants call me and I have seen the forming of this world and others and the destruction of civilizations. I was here before Atlantis fell and when gods and men walked the earth together. Serve me and I will bring unto you dominion over all things upon this world. Sunder the peace of this land, for that is not the rightful state of man. Sunder the peace to pave the way for my coming and all will be yours. Give me an offering and I will give you a world."

Mordred could move now but did not run away in fear. He

looked down at the rock platform and saw the sacrificial knife shining before him. He grasped it in his right hand. Mordred would give this great being the blood it wanted. Mordred heard the sobs of the youth. He turned and, with a determined step, crossed to the abbot and plunged the knife into the old man's heart. The abbot stiffened with the impact and his eyes flared with the injustice of it all and, as he died, Mordred kicked his slackening body into the dark waves.

He bent to a knee and lowered his head and thought, "My will is yours," and within his mind he heard the answer, *As it should be.*

The seawater rushed from the cave and the pressure rushed from his head with the frothing water and when he looked up the ocean was clear.

Mordred crossed the causeway and his armour was bright in the sunlight. Behind him rode the youth on Dunstan's horse and the young man held his head high. On the tidal island the monastery burned and the flames were a signal of things to come. Mordred crossed the causeway and he began to plot how to bring down a king and bring war to a peaceful land.

CONTRIBUTORS

Dylan Freeman lives in northern Ohio and has been writing as part of the SCP Foundation collaborative writing project since 2012. He has since become one of the most prolific authors in the project, with over 150 individual works authored or co-authored. Outside of writing, he enjoys studying history and literature. *The Death, Drowning and Revival of Sir Dinadan* is his first professionally published work.

Richard Sheppard is a writer, academic, restauranteur and podcaster from the United Kingdom. His fiction can be found in previous the previous 18thWall anthology *Sockhops and Seances* and in Egaeus Press's *The Book of the Sea*, he has also published academic works on Mary Shelley and Wes Craven. He is also the host and co-producer of the *Hallowed Histories* podcast and *The Constant Reader Podcast*—the former deals with local folklore, the latter with the life and works of Stephen King. He lives in Norwich with his wife and cat.

A professional author since 2007, **Josh Reynolds** has over thirty novels to his name, as well as numerous short stories, novellas and audio scripts. Born and raised in South Carolina, he now resides in Sheffield with his wife and daughter, as well as a highly excitable dog and something he hopes is a cat. A complete list of his work can be found at https://joshuamreynolds.co.uk/.

Edward M. Erdelac is the author of fourteen novels including *The Knight With Two Swords*, *Andersonville*, and *The Merkabah Rider* series. His stories have appeared in dozens of anthologies and periodicals ranging from *Tales From Arkham Sanitarium* to *Star Wars Insider Magazine*. Born in Indiana, educated in Chicago, he lives in the Los Angeles area with his family. News and excerpts from his work can be found at http://www.emerdelac.wordpress.com

Simon Bucher-Jones, has been writing stuff for almost the whole of his life, and persuading people to publish it for twenty eight years. Eventually he hopes to be good at it. He's best known for *Doctor Who* tie-in fiction, writing *Black Archives* analysing the tv show, a cursed play, poetry, and novel mash-ups co-written with Dickens and Wilkie Collins. He lives on the Isle of Wight and writes part-time. The rest of his work has included scare acting every Halloween at the award winning Terror Island, and voicing Marley's Ghost for a locally produced web version of *A Christmas Carol*.

Ethan Sabatella is a writer of sword & sorcery fantasy, historical fiction, and cosmic horror. He cites Celtic language, history, and mythology as the primary sources of inspiration behind his stories. The plots of his stories often focus on warriors overcoming martial challenges or encounters with hidden ancient, primordial forces. They also encapsulate themes of brotherhood in the face of danger, loyalty, and survival. Ethan's previous work has appeared in the anthologies *City in the Ice* by Hiraeth Publishing and *Monsters & Mayhem* by Eerie River Publishing, the sword & sorcery magazines *Broadswords and Blasters* and *Whetstone*. When Ethan is not writing, he practices Historical European Martial Arts and creates content for tabletop roleplaying games.

Timothy Williams lives in the wild state of Texas with his loving family, who may or may not be held hostage by a blind dog who is also a criminal mastermind. When not saving the world from unspeakable evil he can be found at his day job of which the less said the better. He enjoys reading and watching TV and just about any other activity that keeps him indoors and sedentary. This is his first published bit of fiction.

Tim Mendees is a rather odd chap. He's a horror writer from Macclesfield in the North-West of England that specialises in cosmic horror and weird fiction. A lifelong fan of classic weird tales, Tim set out to bring the pulp horror of yesteryear into the 21st Century and give it a distinctly British flavour. His work has been described as the love-child of H.P. Lovecraft and P.G. Wodehouse and is often peppered with a wry sense of humour that acts as a counterpoint to the unnerving, and often disturbing, narratives.

Tim has had over ninety published short stories and novelettes along with seven stand-alone novellas and a short story collection.

When he is not arguing with the spellchecker, Tim is a goth DJ and a co-host of the *Innsmouth Book Club* podcast. He currently lives in Brighton & Hove with his pet crab, Gerald, and an army of stuffed octopods.

https://timmendeeswriter.wordpress.com/
https://tinyurl.com/timmendeesyoutube

Tim Hanlon has been a History teacher since the dawn of time. He tries to follow the tenets of Stoicism but generally fails. Tim's interest in Arthurian Britain began with the novels of Rosemary Sutcliff in his early teens and continues to this day. When not reading or writing, Tim enjoys craft beer, boxing, and getting caught in the rain.

DID YOU ENJOY WHAT YOU JUST READ?

If you enjoyed this book,
please review it on Amazon and GoodReads!

It's the best way to support the author.

For fantastic fiction, in-depth articles by your favourite authors, open submissions, and more, please…

VISIT OUR WEBSITE
18thwall.com/

LIKE US ON FACEBOOK
facebook.com/18thwall/

FOLLOW US ON TWITTER
@18thWall

We'd love to hear from you! You help make these books possible.